Adam Klein studied creative writing at the University of Iowa and San Francisco State University. This work has appeared in *Men on Men 5* and *BOMB* magazine. He is also a musician, recording and performing with his band, *Roman Evening*. He lives in San Francisco.

tiny ladies

Adam Klein

Library of Congress Catalog Card Number: ????

A complete catalogue record for this book can
be obtained from the British Library on request

First published in 2003 by Serpent's Tail
4 Blackstock Mews, London N4 2BT
website: *www.serpentstail.com*

Printed by Mackays of Chatham, plc

10 9 8 7 6 5 4 3 2 1

I

Tiny Ladies

Every word I say has chains round its ankles; every thought I think is weighted with heavy weights.

Jean Rhys, *Good Morning, Midnight*

For some people, trouble runs so deep in them no part is left unaffected. You spend your time trying to help them fix a thing here or there, but they cut you like a handful of shards. People are fragile; once they're broken you can't piece them back. Not that anyone has the time to try, at least not those of us working for the state. We're wearied by quotas, the endless cycling of people through the system. Concern is invariably measured, and that, they will tell you, is how it has to be. The world generates more need than satisfaction; there's simply not enough to go around. Be cautious with care. Sparing. That's what I've learned, and I'm happy to have learned it.

Frances says, 'Carrie, you don't have to tell your story to get your clients to share theirs.' I don't answer her. What she says is not unfamiliar; she says it with brusque concern. But her reminder is crushing. I have been a caseworker for seven years, and it always comes to this point – a vantage point – of who sits behind the desk and who is in the chair. It's give or take, and you can't do both.

That, of course, raises another point: only the blind are willing to lead the blind. And often they don't want to. Just because someone's had a tough life, some struggles of their own, doesn't make them empathetic. Empathy is hard won, rare. Frances finds empathy dangerous, disorienting. But if you've survived – even if you don't know how – you might have something to offer someone who doesn't believe they can survive. You're a kind of example, a museum piece. Something suddenly valuable in you, admirable. When I walk into the office, I can't help but think of my co-workers, at least the good ones, as artifacts; they seem removed from their lives except to exemplify their history, convey its lessons. Their bad choices make them good counsel.

I started doing casework in San Francisco. They interviewed me before a panel of eight representatives from various field offices. They put a heavy, gray, reel-to-reel recorder at the center of the table and sat sipping from Styrofoam cups.

'Why do you want to work for the Department of Social Services?' a young woman asked. The left side of her face drooped, as though she had had a stroke or had been in some kind of accident. She was hard to understand, but I didn't ask her to repeat herself. When I smiled at her, she averted her eyes, so I stopped smiling. Through most of the interview I sat quietly, looking at each of the panelists' faces. Their inquiries were strangely laconic, their silences more demanding than their questions.

Feeling pressed to respond, I answered, 'I feel guilty not helping people who need it. When I needed it, someone was there for me.' They suddenly stiffened as though to dam a flood of potentialities in my answer. Their expressions turned unenthusiastic, like a wary parent, a distracted police officer. Just the facts, ma'am. They had done this for years; they asked their questions, biting them off before they could provide revelations. Not one organization in America can ask the pertinent questions. And if they stumble on one, just by accident, there's an automatic shutdown in the person who has asked it. The parts just settle and turn off.

So when I got the job, and they told me about the pool of two thousand applicants, I said, 'You've made a mistake.' But I was wrong. They didn't want any more than what they got. They sent the recording to Sacramento, where my answers – and my silences – were impartially scored. If they'd made a mistake, it was not irreparable. There were 1,999 people waiting for my position.

Now, in Iowa City, the expectations are considerably different. I hurry into work clutching files. My co-workers, four of them, are at their desks before 8 A.M. I say good morning to them, making sure they hear me. They are sensitive about these things. If I brush past them and don't speak up, they talk about it. Frances says, 'Treat it like another part of the job, being nice to them.'

I look out at the lobby. Empty. Some days only one or two people make it in. In San Francisco, my caseload was never under fifty. People took numbers, sat on hard plastic chairs waiting to be called. Selfish of me to think that was better. Frances, when she hired me, told me this wasn't a busy office. 'Iowa City is hardly a city,' she said. 'Still, people have problems here.'

Frances is black; she's a heavy woman who wears a base too light for her skin. She smokes incessantly, often with the patch on. She smokes until she's dizzy, sitting outside when it's warm enough, with her head in her hands. 'It's not easy to close a case here,' she said during our interview. 'It's a college town mostly. Students come in when their financial aid doesn't cover them. They want food stamps, that's about it. Your job, really, is to keep your stats.' She looked at me with surprising concern after laying out such cynical objectives. 'Are you sure this is the right place for you? I know you've worked with much tougher cases.'

I didn't say anything about Victor, about what came before, and how an easy caseload would inevitably present challenges for me. I made my job in San Francisco practically impossible; I could do that anywhere. She never asked me why I left San Francisco. I don't think she called my references. She took me on face value, and I'm glad she didn't tell me what she read there. But I've never known her to do anything that rash since. Even after three years of working here, we still seem to be stumbling around that first encounter; I sense her regarding me with a concern that borders on distrust, and I either feel indebted to her or humiliated by her attention.

I start going through the files on my desk. Last name first. Social security number, and on and on. Jones. Gloria. November 9, 1989. A week ago, but I can't imagine her face, so I read on. Mother of two. Court case pending. Substance abuse. I remember her now. She looked anorexic, her eyes enormous in her face. Her education was minimal. She wanted work as a home health attendant, emptying bedpans, cooking up oatmeal. She had less than a week clean. She was still shaking.

She never made her follow-up appointment. One of those people who gets clean on New Year's. Not my failure, I tell myself, as though I'm new to this and need to justify the incompleteness of case files, of lives. I know what it means to sit on the other side of the desk, to spill your life out to someone you've never met before, thinking they're the last safety net, the last hope. I know what it means to sit shaking in a chair, listing your skills to a skeptical job developer. But that experience doesn't keep me from feeling a sense of personal defeat when I come upon the abandoned cases, the early terminations.

Frances is on the phone behind me, talking to her boyfriend in Washington. They're planning to build a home in Virginia. She whispers, but just loud enough for me to hear her making plans.

She's starting a new life. It makes her purposeful and energized. I've felt that way every time I started over. Except the last time, when I left California. Then, I just felt tired.

The door swings open, letting a chill wind whip through the office. As though we've planned it, none of us makes a move to admit the young woman who takes a seat on one of the orange chairs in the lobby. We push files aside, lift our phones to make calls. We're adept at looking busy; we do it as a defense. We prepare a front of orderliness to address whatever chaos we might encounter that day. Eventually, I stand up and call her to my desk.

She has hair like a rooster, pomaded so each strand looks thick as a pencil. It's cut short, exposing her face. She doesn't wear much makeup, but I continue to look at her, drawn to a kind of toughness and sadness that is its own shadow. I ask her name, a litany of questions before we begin.

'My name's Carrie. What's yours?'

'Fisher. Hannah Fisher.' She answers indifferently.

I ask who referred her, and she responds with a name I don't recognize. Then she just says, 'The hospital.'

I know instantly what she is alluding to and write the words *South Wing* on a post-it. Sometimes writing informal notes – rather than composing longhand in their files – keeps them from embellishing too much. When I'd first met Victor in San Francisco, he used to lean over my desk and dictate, tell me when I'd left out something he considered important. I'd become a kind of biographer in his mind, even though no one would read his file, except maybe the police a few years later. I wonder now what I wrote in it and whether they noticed the dangerous attention I gave him, the fond slant my notes could hardly have hidden.

I look at her while leaning forward in my chair and giving one nervous tap of my pen to the blotter. 'How'd you end up in the hospital?' I ask.

She looks at the pen for what feels like minutes. 'My best friend died last winter.' She meets my eyes and smiles for the first time. 'I think I may have had something to do with her death.'

I recognize but can't place her, and begin to consider my limited spectrum of activities in town. I don't see her face in The Deadwood, a dark-paneled bar I sometimes stop in; or Pierson's drugstore with its fountain in the back; or the Bijou theater. I imagine myself walking in and out of these places alone, and Hannah Fisher doesn't appear in any of my recollections. My time outside of work seems suddenly full of dark and aimless meandering, untouched by any interaction. It's distressing not knowing anyone here. Only part of it intentional.

'Do you mind if I smoke?' she asks.

'We'll need to go outside,' I reply. 'I'll join you.'

Outside, I realize how young she is, maybe twenty-five. Her hand trembles while she lights her cigarette, and when she looks at me I notice one pupil more dilated than the other – a reaction I've seen before in people on the drugs they give at the hospital.

'Do you mind if I have one?'

'Oh, sure.' She says this flustered, sorry for not offering. She rummages her purse, then the pockets of her winter coat before she finds them.

'So, they must have mixed some strong cocktails for you at the hospital?' Her dilated eye is almost vibrating.

'I beg your pardon?'

I explain how South Wing patients sometimes call their pills cocktails.

'I wasn't there too long, but I did like the chloral hydrate.' She laughs briefly.

'In the old days they called them Mickey Finns.' I say it, gloating a little, something my father taught me.

The sky is still dark, and I think it will be another impossibly gray weekend. There's a fine snow over the cars in the parking lot and over the fields stretching away from us. She turns to look out over the faint snowdrift, and her profile is startlingly beautiful. Her green eyes and orange hair are sharply contrasted, cut out against a sky the color of purple contact paper. She turns to look at me, exhaling smoke from her nose.

'I noticed the pictures at your desk.'

'I've been collecting them, cutting them out of books. I've had some of them since I was a child.' I remember sitting by the canal near our house paging through heavy art books. My father sold them, but he wasn't a bookseller. The books were one of his many occupations. He had a trucking job when he married my mother, but when I was ten years old he lost it. He went to jail, came back, and went to jail again. We call it recidivism.

'Someone always needs something fixed,' he'd say, and that's where he came in. Most of the books he'd get from people who had died, or the Salvation Army drop box. Sometimes, if he saw one cheap in a used bookstore, and he knew its value, he'd buy it and sell it for what it was really worth. That's another thing he told me: 'You've got to learn the real value of things.' There was no shame in picking around for what others – through either laziness or negligence – discarded.

I'd sit under the bridge where the sounds of the canal magnified, damp sounds you felt in your bones. If I found a picture I liked, I'd scramble out from under the bridge wiping away the pebbles and dirt embedded in my knees, and open the page up to the sun. My eyes would adjust slowly, and then the picture would assemble itself. The pictures I'd look at the longest depicted women in the midst of battle: *The Rape of the Sabines* or *Liberty Leading the People*.

'I love nineteenth-century painting,' I say to her. 'Do you like painting?'

There's a dead silence, a windless snowfall. At the mention of painting, I notice a flash of curiosity in her eyes.

'That's what I was in school for,' she says, dropping her cigarette in the snow. 'I finished last year.'

'Do you still paint?' I ask.

'A lot of people at the hospital liked my yarn and felt work.'

It takes me a moment to discern her sarcasm. 'I guess that was a stupid question.'

'No,' she says in a careful, correcting voice. 'It's not stupid. I just don't think of myself as a painter right now. Besides, I have a hard time believing it matters to you one way or the other.'

'It does matter to me. I'm here to help you if I can.' I watch her light another cigarette.

'People shouldn't burden each other.' There is something disheartened in her tone, as though trying to convince me of this is too much. She looks at me squarely. 'You're awfully young.'

'No, I'm not. Not really. I'm twenty-nine, and sometimes when I look at myself I see someone older. I have these dark rings, for instance.' I point to my eyes. 'They're genetic, but they say something about my life.'

I notice Hannah has them too, but I don't point this out to her. 'Where are you from?'

'Sioux City,' she answers. 'I came to Iowa City to study painting. I got my MFA here last year.'

'And you decided to stay?'

'My friends expected I'd be the first to leave. All of them have moved on. They'd be shocked to know I couldn't.'

That's how these college towns are. If you're not connected in some way to the university, you immediately become the town idiot, delivering newspapers, chewing your own tongue. Or you've had some misfortune no one's ever asked about, but everyone knows. You carry this dark aura with you, and people watch you a little closer. It's not difficult for me, having never attended the university. I drove in from San Francisco and decided to stay. Anything they might say about me is true.

Hannah Fisher, however, does not belong here. I trust my instincts on it.

She stubs out her cigarette, and we go back inside. I continue for a moment to write out her case notes.

'Do you want to tell me about your friend?'

'Not really.' She laughs, picking up the taxidermic baby alligator I've carried for years. 'You have the strangest things on your desk.'

My father first took me down to the canal after a particularly dry summer. The water level was low; the canal was like a long skeleton baring itself. He carried a big branch, turning over old cans and plastic bottles, pieces of clothing.

'Why would someone take their clothes off here?' I asked him when we chanced upon a muddied pair of panties.

'Probably to go swimming.' He raised them up before us on the end of the branch.

'Why didn't they take them when they left?'

'This little girl must have lost 'em,' he said. I could tell he was thinking about her, so I started thinking about her too. I thought of the girl who wandered the block eating the prettiest flowers. We had angels' trumpets growing at the side of our house. My mother cut them with scissors and threw them into the trash. 'One day that girl is going to die on somebody's lawn, but it won't be ours,' she said. I called her the 'Poison Girl' from then on. That's who I thought about when I saw those panties on the end of the stick. Perhaps she'd eaten those flowers before she went in, paralyzed by their poisons or succumbing to the delusion she required no air. I imagined her body falling slowly through the murky water and settling on the soft bottom.

We were just about to move on when my father discovered the alligator, a tiny little guy wriggling alone in the mud. My father immediately grabbed him up and looked into his half-lidded, perfectly round eyes. His legs paddled as though he were still moving his way over ground. 'Smart little fella,' he said. 'He ain't supposed to live here. This guy was probably flushed down someone's toilet and has been living on his wits ever since. You want him?'

We took him home, and my father went into the shed and brought out an old grill, splashed some water in it from the hose. I went around the backyard pulling out grass, clumps of dirt, rocks. We put him on the patio. My mother had just gotten out of bed, though it was well past noon. She gathered her night robe around her and looked in. 'That's the saddest thing I've ever seen,' she said, and though my father insisted it was a great life there in that rusty black drum, the alligator did look sad. Sad and confused, sitting on a little rock with mud and grass and sooty bars overhead.

We rarely had pets growing up, but I remember the Wallaces' horse. Sometimes they kept him overnight in their backyard, and I'd sit and watch him from the window, gracefully bending forward and eating out patches of the grass. He belonged to Karen Wallace, who was a few years older than me and who used to charge me money to pet him, so I just watched him over the fence when Karen was asleep. I remember the commotion, too, when that horse got loose at 3 A.M. one morning – my father out in his shorts with a flashlight, my mother standing beneath our yellow porch light. It was my father who brought him back; he rounded the corner cocky as a hero and put the horse behind the Wallaces' gate. My father always said that the best way to calm an animal is to look in its eyes.

I often look in my clients' eyes, angle my chair to sit a little closer to them. Frances says I get too involved. She prefers an impartial interrogation. I don't think looking into a client's eyes is necessarily coddling; many of them are unnerved by it. So I don't look into Hannah's. I just tell her, 'That's from Florida – where I grew up.' I take the alligator from her hands and run my finger over the little, bared teeth, the hard ridges down its back.

I put it back down near my pen holder and bottles of White-out.

Hannah looks amused, thinking about something.

'Ellen was . . . mischievous,' she says. 'She was always surprised by the trouble she'd find herself in. I think that's what I liked about her, at first. She seemed so lawless. Naive, but brash at the same time.'

'How'd you meet her?' I ask, sensing immediately that this is about her friend who's passed.

'She was in painting class with me, and I liked her work. She painted these almost primitive self-portraits engaged in petty crime – shoplifting, pouring coffee on an unsuspecting lady, perched in a tree with a slingshot. Really funny paintings, some of which I still have.

'I talked to her once about them. I think I just said something mildly encouraging, like how funny they were – nothing really critical. Then, a couple of days later, I found this box of home-made cookies she'd baked and placed on my front doorstep. She'd made a box for them with miniature paintings on each side, and all the cookies were glazed and decorated with different color icings and silver candies. It was an amazing effort. And I remember thinking she must have followed me home, which I found kind of childish and flattering. I knew we'd be friends.'

'The last time someone followed me home, it was an ex-felon on my caseload.' I don't tell her that I invited him, that I was an ex-offender specialist in California. No. Why should I tell her about Victor? *You don't need to tell your story . . .*

'That sounds a little scary.' She loosens her scarf and draws it from her coat. She carefully drapes it over the back of her chair, but she keeps her coat on.

'Well, fear was something I had to learn. I'm better at it now.' I recognize stability, what some might call common sense, as something Iowa affords. I remember San Francisco – my whole life, really – as demanding something else from me: blind courage, perhaps. I have some simple things now that I can depend on: a quiet cottage; a loving dog; this job that many of my co-workers plan on retiring in; a checking account and a little savings. And my car. God bless my rusty old Valiant.

This is what I'd suggest to Hannah: a safe place, a few simple amenities. Though I'm sometimes afraid of the quietness of my life – how the walls sometimes whisper, conspire – I prefer it to what came before. What came before is always on the tip of my tongue, but I'm no longer in its mouth.

She leans forward over my desk, cupping her face in her hands.

'Did you get some kind of training to do this work?'

'I'm not a therapist,' I tell her. 'I had some training when I worked for the state in San Francisco. I'm a case manager. I'm primarily here to make referrals, coordinate some kind of plan for you.'

'I'm good at planning myself,' she says. She leans back and inspects me coolly. 'I'm very quick,' she says, clutching my stapler and pointing it at me. 'I'd probably be pretty good at your job if I wasn't so fucked up.'

I put her file aside and move my calendar to the front of the desk.

'I don't doubt that you might be good at this,' I say. 'But for now we might just want to concentrate on one thing at a time.'

We schedule an appointment for the following week, but I notice her drumming her fingers on the chair, shifting in it as though she has something else she wants to tell me. I look up at her once I've written the appointment date on my business card.

'Is there something wrong?' I ask.

'I was just wondering if you might really be able to help me,' she says. She looks off for a moment, then stares into my eyes. 'I'm not comfortable asking too much of anyone. I have a way of screwing things up, you know?'

She stands up abruptly. 'I enjoyed meeting you, though. I'll see you next week.' She walks out the door before I notice her scarf piled by the leg of the chair. And then the phone rings with the day's first cancellation.

The road home is desolate and lunar, a little wooden fence and railroad crossing. Nothing else for a few miles. I put a cassette into the tape recorder I keep on the front seat, and the Byrds' *5-D* scratches its way out of the box. *Oh, how is it that I could come out to here and be still floating and never hit bottom and keep falling through . . .*

I light a cigarette and look over at Hannah's scarf on the seat beside me. I pull up to the little cottage I'm renting, with its shrunken path, the insulating, waist-high wall of snow up to the doorway. It seems like an entrance to an igloo. How I arrived here is a question that persists for me, but the place is so remote I no longer seek out an answer.

I have to keep the porch light on all day so when I get home from work I can make my way up the path. I haven't shoveled it in the past few days, and the mottled ice is slippery as the back of a prehistoric fish. I spot King in the window, my beautiful white Samoyed, fogging the glass with his panting. I picked him up on my way to Iowa, riding on the highway at 2 A.M. in a terrible storm. I saw him running along the side of the road, just a strange white flash at first, a dwarfed ghost. Then I saw him turn in someone's headlights, stilled there with his mouth and eyes wide open, a terror and incomprehension that made me brake danger-ously fast. I had only to open the back door of the car and he jumped in, wringing wet, overly excited for the next three days.

For a while we lived in the car together. Once I got this place, we slept on the floor – just the dog and me – with a few layers of blankets. I had some cocaine left, and I was shooting it, cramped by paranoia, visions. I thought of them as visions. I imagined Victor outside, as patient as any judge. I spent the first nights convincing myself of the impossibility of his having followed me. But when you pull yourself out of a place as low and desperate as the one I'd escaped, it's easy to imagine things and hard to stop.

King would cower in the corner, and I'd spend hours peering from the windows, hiding from shapes the shadows took on, or trying to coax him to me, staring into his eyes as though I could communicate with him – some crazed Dr Doolittle. At one point he lunged through the screen door and ran out to the pond. I ran after him, calling to him in my underwear, eyes dilated like black lakes themselves. I saw him out in the water; I was paralyzed with the certainty he'd drown.

He didn't drown. He eventually came out, shaking with cold, and afraid of me. I began to get a hold on myself, approached him carefully and dried him. That was the last time I did drugs. I gathered up all the syringes and paraphernalia and dumped them into a milk carton, threw it away. Two weeks later, I interviewed for my job with the Department of Social Services. I was wearing a belt with my teeth marks in it. Once I got the job, I threw the belt out too.

I got the job three winters ago. I'm still trying to convince myself that it's possible for life to move at this pace. Maybe it has something to do with my not using drugs, the tentative return of sanity, but the days have a dream length, entire lives played out in the inching forward of a clock hand. And only recently have I come to appreciate each day's slowness, a languor that makes me wonder if I didn't drive into some lost or swallowed-up town, where sands move backward through the hourglass, the past reassembling itself, ready to fall again in different configurations.

This two-bedroom cottage has a peculiar warmth. I appreciate its accumulation, a kind of organic decorating that seems to have happened without my intervention. Some of it was here when I arrived – the lamps and a couple of the rugs. I purchased the furniture almost entirely at the Mennonite store: a used '50s sectional and a recliner with a worn plaid cover, forest and pale green. Now there's a nest of King's white hair in the lap of the chair. His toys are here and there, and records everywhere.

I take King out behind the house. He loves the snow and runs over the slick surface of the frozen pond. I worried at first, fearful of a break in the ice. Now I just assume that dogs have some kind of sense about these dangers. Animals know trouble; you can see it in the eyes of the alligator on my desk.

I don't follow King out over the pond, but pack my heels down along the natural embankment, admiring his bursts of energy. He's a beautiful dog, healthy and with a full winter pelt, but there's something sad about him too. The image of him running along the highway remains there for me, and I hug him sometimes too tight, and give him too much love and talk embarrassingly like a child with him.

I look away from King and scan the flat landscape, the one large hill like an Indian grave that casts a shadow up to the door, the few dead trees and the abundant snow pillowing the roof of my house and virtually camouflaging it. I rarely recognize my loneliness anymore, except in this silence. And it isn't silence, really. I hear an owl, the wind, and my breathing. I bring my mittens to my mouth. The heat of my own breath is a comfort. There was a time when this weather would have killed me, when I couldn't find any warmth in my body, bone-thin from drugs. But I like it now; it points to the change in me.

When I turn away from the cottage and the pond, the white seems to go on forever. I often think of Jack London stories when I come out behind the house. My father loved his stories; he read them while incarcerated, dreaming, I guess, of some other wilderness with its other justice.

It is after 7:30 P.M. I cross the floor, back and forth, looking at the phone, sick of smoking. I pull my large bag from the couch and draw out Hannah Fisher's file. The notes I meant to transcribe are there on post-its. I think of rewriting them – fleshing them out – but with what? Her features are strong. She's Jewish, I think. She's guarded. There's something almost willfully vacant and affectless in her speech, and at other moments she exhibits an unrestrained enthusiasm. I wonder how much of it is the drugs, and how powerfully her past is pitched against her. And what are her odds? No odds for someone up against the dead. I think of Janine, and how my leaving San Francisco only made her more present. I can't be impartial about guilt or ghosts. I live with them, their limits. It is Janine who keeps me from knowing anyone here, not my other fears. It's atonement she exacts. Stay alone, Janine says. Be cautious with care. Don't think of calling Hannah; she's more trouble than you know.

I get in the car and drive through Iowa City, past its fraternity and faculty houses, the gold dome of Old Capital glowing like a captured sun. These sights carry all the hushed solemnity of my first encounter with them. When I first arrived, I'd driven so long, pushing myself past exhaustion, past the life that chased me here.

I lived with Victor in a small hotel in San Francisco's Tenderloin for two years. Life began and ended there; there was no larger picture. At the very end, I lost my job and Vic went back to his old ways, nothing like he'd been at our initial interview when he was just out of prison and certain about too many things. He'd become unpredictable and dangerous, the behaviors he'd warned me about but that I thought were just boasting. And though I fled because of him – the desperation and plotting he carried into our relationship, and how he involved Janine – I know I scared myself too. I was too hungry for everything, and too accustomed to crumbs.

I drive west up streets with small houses and large porticoes, and away from the area where students are walking, encumbered with too many books. Their down coats make them look comical, balloon-like, as though they could rise a few feet off the sidewalk. But on the side streets, apart from the vigil of porch lights, there is no movement or sound. I pull into a driveway that hasn't been shoveled. There's a birdbath submerged by snow in the front yard. I gather loose cassettes and put them into their covers, suddenly in no hurry to talk to Gina. Then I look up again at the house. The lights are on in all the windows, but still it emanates a kind of darkness. Some places reveal their troubles as plain as the people who tenant them. This is Gina's house; it sinks a little on one side, and the screen door is patched with a green mesh.

I met Gina at The Deadwood bar shortly after I arrived in town. She was saving her money, she said, to get out once and for all. She provides massages to older men in the city. She shared this with me within the first few minutes of our introduction.

'I don't mind giving a hand job when I have to. It's easy. Only complication is that I'm a dyke.'

Rachel, who has been working with Gina recently, is sitting on the couch when Gina opens the door.

'Good to see you,' she says in her gruff, warming voice. Rachel waves from the couch. She is wearing a pair of red vinyl pants and a black rubber bra. Gina's wearing jeans and a tank top. I like both of them, but I'm not sure what they think of me. I know they distrust me. That's the thing about girls like Gina: they'll tell you everything they think you want to know. I do this and this for money, and it doesn't trouble me. Compromise for the long-term goal. My head's here. My body's here. My sex is hidden. They tell you everything right up front, and you think it's a test. Can you love me? That's what you think they're asking, so you just smile. You're very broad. You're very accepting. But they don't really want you to love them, all bashed up. They want you to look deeper, to find the qualities they've put in reserve. And they're really like hoarding old ladies that way, underneath the wild looks; they put the finery away and just bring out the chipped stuff, until they forget they've got it.

Though there are only a few bottles of beer and a wooden bowl with pretzels on the coffee table, there is the feeling of an impending party – the two of them waiting for their first guest to arrive. I immediately want to put my coat back on and leave. Rachel rubs the couch where she'd like me to sit. 'Come here,' she says. 'I was just asking Gina, if you were an animal, what kind of animal would you be?'

I remember the party we threw for my father when he returned from prison. We celebrated his return, but it also marked the end of a struggle my mother and I endured for the two years he was gone.

Six months after my father's incarceration, my mother had me begin a series of what she called 'crash diets.' Oddly enough, she believed that naming them this way would make me feel encouraged about joining her in them. She'd say, 'Next week we'll go on a crash.' That meant we could drink as much tap water as we wanted and split a can of Campbell's soup once a day. We picked oranges from the tree in our backyard – small, sour, and still green at the tops – and ravaged them, skin and pulp spit out in our hands. My mother would create elaborate stories about the healthfulness of a fast, and when I was sick, diminished from lack of food, she would insist that was a sign that the toxins were working their way through me and that I'd soon be as good as new. Once she insisted we eat only white foods: bread, milk, rice, angel food cake. I waited anxiously for my shit to turn white, to be restored to the pre-toxic state she seemed so certain of.

We didn't talk about money. She contacted her mother, just once, and I spoke to her for the first time in my life. My grandmother asked the kind of questions you expect of a substitute teacher: How old was I? Did I like school? What did I eat today? We received small checks from her each month thereafter. On the memo, she wrote 'For Carrie' in careful script.

Sometimes my mother spoke to my father on the phone, either shouting or crying. But during the time he was gone she never spoke harshly about him – nothing as tangible as anger, or the inevitable guilt she must have felt in her dull complicity. He was apprehended for grand larceny, and of course she knew about it; it was a restaurant she'd worked in years before. He went right to the safe. The mouse, the cheese. We went to eat there a couple of times before he did it. I was ten years old, and they talked over my head.

What kind of person eats dinner in a restaurant they've been fired from? Who eats dinner in a place they plan to rob?

They always talked over my head, but it wasn't their words that were hard for me to understand. It was their reasoning.

My mother said of my father: 'He's just who he is,' or 'Who can say what's wrong or right for anyone else?

'We've just got to tough it out,' she'd muster, weakly smiling. 'That's what family is all about.'

After he'd served his time, we had our party. It was 1972, and I'd just turned twelve. I helped decorate with drawings I'd done for weeks in my room. The one I was most proud of had prison bars; handcuffs simplified to a figure eight or an infinity symbol; and the traced-in background of Samson's temple crashing around a less finished image of my father. I traced the ruined temple from the cover of a Bible stories record he'd bought me from the supermarket. My mother reluctantly taped my drawing to the refrigerator. I helped her with streamers and a banner that read: 'Welcome Home.' All his friends brought liquor, mostly beers, and I remember the refrigerator stocked full for the first time since he'd gone. My mother was drinking long before he arrived, nervously talking to his friends and arranging things, but the place looked bereft.

When he finally showed up, he seemed strangely improved, healthier and rested. My mother looked desperate and old standing beside him, so that I felt bad for her and ashamed of her too. He had incredible energy and lifted me high above his head and spun me so close to the light on the ceiling I had to hold my breath and close my eyes, imagining a shower of glass shattering around us. When he put me down, I stood woozily before him, strangely overwhelmed with tears on my cheeks that he brushed away with the back of his knuckles.

My mother got drunk, interrupting conversations with comments no one could understand. They tolerated her briefly before sidestepping her. 'You stay up with me,' she said after my father had sent me to bed. 'Let's show everyone what kind of fun we can have together.' She hollered out to Ernie to put on a record and swung around to grab my hand and guide me into the center of the living room. She danced until she was dizzy, falling backward over the coffee table, then quickly picked herself up, pushing off anyone attempting to help her steady herself. 'I don't need you,' she snarled at my father. 'We had a fucking ball. We had the time of our lives!' She said this with such force and rage, she threw up. Then he carried her to bed.

I've seen Gina that drunk and that angry, and when she feels alone it's tantamount to a betrayal by anyone who has ever known her. She and Rachel are listening to Madonna. They think it's perverse to participate in the mainstream. They play it too loud; even their parrot looks irritated, gnawing at the bars of his cage. 'Bitch, bitch, bitch,' the parrot says, looking at the three of us at once. I lower *Like a Prayer*, and make it more prayerful.

Gina was raised in Cedar Falls. Her parents divorced when she was five years old. Her mother never sought custody. Her father owned a farm, then he went bankrupt in the early '80s. Gina has a scrappy practicality despite the danger she's courted since she left home at the age of seventeen. It's not difficult to imagine her in a pair of overalls, fixing a tractor off the side of the road. She was a hard drinker under her father's tutelage. 'I'd sit across the table from him,' she said, 'and we'd just drink whiskey, competing with shots like we did when we were arm wrestling. I beat him in either sport. It wasn't hard.' She worked construction for four years until she was thrown off the crew for drinking. Then followed the years of prostitution, during which time the drinking was an asset.

'A gazelle,' she says, turning to Rachel. 'That's what I'd be.'

'What the hell's a gazelle?' Rachel asks.

'It's some kind of bird. I haven't seen one,' Gina says. 'But it's a good name, isn't it?'

After a moment, Rachel explains, 'You've got to be something you know. Or at least something I know.'

'What brings you out on a cold night?' Rachel asks, handing me a beer.

'She's bored. She has no other friends. She's a lone woman in a world of brutes.' Gina moves closer, puts her arm around me. 'Just kidding, kid.'

She exudes a kind of masculine confidence, and when she puts her arm around you, it's as though she's drawing you into a huddle. You're on her team.

'No,' I say. 'I was just thinking how true that is.'

She laughs. As though it's unthinkable. 'We're not exactly

jumping tonight. We could use a few brutes. So I guess it's ladies' night.' She moves her eyebrows up and down. Hoot owl, I think.

'You're not drinking,' she says, in her well-humored scold. 'Ladies' night's a drinking night. No little dicks to massage, right, Rachel?'

Rachel pulls at her beer. 'Uh-huh.'

'Are you working on a performance?' I ask Gina.

I've always felt with a little encouragement she could make a name for herself as an artist. After I first met her, she invited me to see a performance she'd put together for a class she was auditing. I bent down and looked through a peephole where she was tied to a rotating stage in a bunny outfit, whipped by women holding links of sausage. That performance stirred things up, and her teacher told her she was one of his best students and tried to encourage her to make it to class more often. Then the *Daily Iowan* ran an interview with her. I remember reading it at work. The interviewer asked her about the difficulties of doing a personal piece like that. She said the only difficulty was cutting the peepholes out of the wooden panels. I laughed out loud, remembering how rough they looked, like she'd scratched them out with her nails. 'I have no difficulty in putting myself out there. Personal shit's easy. It's the only thing I know,' she said.

'My whole life's a performance,' she reminds me. 'I don't need any more classes.' She lights a cigarette and crawls over the floor, laying her head in Rachel's lap. 'I just wish all these fuckers would pay me for my brilliance.'

'Jesus Christ, your head is heavy,' Rachel says, but doesn't push her off. She strokes Gina's head absently.

'All them brains,' Gina says. 'They make my head heavy.'

'Yeah, well, you're making my leg sweat with these fucking pants on.'

'They look like upholstery,' Gina says. 'Like something that would cover a bar stool.' She laughs hoarsely and claps her hand on her thigh.

'Great,' Rachel says, pushing her off and standing up. 'You would know.' She pretends she's upset, but there's something so genuine and tacit between them I feel slightly envious and out of the loop.

You never find that camaraderie in an office. Sometimes I miss it. Though not often. Because I've renounced this life – if only by working at a regular desk job – they assume I judge them. There's a nerve exposed, as poised and sharp as a whip. I want to tell them about the places I've worked, how and when I started, where it took me. But I think it would come off like bragging, an attempt to connect with them in a way I no longer need to. With Gina, I am always asking myself what it is I need from her. Authenticity, perhaps. But that's always trouble.

A man comes to the door; he must be sixty years old. Rachel lets him in, but Gina, who has risen from the floor, takes control of the situation.

'How you doin', Pops?' she asks. 'Let me grab the coat.' I put my hand over my mouth, not sure if I want to laugh or choke. And it's not that Gina does anything peculiar. It's just the part where you try to make it seem natural that always gets me; it makes the living room – with Gina's self-portraits, which are too dark and brooding even for her, and the framed poster for Pabst's *Pandora's Box* – seem too revealing and human, like she's saying, I've got a brain and a personality, and the moment you're gone I'll get on with my *real* life. And, of course, why should he be interested in that?

The man looks at me while she removes his down jacket, and for a moment I think he's concerned about my presence, not recognizing my face. Then it occurs to me he's interested in me. I recognize that look but can't connect to it. How far I've come, how far I've run – from that crap. But the man doesn't take his eyes off me, despite a discreet movement I make to divert my eyes from his gaze. He stands there with the austere patience of a doctor who has come to report on the prognosis of my disease. I stand up to gather my coat. I think of a game I used to play. The moment he looks at me, I'm dead. I have to dodge him. Him and so much else.

'Don't I know you?' he asks. I look at his eyes for the first time, and though I recognize no malice there, I hate him – his sad, selfish eyes that honor his loneliness above anyone else's.

'That must have been some other girl,' I say. I look at his Osh Kosh overalls and think: I don't do barnyards.

'Wait a minute,' Gina says, clutching my arm. 'Rachel's going to take him. That OK, Pops?'

The man looks shyly at Rachel, and nervously reaches out to shake her hand. The deal is struck with a farmer's equanimity.

'C'mon,' Rachel says, in a voice already tired despite the slowness of the evening. 'Right up here.'

After they've gone upstairs, Gina lures me back to the couch. 'What are you frowning about?' she asks, tentatively frowning herself as though her mimicry will help her understand me better.

'Did you ever see *Walk on the Wild Side*?' I ask her, thinking of Rachel and the man in overalls walking behind her up that creaky staircase. I begin to talk about it, but Gina seems uninterested, and goes off to the kitchen.

She returns with a beer for me. 'Sit down for a while,' she says, and I join her.

'How's work?' she asks, after putting a bottle intently to her lips and taking a long swig.

'Fine,' I answer. 'I had a woman come in today,' and I start to tell her about Hannah. I don't mention her name. 'She's interesting. She's really confused,' I say, embarrassed by the strange pull her story has on me – the one she's not told yet – 'by her friend's death.'

'Not Hannah?' Gina asks. 'She worked for me.'

I sit there, wide-eyed, feeling very stupid and guilty for talking about her.

'She worked here just before she got herself locked up.' Gina faces me, puts the bottle down. 'I liked her a lot,' she says. 'But she's always been troubled. Her friend was killed by one of the professors at the university. He was having an affair, and he killed her when it got too messy.'

'Why does Hannah think she had something to do with it?'

'I don't know. Maybe because she saw it coming and didn't

do anything about it. Hannah's an Iowa City legend,' she says consolingly. 'Everybody knows her, or about her.'

'I didn't know,' I say, trying to figure out why I feel so betrayed suddenly. It's such a silly thought: *I thought she belonged to me, but she belongs to everybody.*

Gina goes on, though. 'I know she was in this sorority a few years ago, and she got drunk one night and stood at the top of the stairs while a mixer party was going on, and she threatened to slice her breasts with a knife. A huge knife. Then I guess she locked herself in her room when the police came, jumped out the third-floor window and didn't return to school until a couple of semesters later. That story made its way around, but it didn't sound that crazy to me. I mean, drinking does things to you. I thought she was pretty balanced. She just temporarily wanted to get rid of her tits.' She laughs, looking down at the beer stain on her tank top.

'Jesus,' I say, leaning back into the couch and closing my eyes for a moment. 'I thought Iowa was supposed to be simple. I thought I left the craziness behind.'

'There's no escaping it,' she says with the certainty of someone not running. 'This kind of stuff happens anywhere.'

I think of the paintings I've collected – (snipped from art books – how I've always wanted to be able to look at these horrors with Gina's detachment.

'How did her friend die?' I ask.

'She was thrown down the stairs. Her neck was broken. Her teacher admitted it when they finally caught up with him. It happened in his studio.'

'The poor girl,' I say. 'That's awful.' The story really disturbs me. It's too close. I don't try to explain it to Gina. 'People are capable of anything.'

Gina stubs out her cigarette. 'I used to worry about stuff like that, but in this business it makes you too paranoid. Now I figure whatever happens, happens.' She takes another pull from her bottle.

'What are you supposed to do for her, anyway?' she finally asks.

And I think: She's ready to pounce now. She knows I'm upset. She knows I'm already too attached, so she's going to harangue me until I've toughened up. She scolds me for being sympathetic or overly concerned, then demands I respond to her every mood and crisis.

'Well,' I say – and there's that awful measuring – 'maybe I can help her get clear on how much of it was her responsibility.'

'Maybe she's as clear as she's going to get,' Gina says, agitated by too much or too little beer, or too little skepticism on my part. 'Maybe she is responsible.'

I see she's baiting me, playing devil's advocate. I look at her for a moment, considering whether I should tell her she's had enough to drink, but think better of it. It's not her drunkenness but my sensitivity that's making me so uncomfortable. She follows behind me as I gather up my things and make my way to the door.

She grabs my arm while I unlock my car. 'Maybe you can help her,' she offers. 'Anyway, it's worth trying.' My walking out has affected her. She sounds humbled and genuine.

'You didn't need to go after me like that,' I say. 'I've been doing this work for a long time, and I can assure you I'm not going to get too attached to be effective, and I'm not going to take the responsibility if she can't be helped.' And I'm thinking: The peep-hole is the easy part. It's what people don't exhibit that's so difficult.

She looks taken off guard for a moment. 'You make me worry sometimes, that's all.' She hugs me close, but I know her feelings are mixed, and that soon the bad ones will overtake the good. As I drive away from her, I feel an overwhelming pity for her mixed with a pity for myself, for Hannah, for her dead friend who presides over each of us, making the cold so much colder, and the white so much whiter.

2

I arrive home and find the box Hannah has left for me. I hesitate before picking it up. Because I remember this was the dead girl's gesture — at once an intimidation and a seduction. And I am unsure of why I feel I know Hannah so well: It could be the folder still open on my couch, or the exchange I've had with Gina. And I wonder why I brought her up, why I inquired of Gina those secrets that Hannah would no doubt confide. I turn the box in my hands; the drawings are pastel-colored snowflake patterns, some intricate and star-like, some just dashes, a code. And inside are butter cookies brushed with sugar, red and green. I take them inside and King bounds up from the braided carpet, tugging at me with teeth and paws. I take off my coat, shaking the snow from it, and sit on the couch to take off my boots. I walk to the bathroom and draw the bath. I can hear the wind outside, and watch it playing with the snow, lifting it after it's fallen, like another life, another brief fall. I take out a cookie and look it over before putting it in my mouth. I think I'll tell her she was wise to leave them at my house. We're not allowed to accept gifts from our clients, and in the office I'd have to turn them down.

I fall asleep in the tub, and wake up startled, unable to shake the residue of a dream: a policeman taking each of my fingers and bending them back. In my hands are two rocks, about the same

size and weight, and I can feel the chalk from them on my fingers.
I plunge my fists into the bathwater, which is already cold.

I close my eyes again, using the rock to draw a starting line.
Right foot first. Always the right foot first. And there are good
starts and bad starts. But rarely is there a game where the starting
line is the finish line, unless you play it wrong. Or you've had very
bad luck. Or someone has forced you to take steps backward.

Let's say I had a normal start and about as much luck as you can
manufacture.

On the weekends, I take baths while the sun goes down. I hate
the dark and turn up all the lights before the sun sets. I draw my
bath and step in when the light's just getting orange and fall asleep
every time. I wake up with the windows black and all the lights
burning. I don't look out the black windows; there might be
someone looking in. Horrible, glowering masks. Daddy's friends,
practical jokers. Let's put the masks to the window and scare her,
make her jump.

We lived in Sweetwater, Florida, not far from a black ribbon of
canal, almost currentless and full of dark life. 'It's not your business
to go there,' my mother warned. But it was as if she knew of its
attraction, a murky light like emissions from an ancient sub-
marine, or the wide blind eyes of fish that never surface. Imagine
not craving light, swimming in black panes, masks that hold no
terror for each other.

There were bridges over the canal, and porous jutting stones in
perpetual shade beneath them. The canal waters would lap and
eddy the ledges I'd sit on under the bridge. There was always the
terror of water rats or moccasins and the water itself, carrying
trash on its oily surface. There I'd spend hours just being in an
unknown place, sometimes smoking cigarettes I'd pilfered from
my mother's night table, or looking at my father's books in the
dim light.

And when my father was gone, I would sit for hours watching
from our front window the neighbors watering their lawns, gathering in loose and fluid association. I wondered deeply about

other people's lives. But always looking out a one-way glass. They looked in and saw themselves, so why look at all? My mother warned me of our neighbors – not only the girl who put flowers in her mouth, but the nosy ones who inquired too earnestly whether my mother was ill and what my father did for a living. I had no answer for these questions but ate the lunches they made for me and swam in their pools. Their houses had different feelings about them: family areas and bedrooms that seemed exclusive, displaying their abundance of folded clothes, working televisions, and neatly made beds.

Once, when I'd gone to visit Scotty, the boy across the street from us, I overheard his mother ask him if I'd used the bathroom. Later, when I came in early from the pool, I found her scrubbing out the toilet wearing long, green rubber gloves.

And was it wrong to find the thought of cleaning comforting almost fourteen years later, during my hospitalization? A nurse who comes in and disinfects everything while you lie on your back, but the dirt is in your blood and your memories?

Drip, drip, drip. The detox baths. How many have I had, waiting for the poison to sweat itself out? Pre-toxic states. Were there ever any?

And what did Rachel say the rules were? You can't be something you don't know? And who is this woman in the bathtub after the water's gone cold, afraid of the windows? She is a fugitive everyone forgot about. If there were justice, she'd be dead. Maybe she is dead, and no one's told her.

My mother was once pretty. There were a few pictures of her, unglued, stuffed between the black pages of a photo album. She hated those pictures, but she kept them. She hated everything she kept, and loved everything she lost. Her real face, the one not in the pictures, the one no one took a picture of, was lined and fissured, the skin pulled taut between poles, having and not. Her smile was pained and rare. Her love for me was my first encounter with tragedy.

'Having you was the best thing that happened to me, and the one thing I didn't deserve.' She said these things when I was young, when she could afford the generosity of emotion, applying it like a tincture, from a dropper.

She would lie in bed, holding a small hand mirror. 'You do a nice job with that makeup,' she'd say. 'I like it to look natural.' Though it was rarely natural light she would venture into. She'd stand outside in her nightgown amid the motorcycles and under the moon, smoking her Old Golds. Sometimes she couldn't stand still, and I'd watch her erratic gestures as though she were possessed, kicking pebbles and dirt in our parking lot, or wandering over the grass in the yard. I remember the record cover for *Hullabaloo* – a woman in go-go boots, navigating her way through pools of colored light. Somewhere snuffed out, beneath my mother's paste-white skin and perpetual sunglasses, the lurid sensuality of the late '60s lingered like smoke after a party.

She'd dance to Ike and Tina Turner. She loved Tina's voice, the spectacle of her and the Ikettes on television. *Do I love you, my oh my, river deep, mountain high*, she'd sing. She'd call me into the living room to join her. 'Dance with me,' she'd command over the music. She was particularly good at the funky chicken, lifting up on her toes and bending her knees inward with a strange rubbery smoothness. I learned that dance in a dream and awoke with the skill strangely acquired. When she danced with me she seemed more like an older sister. She'd wail out the lyrics of *Dust My Broom* while she cleaned the house, letting me spray the lemon-scented dust wax before she wiped it with one of my father's old T-shirts. She had red, wavy hair that she wore beneath wildly printed Peter Max scarves. She wore her eyebrows tweezed thread-thin.

She could fall into deep moods that seemed to shut the entire house in darkness. There were countless days when she wouldn't leave her bed. Her demands became frequent and excessive. I would do my best to fix her food, but she rarely ate. 'Oh, honey, just pour your mother a drink.'

She'd ask me to organize the valium in her pill case, the plastic sections embossed with the first letter of each day of the week. I remember that pill case better than most things I treasured; it was a lemon-yellow plastic and its upraised letters were like a Braille I'd run my fingers over while talking to my mother in her sunless room. I suppose keeping the pills organized that way was her ineffective attempt at controlling her intake. By midweek, there was nothing left in its finger-deep days.

Sometimes I'd slip pills from her, taking them alone and falling asleep in a neighbor's tree house. I didn't like the way they made me feel, rubbery but not like dancing.

'If I knew it was going to come to this, I would have killed myself a long time ago.' When your mother says it, there's no need to repeat it, even to think it. I tried to imagine her expectations, the impossible things that left her so defeated. I'd pore over magazines in which kitchen floors were the blue of prized marbles. I'd spread out magazines on her bed, but they did nothing to console her. Her vision of well-being was inaccessibly lodged within her, a darker room than the one into which she invited me.

There are good fears and bad fears. In the hospital I looked at my own arms against the white sheet, under the overly bright lamp, arms that seemed to reach out for fire without the normal inhibitors. I remember my father's hands on my wrists, pulling me out of sleep. I slept like the dead. I slept through the endless waking and shifting of figures in our house, bottles and bodies dropping to the floor.

The moon was still out. 'C'mon, honey, get dressed.'

'We're going on a drive and Mom's already packed your bag.' My father leaned in the doorway.

She stood beside him with a round, pink suitcase all zipped up. I was surprised to see her out of bed, not just because it was 4 A.M., but because she'd been depressed all week. Now she seemed oddly energized. I noticed the makeup on her face: eyes drawn with blue liner, and her lips a creamy orange. She walked me into the bathroom and washed my face with her violet soap.

'Your dad's got some important business to do, and I want you to keep him company. You want to borrow my headband?' She took a large brush to my hair, and I pressed my face into her breasts. She smelled of Charlie and cigarettes. But why was she treating me like a child? And why was I acting like one? I was almost fourteen.

'Try not to ask your father too many questions and don't get in any trouble while you're away,' she said firmly, detangling my hair section by section. I wondered if my father had finally decided to do something – the thing that would keep her from spending whole days in bed. Another scheme, I was certain, but I had no idea how desperate they'd become. And then I heard Jim was coming.

Jim drank too much. He punched me once when I insisted I was tough enough to take it. He didn't hold back. My arm stung and went numb, and by the next day it looked bluish where he'd done it. The thought of traveling with him depressed me.

My mother said she'd have me excused from school for the week. When my mother's mood was good, I loved her moodiness. She'd come out of her depressions as though out of prison, hungry for life, generous to the point of recklessness. I knew she would have to explain my absence from school. The last time, she took me with her when she spoke to the principal. I stood beside her, engulfed in her shadow. The principal had long since ceased to discuss my potential for learning. He was now determined not to recognize me, as though absence were my fate. My mother assured him this would be the last time. I thought she sounded as though she were pleading or trying to seduce him, and I looked away from them, embarrassed.

I'd traveled with my father before, short trips 'up and down the line.' We'd been to Georgia and Tennessee. I was too young to take much interest in whatever business he was doing. I'd wait alone in the car, sometimes for hours on end. As a reward, he'd let me drive, sitting in his lap and carefully turning the wheel while he braked and accelerated. We rarely stayed overnight in a motel. Those were particularly special events. Once we slept in the truck in the parking lot of a Motel 6. Before we left, he let me go swimming in the pool. No one was up, and I had the pool all to myself. I walked from the shallow end until I was on tiptoes, not even a third of the way to the other side. I remember just trying to float there, somewhere between shallow and deep. I wished my father were with me instead of in the truck. I would have ventured further. Instead I got out of the water, cold and without a towel. I looked at all the rooms with their drapes closed and wiped the water off my arms, shivering.

I put my feet up in the bath and adjust the knobs with them. Hot water, so I can sweat these poisons. Though there are no drugs in me now, I still run the water too hot, trying to get the blood and the memories clean. I slide down and let the water fill my ears. And I remember letting the air out of my lungs, and settling at the bottom of a hotel pool, imagining myself slipping through the grate over the drain and surfacing somewhere else altogether.

'We're off to New York,' my father said excitedly. He meant upstate. He put a dirty fingernail between his teeth when he was thinking.

Jim lived in southwest Miami, not too far from us. I was already hungry, but I didn't say anything. All the restaurants were closed. The moon was still out, and along 8th Street the trees rose up like dark arches. I opened my window and hung both arms out the window. Once I'd taken a bus with my mother to Dadeland Mall and an old Seminole Indian sat behind us in her hand-stitched skirt. I felt her touching my braids and turned around quickly to catch her at it. My mother turned too. 'Such a pretty girl,' the old lady said. 'Pretty hair.'

'You want her?' my mother asked. She was holding her compact in one hand. 'You can take her.' They both laughed.

'I want to go with her,' I pleaded.

'You see,' my mother said. 'She has no loyalty. She can't be loved enough.'

The Indian woman seemed not to understand or even to be

listening. She smiled, and her teeth were full of gold. It terrified me, and I quickly turned and grabbed my mother's arm.

Sometimes I wondered what life would have been like if she had taken me, if my mother had handed me over because the woman liked my pretty hair. And wouldn't that be lucky, to have people look at your hair, and not your eyes that won't shut up. No, your eyes always give it away. Or your arms that seem to reach out regardless of risk and are marked for it. Because you can't be loved enough, but you can be loved too little. And whenever we'd get on a bus, I imagined we'd see the lady again. And this time, I thought, I could look into her mouth.

My arms out the window: chin on one, eye cocked as though through a sight. I imagined scooping up the houses and mini-malls that flashed by; then I crumpled the shoddy architecture like pieces of newspaper. As we got closer to Jim's house, I moved toward my father, face against his plain T-shirt.

'Find a station,' he suggested, and I moved slowly over the blasts of talk and jingles. I came to a station playing Bloodrock's *DOA*, and my father held my hand still. 'I like that one.'

I remember, we were flying low and hit something in the air.

Jim's house sat behind two stunted palms and high grass, crooked awnings like poorly sewn patches. My father drove into the yard, jumped out of the truck, and made his way to the door. Jim answered, rubbing his eyes, still in his underwear. I saw the leg then for the first time without the floppy green combat fatigues covering the stump. His body seemed to end and begin there, so brutally it took the wind out of me. He carefully leaned his crutch against the doorway. I pulled my leg up on the seat and sat on my foot, staring at my own knee dropped down to nothing, but it started to hurt so I let it go.

I put my head on the dashboard and stared at the snow dome mounted there, a few drifts around the Florida water-skiers. I heard the door open then, and Jim was in beside me, laying the crutch into the truck bed.

He and my father started talking over me, Jim opening the window when I shooed away his smoke. It didn't really bother me. In fact, I'd been smoking a lot by then, lying back on my bed with that sick, spinning feeling I decided was the best part. And I could just stare at the burning end without thinking, without hearing the records skipping in the living room, the arguments that went ceaselessly on.

My father warned me not to ask about Jimmy's leg. But it was the only thing I wanted to know about. I wondered why he'd cut one pants leg short, and whether he still felt the leg in some unusual way – the way people feel ghosts. I also wondered if anyone loved him now that the leg was gone. How could they? Though I guessed he was handsome, all bashed up.

We were driving along the expressway and Jim pointed out the Coppertone sign with the little girl on the beach, a dog biting her bikini bottom and pulling it down, exposing her tan line and her butt.

'You know what to say to the dog that tries to do that to you?' my father asked.

'Shoo!' I said, laughing.

Jim said something like 'There's gonna be a lot of them dogs after you, Carrie.' He turned up the radio. 'Man,' he said, 'this song always brings me back.' Neither my father nor I asked where to. *I ain't no fortunate son.* No, of course not.

The sun was just coming up, and my father suggested we stop at Krispy Kreme Donuts. The thought of food made me happy.

My father went to the bathroom, and Jim and I sat across from each other. Dough was punched out at the top of a tall conveyor and dropped into a large vat of oil where they puffed up and floated like inner tubes until someone scooped them out. 'You sure eat slow,' he said. He wiped his mouth with a napkin and smiled at me.

'Making it last,' I answered. We both laughed, strangely intimate as though we knew some kind of secret about each other. But I knew none of his secrets, just that there was something shy in him and that he probably killed someone.

He sat close to me in the truck, and at one point I felt his hand on the back of my head, tenuously touching my hair in a way that made me want to laugh. I closed my mouth tightly and looked straight ahead. I didn't move an inch. We drove for hours that way.

'Too bad you never tasted combat.' Jim reached over me and lightly punched my father's arm. 'You're one lucky bastard.' You could tell Jim didn't think my father was really lucky. He was lucky like those Washington people, like everyone who watched the war on the nightly news. Fortunate, like everyone the song indicted. My father didn't respond right away.

Finally he said, 'If you think being locked up is some kind of vacation, I probably shouldn't be doing this with you. If you think prison was the lucky break that kept me out of Vietnam, I'll just turn this truck back around and drop you off and that'll be that.' I always felt mad when my father mentioned prison; he'd first disappeared when I was eight years old. I expected he'd go back; it made my attachment to him fretful and melancholy. We all sat silent. After a while, I reached over and touched Jim's hand with my own. I don't know why I did it – it was like prodding an animal, just to see it move. I didn't touch my father because I knew that when he was in a mood he didn't want anyone to take him out of it.

Jim looked at me and smiled real briefly, so my father wouldn't see. And I remember feeling both amazed and proud of the fact that I could shift that darkness in him, if only for a minute. Then I felt guilty that I couldn't change my father, and hadn't tried.

We stayed in Georgia, then in New York, in dirty motels without pools. In Georgia, my father and I shared a bed with a burned, brown comforter. The room had beige walls, swirls of plaster, and cockroaches so bad we had to keep the light on while we slept.

That night must have begun something inside me, something like a romance with my father, whom I gazed at in that sickly yellow cast as though he were already lost to sepia. His arms had tattoos the color of blueberry stains, some as indecipherable. When I pressed my head to my sleeping father's armpit, I felt a surge of shame and excitement. He didn't wake, and I clung to him long enough to watch the cockroaches adjust to the light and move out over the carpet.

What can I say? You get accustomed to dirty rooms, and the covers fold like your father's arm over you, and you can stop your heart from racing. Just for a while, you can relax when you think it can't get worse than this. If I ask myself now what Victor offered me, I'd say that kind of peace. The deep sleep after trauma. The comfort in knowing you'd seen the war, and it couldn't get worse.

In another motel we stayed at, my father knew the man in the cashier's cage. The man had a face the color and texture of handled dough, a red mustache and green eyes. He wore a black hat, an opened black shirt and heavy gold chains, an Italian horn. His name was Tony. He came out of the cage to hug my father, and I noticed his fat freckled hand striking my father's back while they embraced. They talked a little before I noticed Tony's eyes, drifting, unfocused. He walked us down a hallway. This room was smaller than any room we'd stayed in, with no curtains and a punched-in screen on the window. Outside the window was a small pebbled alley, about as wide as an air chute, littered with trash. I hated that room. It smelled like salami and stale cigarettes.

Jim slept in the room next to us. I heard him breathing with my ear against the rough wall. He taught me Morse code. He said that two knocks on the wall meant 'You're pretty.' He did it a couple of times, then stopped. But I kept listening.

Later that night I heard a knock on the door. I pretended to sleep. My father and Jim whispered through the chain on the door, then Jim came into the room. My father took a syringe from him and began tapping the top of his own hand. Jim held a spoon over a lighter. I was squirming in bed watching my father move the point in and out of the top of his hand. 'It's like alligator skin,' he complained. I remembered our alligator in a mason jar, and how my father and his friends had filled it with whiskey one night. Even squeezing my eyes closed wouldn't make the picture go away. I moaned and turned my face into the pillow. My father said, 'Honey, it's all right. Daddy has to make himself well. You just lie there and keep your eyes shut.' When I opened my eyes again, Jim was putting the syringe into a large vein in my father's neck. I saw the color drain out of him. His eyes went reptile.

There are good fears and bad fears, good starts and bad ones. I knew I was afraid of these things the way others were, the way I was supposed to be. What I didn't know was the part of me these sights awakened, older, without fear, almost without feeling, except, perhaps, sexual feelings. The fat freckled fingers of Tony, the explosion of blood in the syringe, the smell of my father in these crummy rooms – against these I held my legs firmly together, the images locked inside me, not in my head. That night, flecks of snow came in through the hole in the window screen, the alley filled up with a dazzling white blanket of snow, and my father's hands, callused and heavy, marked by these intricate pricks, ran up and down my arms until I'd fallen asleep.

In the morning it was Jim who woke me, tapping lightly on the door. 'He's asleep,' I said, letting him in. Jim sat quietly on the bed beside me. He put his hand behind my neck, and I felt a chill pass through me. 'Hold still,' he said. I looked at his face and saw his whistling tooth, his kind but somehow vacant eyes. His hand went under my T-shirt and over my back, not like my father's, but pulling at the skin, and then up under my arms and to my breasts. I thought I had to pee, but I didn't dare move. Behind us, my father remained sleeping, sound as the dead.

Jim became more insistent, breathing close in my ear and moving one hand down between my legs. I watched it there as though it were detached and almost funny, working at the buttons of my shorts. 'Come into my room,' he whispered hoarsely. That's when I began to feel dizzy, my heart jumping the way it some-times would when I raised my hand in class. A wrong answer. So I didn't answer, I followed.

He lifted up his shirt. A thin line of golden hair ran up the center of his chest and spread out under his collarbones. We were on his bed, identical to the one my father slept in. He laid back on the bed and unbuttoned his pants, pushing them down just to the point where his leg ended. His penis was stiff and pliant as a diving board, and with one hand he'd press it forward and watch it spring back.

He said, 'Just put your mouth on it.'

As a little girl, able to press my face to the hearts of most full-grown men, I noticed detail a lot, and details excited me – the hair on men's chests that often smelled sweeter than you'd expect, the hair on their hands that took hold of mine, the heavy gold flexible watchbands and forearm tattoos of my father's friends. I thought of the girl eating the flowers, the impulse to put beautiful things into your mouth. I thought of my mouth full of the fingers of my father's friends.

I listened to Jim coaxing me. I felt his hand on the back of my head, suddenly not coarse at all. A desire that had rolled around in me now came open. This thing we'd talked about, worried over, behind portables at school – sex – it was like I had done it long before, knew it like my bedroom, my private drawers.

'Take your shorts off,' he said, letting his own pants fall to the floor.

I got real still and looked over his shoulder at the lampshade, wrapped in plastic like a shower cap. Scrub nurse, dirty room.

The leg was oddly transfixing, shaped long like a breadfruit with a bone in it. I wondered what it was like to live with an absence like that, and whether it always made him think of the war. It made me think of television, horror shows you watch through the spaces between your fingers.

He looked at me, then. He hopped around the side of the bed, and at that point I laughed aloud. He was like a strange Easter bunny delivering this carrot.

'What the fuck are you laughing about?' he asked, falling down beside me. He didn't want to know what I laughed at. I couldn't have told him then, the way I could now. Knowing laughter. That's what they call it. Knowing, helpless laughter.

I felt his fingers inside me, so different from the way I did it when I was alone. He crawled on top of me, and I felt him pushing his penis between my legs. Though this was something I wanted, I felt paralyzed by the pain of it, the bluntness of the act. I felt I'd done something wrong by laughing at him, so I didn't dare scream.

On and on, but I continued to nod my head yes when he asked if I liked it. My whole body shook with pain; I feared biting my lip because I thought I'd hurt myself. I spread out under the pain like a map, him striking impossibly at me. But I also thought I enclosed him somehow, contained him. That's why the blood startled me – coming back to my own body when Jim raised himself from it.

'It'll be better for you next time,' he said.

'Uh-huh,' I answered, moving away from the stain on the brown comforter.

'I'll clean up in here. You go wash up in the bathroom.'

I walked in and closed the door behind me. I took a washcloth and blotted at my thighs. An emptiness kept creeping in, as though a part of me was being pulled out of the room by the fan above the mirror. It wasn't a sadness you cry about, so I didn't. It's strange, but I thought more about my father than I did about Jim, his blood and my blood, the secrets we'd made of it. And I think I may have thought myself a woman then, because that was what the sex thing was about. But it was also something that tied me to my mother – a disappointment that sounded wrong if you talked about it, like you'd gone crazy on pills. A bigger part of me wanted to pretend it hadn't happened, so Jim and I could go swimming sometime and there wouldn't be any embarrassment between us. Banish embarrassment, be cautious with care.

My father tiled our bathroom floor just after he got out of prison. Gold-sparkling pink and white tiles swimming in grout. They were small tiles, designed really for sink tops rather than floors. I would take off my clothes and lie on them, the roughness of the grout interrupted by the cold smoothness of the tiles. I imagined it like a grotto: the sound of water running into the bathtub and the moisture between the tiles. I looked at Titian's *The Bacchanal* and Bosch's *The Garden of Earthly Delights*. Otherworldly nakedness. I'd look at the impressions the tiles left on my back, large scales, a new kind of skin.

I left Jim's bathroom reluctantly. I wanted to lie down in there, but there was water on the floor, and I wasn't sure if it was from the washcloth or if it was coming from the bottom of the toilet.

'It's been a long time, baby doll,' Jim said as I got into bed beside him. I wondered how long, but didn't ask. Since he'd lost his leg? The war settled between us, silent, evacuated, as I nuzzled him, lips grazing his neck. I wanted him for the tragedy he lived, and the tragedy his silence attempted to protect me from. I loved the obviousness of his secrets, his determined loneliness. 'You know you can't mention this to your father,' he said. I felt certain and confident around this secret – that as long as I held it, it would continue to shape us both. 'Of course,' I answered.

'You should go back,' he said, pulling a cigarette from the pocket of his fatigues.

I looked at my father. He'd turned over in sleep and had both palms up. By going into Jim's room, I felt I'd lost my place in this one. I couldn't rejoin him on the bed – it looked so small, and he looked smaller on it.

I left the room and wandered up and down the halls until I came upon the ice machine buzzing quietly under the stairs. I put my hands in and kept them there. I pulled them out blue and wet and tingly. Then I shoved them back in and kept them there until they went so numb my eyes watered.

I think of stepping out of the bath, but feel suddenly exhausted, as though the tub were filled with lead. I stare ahead at the faucets, at the peeling paint near the molding, and remember the apartment I shared with Victor: a stark bathroom, fluorescent light annihilating its surfaces.

'You're too cold,' he said.

'I can't do this! I have no veins!' I threw the syringe and heard it skitter on the floor. He picked it up and held it between two fingers. 'Take a hot bath,' he said, 'and you'll see your veins come up.'

He sounded so reassuring. I looked into his eyes and knew he could take care of me, even if I sometimes worried how we could possibly go on with even our bodies as adversaries.

Jim and my father left me under the orange awning outside the motel's cramped lobby. I walked the full length of the motel looking into windows and doors left ajar. There was a foreign family in one room, all of them packing with a spirit at once chaotic and unified. Through another window I saw a woman stretched out over her perfectly made bed, staring intensely at the ceiling, her arms stretched over her head as though on a rack. Waiting is like that, and you hear the gears going *click, click, click*.

There was nowhere to go around the motel. Beyond the parking lot, with its two chained dumpsters, there was only a road through some trees that connected to the highway. The only food available to guests was a restaurant a couple of miles away, or the vending machines that had cans of ravioli, hot coffee. In the lobby was nothing but the cashier's booth and a television flickering behind the counter. The man behind the counter did not want to talk to me. He had a thin mustache, spit when he talked. 'Go play in traffic,' he said. Very funny, I muttered. I stood there waiting until he said, 'Go away now.'

I went back to our room. I thought of Jim and stretched out on the bed much like the lady I'd seen in the other cell. I rolled my head on the pillow, listening to the air rushing in my ear as it changed with my movement. My father once told me you could hear the ocean in the sound of a conch shell. I wondered what sound I was hearing in the pillow. Perhaps it was the sound of the secret Jim and I kept, or the ones belonging to the people past and present who'd slept in these beds, stepping over doorways and into each other's private universes. I fell asleep that way, as I often did, with my thoughts thrown out like a net, too wide to gather anything but the shadows crawling over the room, the indistinct sounds from the other side of the wall.

'Look at your arms,' the nurse said. 'Why would you want to go and hurt yourself like that?'

'I didn't know I was hurting myself.'

And a long bath brings these things up, deep channels, canals where the trash flows on the surface.

My father woke me up. Jim stood discreetly in the doorway behind him. They were amped up. The air around them was like cellophane.

'C'mon, we're going now.'

I noticed it was dark outside the screen window, the room cold enough to make my father's teeth chatter. I rubbed my own arms, looking for the suitcase my mother had packed with a flowered windbreaker. When I caught Jim's eye, my arms seemed suddenly not mine, hard plastic like a doll's. He appeared to waver on a shore of regret — impossible not to share it, it came between us cold and impassable as a frozen lake, his eyes bluer in its reflection. I put the windbreaker on and snapped it up with an attention that gave us both a momentary respite from each other.

Jim was talking excitedly to my father while I gathered my things. He'd figured it out, he said; he did the numbers. The heroin could net them 30,000 dollars. *Real money*, that's what Jim called it. Then he burst out laughing.

That's when my father decided to get the monkey.

The monkey belonged to Jim's ex-girlfriend; she'd had him for some time and couldn't find anyone to take him off her hands. She also lived in southwest Miami, but a part that was barely developed.

'Monkeys are just like little kids,' my father said. 'And this one's supposed to be real friendly and smart.'

Jim said, 'I don't like pets that mimic me.'

My father talked about understanding the monkey mind. The thought of that money had him imagining a kingdom of needy animals over which he would preside. 'Maybe we'll start up our own farm for animals people don't want anymore.'

There was a sign outside the Quality Inn boasting its swimming pool, color TV, and air conditioning. We had another two days of driving ahead of us.

There were curtains that ran from the tops of the windows to just above the carpet. When I pulled the cord I could see the pool, glinting with the last pink rays of sunlight. No one was swimming.

My father was stretched out on his bed, hands behind the back of his head.

'Want to sit with me?' he asked. I sat beside him. 'Do you like it here?'

I looked around the room. The other bed was perfectly made, not a wrinkle in the beige coverlet. 'What's that?' I asked, already getting up to investigate. 'Glasses wrapped in paper,' I said, laughing. 'We should wrap our cups at home, just when company comes over.'

'Maybe we'll take more trips, just you, your mother, and me.'

'Can Jim come?'

'Sure, if you want.'

I nodded, rejoined him on the bed. 'Can you grab that bag for me, baby?' I pulled his suitcase up between us. From a side pocket he withdrew a small zippered pouch. 'You going swimming?'

'Will you come?'

He was already making his way to the bathroom, pouch in hand. By that time, I knew what he was going to do. 'Don't do that,' I whispered. 'Please.'

'Don't worry about me,' he said, turning for a moment in the doorway. 'I'll meet you later.' He ran a hand down my cheek and closed the door between us.

I went to my bag and opened it despondently. The world that occupied my father in the locked bathroom felt like it had dismantled itself and floated off, leaving me in this strange bedroom with its unmarked surfaces and sterile glasses. I pulled out the bathing suit my mother had packed for me, and immediately went to the door that connected Jim's room to ours. I knocked on it furiously until he answered.

'Where's your dad?' he asked.

'In the bathroom,' I said miserably. 'Again.'

'You want to change in here?'

I walked through the door and put my face against his chest.

'Not now,' he said, moving away just slightly. I felt *now* pressing on my heart like a heavy, flat stone. I felt the air go out of my lungs. My face reddened; I felt lifted, somehow, from a special place I'd occupied, unsure of what I'd been replaced by. *Go play in traffic, take a long walk off a short pier . . .*

Neither Jim nor my father came down to the pool that night. After an hour, I walked up the stairs, let myself in. My father was still in the bathroom. When I knocked on the door, he told me to be quiet and go away. Jim didn't hear the quiet tapping I did on his door; the faint Morse code I'd made said *I'm drowning*. I slept by the pool that night. I imagined the lounge chair settling over the drain, held by the quiet pressure of the water. A wind came up, and it was suddenly much colder. I could see mountains between the buildings. I snuggled deeper into my blankets, holding them around me.

'You don't trust me,' Vic said. 'You're all fucked up about love. You always think I'm going to take it back, won't give you enough.'

And I sat there shivering. 'No, I don't,' I said. 'I don't think that.'

But things just run out, no matter how much you've got in your supply. No matter how careful you are to make it last. You always use it up too soon.

And then the nurse said, 'C'mon on, honey, it's time for your methadone,' and my cells flowered like open traps.

We drove into Miami in the late afternoon and pulled up to a house sitting off a dirt road. The place had high grass out front and blankets tacked over the windows. There were two cars pulled along the side of the house. We all got out of the truck and made our way to the door. A woman answered. She pulled the hair from her face with one hand. She had the look of an old sharecropper; her face was bony and tired looking. Jim got out of the truck with his crutches. He didn't kiss her, which I'd prepared for. He stood before her, appraising her silently.

'We're here for the monkey,' my father said.

'He's inside,' she said with some relief. She shuffled deeper into the house. People lounged around on threadbare couches near tilting shelves of dusty figurines; those little dwarfed figures looked like they belonged to a Dutch family – something that you might find boxed in the back of someone's garage – and the greasy film over their ceramic surfaces made you not want to touch them or lift them from the shelves. *Let It Bleed* was playing on the turntable through one crackling speaker; there was no talk between the stoned zombies also tilted on the couch.

The woman walked us toward the kitchen, where flames shot straight up from the burners with nothing on the stove. 'God damn it!' she hollered. 'You guys are gonna burn this fucking place down.' I saw the vomit in the sink then, and the woman casually turned the water on it, which made it more pungent.

'Shit, this place stinks to hell,' Jim said.

She turned on him, vehement. 'What the fuck do you want from me, Jim? Lay the hell off.'

She walked past him and lifted a blanket off a baby crib. The crib was wrapped with chicken wire, and inside sat the monkey. Upon seeing us, he leaped to the wire.

'He's a capuchin,' she said, rubbing her nose as though the accumulated stench of the place had finally found its way to her brain. 'His name is Puchi,' and her voice affected a sweetness that sounded unnatural and lewd.

My father squatted down and extended a finger. The monkey's hand reached out through a hole he'd opened in the wire and grasped it.

'He's pretty friendly,' she said, offering her halfhearted sales pitch as though reading it from the back of a card. 'I'll tell you right off, he's not easy to keep. I don't want you bringing him back here next week.'

The monkey's eyes were round and as expressive as a baby's. They appeared almost liquid. But his hairless pink face had the wrinkles of someone old. He had patchy brown fur that didn't look soft, and on the sides of his face two sweeps of yellow hair. With one hand he appeared to pull fleas from his belly. He had a ring tail with sparse hair like a tethered rope. His teeth were sharp and yellow. I could not tell if he was menacing or smiling. If he was like a baby, none of us were close to being a mother.

We took him anyway. My father got him up on his back, and the monkey's tail curled tight around his neck like a choker. The zombies on the couch began to move when they saw my father walking him out. 'Hey, where you takin' him?' one asked. A woman stretched over her chair said, 'That's my baby. They're takin' my baby.' Their voices were weak, emptied out. The bulky furniture of that dark house seemed to have some hold on them. They couldn't rise.

Jim's ex-girlfriend walked out to the truck, a little unwillingly. She looked nervously around, though there was nothing moving down the main road and no neighbors nearby. She held her hand like a visor over her eyes, and I noticed the ghostly green disks barely marked by pupils.

'Are we gonna do this, or what?' she asked my father impatiently.

'Hold on,' Jim said with derision. He hated her. I could see it.

My father pulled a smaller case from his large duffel. He opened it on the front seat of the truck, and I noticed the powder-filled bag he'd already weighed out. He picked it up and pressed it into the woman's hand. She looked at me inquisitively, then turned on her heels and started quickly toward the front door. She called out, 'Remember, no returns.'

The monkey was still on my father's back, combing through his hair with black fingers. Seeing him that way made me suddenly want to touch him. Outside of the house, I could almost imagine him adjusted, flourishing in the light, the green of trees in the periphery. I took his hand in mine, my father bending at the knees so he could move from his shoulders to mine.

'I love him,' I said as he took hold of my neck for the first time. It was love mixed with sympathy, and it seemed to color the vast, blank sky a darkening blue.

I step out of the bath and wrap a towel around myself. Check the mirror. I think: How many sleeping pills will it take me to fall asleep, make my mind a blank? But I don't do that anymore. Tea. I'll make tea. And if I had ironing to do, I'd do that too. Pushing back and forth, and your mind just emptying out. And the Iowa night is flecked with white, like the dust of disintegrating stars. It's like the heavens were grinding the stars down, like the bones of some poor animal.

The monkey mind sees blankets, darkness thrown over a cage. False nights that last days. Hands, big and small. The big hands pinpricked, trembling. The small hands greedy, touching you in good places, then withdrawing. A bowl of beer. The green of a screened-in porch. Behind that – real trees, real wind, real night. All of this withdrawing. Close up there are scabbed faces, beards, pupils wide as saucers or small as fleas. Laughter, screaming, muffled through the fabric. Old bananas, black skins. Patches that are wounds. Chicken wire wound around a baby's bed.

Under the bridge I pulled a boy's penis from a pair of shorts, and with a curious impulse took it into my mouth. The boy had raspberry skin: pimply and lightly haired. He wore gym shorts with the junior high school eagle ironed on them. Underneath the eagle, a yellow box where he'd marked in his last name. For a long time I remembered the name. There had been no courtship, no first kiss or invitation to the school dance. I'd simply heard him sliding down the rocky side of the embankment, then saw him squinting into the darkness under the bridge where I'd been lighting matches and throwing them into the canal. I said, 'It's nice down here.'

At home there were parties all the time. Usually just my father's friends, men I'd known since I was a baby. I used to sit on Ernie's lap, play with Donald's watchband. His arm held me as firmly as a padded carnival seat. But the ride had changed. The drop deepened; the earth seemed to fall away at greater lengths.

My father brought out Patches like a mascot, like the ram they trotted out at football games, saddled with a banner, fearing the crowd. Easier not to think my pet too much alive. Patches – for the wounds he gave himself. *Why would you want to hurt yourself like that?* The nurse was so caring, and so disgusted.

They taunted him until he'd bite, then shove him back in the crib and cover it. My pleading didn't help when they were at that point. I could hear Patches scream. It was a terrible, raging scream. It was inside me. I held two rocks in my hand, about the same weight and the same size. Crush a skull, or write the words *Fuck, Fuck, Fuck* over the sidewalk in front of our house.

At one party, Jim and I talked in my room. He seemed nervous and stood by the door. I sat on the bed.

'You can come in,' I said.

'I'm in.' He didn't move.

'I still think about you,' I said. Breathless girl, catch your breath.

'Try not to.' Then whispering, 'It wasn't right what we did. We can't—'

I just sat there, facing him. I remembered how he treated his ex-girlfriend, never acknowledged her. I felt no pity for her. She was messed up, no good. But I wondered if I wasn't like her, whether he saw me older and changed. Because I had changed, my body alive with needs, so I did things I didn't dare talk about. My face was still pink when Jim left the room, as though burned by a hot, bright light.

I reached beneath the bed and withdrew a cigar box my father gave me. I removed the things I'd saved from our trip up north. I took the matches and coasters, drink umbrellas, hotel soap, and laid them on my bed. I stared at the image of ochre-painted judges on the lid of the box. Who were these men in historical gowns? I imagined them the arbiters of the memories I would keep or abandon. I would purge these memories of Jim, of the trip we'd made, and the judges would make it final.

It was my mother who'd suggested only special things be chosen for the box, items somehow steeped in nascent recollection. The box allowed each item to seem distilled and essential, plucked from the flow of life and weighted against the rest. I kept these tokens in darkness beneath my bed. At night, I imagined the items I'd saved lifted from the box and floating before me, a dream I'd configured.

I later learned the power of removing items. These were star deaths in my personal constellation. Anything loved could also be excised. I followed my mother's example. Her boxes were pill-boxes, and each pill – counted, cherished, anticipated, and consumed – helped her love and forget. The judges were silent.

I gave the apartment keys to Victor. He looked down at them, back at me. So much gratitude in his eyes. I thought: He's not a client anymore and it doesn't matter so long as I can still help him. He can take every last thing. And he did. But he didn't leave, even though he was ashamed. 'It was the drugs,' he said, after he sold my television. I forgave him. He had a beautiful, almost religious expression of defeat on his face.

I smoked cigarettes with other girls behind the portables and had some minor popularity for a while based on a kind of fearlessness and worldliness I had about drugs. I spun tales about my relationship with a Vietnam vet. He had both legs, and loved me too much. I had a world of charms in my purse: makeups that I applied in the school bathroom, a wide brush for blushes that made my cheeks look sore.

I carried groceries, mostly desserts, beers, and medicines, home to my mother. I took over lawn work, cutting away weeds, gathering rotting fruit from our backyard and dropping it into a trash bag. I came home from school at 3 P.M. and sat in a folding chair in the yard, face to the sun. I punched the big plastic buttons on my Panasonic tape recorder, listening to my father's cassettes. I poured peroxide in my hair and watched it lighten in a hand mirror I laid in the grass. I got as much sunlight as I could, but then I'd have to go inside. Just my mother sitting quietly in the dark. If I confronted her, she'd say: 'I'm happy, baby. For the first time in a long time, I'm really happy.' And years later, I was still nagged by how resolute she was in that happiness, like someone grateful for a terrible accident.

She had that spellbound look of all my father's friends, as though life had just sped up. Everything around her was the same, but now she looked at everything as though it had lifted off the floor and begun to spin. She had the strange tics and sleepwalking movements of my father's friends, their bland justifications, their forgetfulness. She was hardened but also thin-skinned. I called her 'mother' now, and the word would stiffen on my breath.

'I'm failing school,' I'd tell her. 'I'm leaving you.'

I'd changed, my face burned and lined like a survivor on a raft. The worldliness that had won me meager respect with the girls at school now seemed otherworldly. It was rumored I'd tried to commit suicide.

On the contrary, I tried to live.

Our first day together was after we'd been close in dreams, after we'd shared hell and heaven and all the places in between . . .

I was singing along with Carly Simon when I saw a police car pull up by our backyard gate. I quickly shut off the tape and made my way over to the officer.

'I just wanted to ask you a few questions,' he said. He wore reflective sunglasses.

'How long has your dad been away?' He seemed nervous asking me.

'For a week.' I was rubbing in the tanning cream, squinting up at him.

'Did he leave with anyone?'

'His friend Jim.' It was that simple – talking to the cop – but I never told anyone about it.

Victor is calm. It's a calm I know can precede anything, but surely it precedes something. 'You keep your mouth shut about this,' he tells me again. 'I did this for us, so we'd have the money. If you say

anything about this, I'll make sure no one can identify your body.'
He says this as he opens my shirt.

The room was hot with bodies, pressed close over matches and
cookers. They didn't drink much these days, and I was glad about
that. I got tired of picking up their bottles, dragging out hundred-
pound bags to the curb. I stopped going to school and took the
time to reinforce the patio screen with chicken wire from the shed
so Patches could come out of his crib. They never used the patio
anymore. And with those few extra feet of space, Patches became
wild again. Even my father was afraid of him, so he became my
responsibility. Despite his fearful presence, I pitied him. He was
covered in large, infected wounds and wouldn't let himself be
touched or bandaged. When he escaped the first time, I felt happy
for him. I hoped we wouldn't find him. But a neighbor appeared
at the door in the middle of the night, unshaven, clad only in a
night robe, and clearly dismayed. 'I think that's your monkey
making all that racket.' He pointed down the street, and there was
Patches perched on top of the STOP sign at the end of the block,
banging it wildly as if disseminating an important message.

Once out, it was harder to keep him. Like the old expression,
give an inch. If I opened the patio screen door, he flew at it with
the force of a grown man. My visits to the school nurse were
always for bites; they were deep and slow to heal. 'Carrie,' the
nurse said disconsolately, 'most people get rid of pets they can't
control.' But we weren't most people, and she seemed to know
that. My mother would threaten to have Patches put to sleep, but
by this time she offered no real threat. Her involvement with the
world went no further than the tip of her tongue. She lived as if by
a dropper.

My father weakly feigned affection for the monkey, as though it
were a crucial choice he'd made and had to stick by. But his
presence seemed to alarm Patches; and I was always called to
intervene.

But I wasn't called that last night; the police were. Patches made
his way out of the screen and was high up in the neighbors' tree.

Both husband and wife were in their mid-fifties and childless. Their faces were like small, hard apples.

It was close to midnight and Patches must have awakened them. I could imagine the old lady looking out her bathroom window and seeing that face – so human, so horrible – and hollering and falling back as though it were her own reflection. Her husband had a broom that he was swatting the lower branches with. She came to our door spluttering with anger.

'You've got to come now!' She said this as though trying to wake my mother. 'Your monkey's escaped again.'

I quickly ran to lower the music. My mother stood on the porch, speaking in her slowed, slurred, unconcerned way. 'Honey,' she finally hollered, 'Patches is out again.'

My father went out shirtless, sweating. He'd been up for the past few days on methamphetamine. He'd started to walk funny. Sometimes he heard voices and he'd tell everyone to quiet down. They were little voices, he said, in the walls and under the house. But usually he could be talked out of it, though you always sensed he was still hearing them, just not telling anyone.

The old lady looked him over in dread. With no shirt on, you could see the mess he'd made of his arms. His body was thinned down, so his muscles looked like little knots. He was stammering, attempting to placate her, which seemed to make her more bewildered and disturbed than she'd been. And he'd begun to smell as strongly as Patches. He said he didn't like the way water felt on his skin.

'I'll just go over and get him. Carrie, you better come too.' I could see he was apprehensive. The monkey had turned on him. Everyone had turned on him.

I followed behind them, surprised to see so many of the neighbors out, as though there'd been a fire. The old man was making such a ruckus; he'd turned on some floodlights over his garage and now the whole scene looked like a movie. I stopped walking when I started to see what the others saw. My father looked stiff and babbling in the light. He was screaming, 'Shut those fucking things off,' but the old man stood there with his hands crossed over his chest, his wife beside him.

'C'mon down, Patches!' my father hollered. He seemed incapable of standing still, turning strangely on one foot, the other behind his calf. 'C'mon,' he was pleading, now more to himself than the monkey. I wanted to intervene but I was scared. I felt the outrage, the disgust of the people around him. I wanted to cry, but I didn't. I felt my face going red and realized I'd been holding my breath. I saw the police car moving slowly down the block, casually, as though they did not want to interrupt this community forum. I heard the voices of the neighbors, tiny voices, muffled and conspiratorial. Two police officers walked to either side of my father. 'Are you intoxicated?' one asked.

That's when Patches fled. We heard the rustle of leaves and saw him moving off to another tree, and another. The police made no effort to follow his movements. 'Sooner or later he'll grab one of those telephone lines and that'll be the end of him.'

The police asked to look through our house, and, as though my father had forgotten what he'd hidden away there, he complied. I sat scowling on my bed as they disrupted my room, opened my cigar box, my busted dresser. The smaller officer had pale skin and black, wavy hair. He talked kindly to me while the other searched. His questions bothered me, though. 'Has your father's behavior seemed unusual to you?' he asked.

I kept wondering what he was trying to know about me. Had I been damaged in some critical way? 'Other people think so,' I answered. But when I thought of the neighbors, I thought, no. Nothing *so* unusual.

This is what I'd say to Hannah: *Why do some survive and some don't? I don't know. Why do some that could survive just let go and stop trying? I don't know. But there's a trick to living, and you only learn it after you've done it.*

3

Faith might be a good neighbor and hang fruit over the fence but something else was needed to wield the arsenic spray.

Janet Frame, Faces in the Water

'I shouldn't have called,' I say, cradling the phone while I light a cigarette. 'I thought maybe we could get a coffee. I was just sitting here, and I realized I wasn't thinking of anything at all.'

'You must have thought of me,' she says. 'That's kind.'

I want to tell her it has nothing to do with casework. It's not kindness, my calling her.

'How's your apartment?' I ask. *These walls talk, conspire . . .*

She hesitates for a moment. 'It's hard to come back here. I can't tell you how many times I've reminded myself, "You're not crazy anymore. You can do this." But I feel like a ghost here, like I died and I have a few moments to come back and inspect my things. I can't bring myself to touch anything yet. Do you think that's strange?'

'No,' I say. I look straight ahead and see a picture of my mother – the only one I've got – and she's standing by the tarred stump of our orange tree, a glass in her hand, and sunglasses shielding her eyes.

'Do you want to get out for a little while?'

'Yes,' she says. 'I don't care where we go.'

Hannah lives above a bakeshop in town, and she stands waiting for me in front of its humid glass. I smell the sugar when I crack my window. She is wearing a blue bomber jacket and a rabbit fur hat. Her hands are crammed into her pockets, and she's bent forward, braced against the wind. She runs around the car and ducks inside, quickly taking off her hat and muffler. She smiles, and it seems tinged with condolence, as though she knows what compelled me to call her in the first place.

'Thanks for the cookies, by the way.'

'Oh, it was nothing. I have an idea,' she says, 'about where we can go.'

I look over at her just in time to see something mischievous in her expression.

For a while, she gives directions and we do very little talking. She has a confidence I didn't recognize in the office. *If some of those caseworkers got out with their clients, they'd find someone wholly different from the person they counsel, and they would shut up with all of their suggestions.* But it makes me uneasy, too, the way things change – people change – when there is no structure.

'There,' she points. There is nothing but plowed-up and frozen ground. It's the vast construction site for the new mall coming in. The winter has been so bad there's little work done. The area is a rough, glassy white.

'Let's get out here,' she says. 'Can I take this blanket?'

'Sure.' It's King's blanket, but that's fine.

I follow her. It's barren and slippery in spots, so we walk cautiously, every so often reaching for each other's arm. It's silent, but not like the inside of my apartment. Inside and outside silences are different. She stops at a massive crane, and without a moment's thought pulls herself up over its wheel and opens the door of the cabin. She puts the blanket down and reaches out a hand to me, pulls me up. 'It can get a little cold in here,' she says, sliding into the driver's seat. 'But we can put this blanket over our legs.'

I close the door behind me. From the frozen windshield, and from this high up, we can see out over the entire lot, and it looks like a calm ocean, frozen still. She turns to face me. 'What do you think? I come here sometimes just to get away. I fell asleep in here one night when it wasn't this cold.'

'It's comfortable,' I say. 'Should I get my tape recorder?' I feel suddenly excited about it. 'We should have music now, the right music.'

I wander back to the car and pull my tape player from the front seat, and *Dusty in Memphis* from the glove compartment. It's cued to my favorite song, *No Easy Way Down*. It was my mother's favorite and now it's mine. The small light in the roof of the car reminds me of when I lived in it. Of course I could fall asleep in that crane. I used to sleep on the side of the road in this car, a blue tarp pulled over me for camouflage. I could do anything, just not again. The car light illuminated the last veins, the new scars. And the maps I could barely hold, too high to trace a line, follow a course. Florida is there. San Francisco is there. And I am somewhere here. Yes, right here. Florida was gauze and heat, canals, slime, bloodsuckers and palmettos, displaced Indians and patriotic Cubans, mini-malls, and prisons. Bloodsuckers. And San Francisco. What was San Francisco? Runaways. And Asian pharmacists who look at you sadly when you buy your syringes and make you sign in their books because you haven't a diabetic card. Yes, their faces are expressive. Even if they don't say a word to you. And San Francisco was casework, both sides of the desk. Isn't there an expression: both sides of the law? The law of care. The bureaucracy of care. But I'm here now. Iowa. No different from Idaho for a lot of people. The *I* states.

I slam the door and the light goes out.

Now I hear my feet crunching over the ice. I see her profile high up in the crane. She can sit perfectly still. She has a sad type of beauty, so that you want to give her something. But then you suspect it won't reach her, so you can only just take her as she is. Faces like hers, there's a kind of determination about them. But it isn't a hard face, just not completely open.

And I suppose there's something of Janine's face in the way she holds her chin out, as though she has to be stoical even when she's alone. She has to stand up to her own thoughts.

I climb into the cabin and put the tape recorder between us, and the music gives our perch a lonelier, alien cast.

'I love this tape,' Hannah says, turning the cassette cover in her hands. 'I didn't know you liked Dusty Springfield. Her voice is so cool, and her emotions so raw.'

Now you're standing alone, and the past is unknown, and there is no easy way down.

'I like music that helps me feel. I don't always experience my feelings until it's too late – when the circumstances have changed and the feelings no longer seem true.'

'I always assume if I feel something, it's true,' Hannah says.

'Yeah, and I'll bet you met a lot of people in the hospital who were as certain as you.' The moment I say it, I'm sorry. She sits quietly thinking about it, or the way my voice changed when I said it, like I was trying to protect something. My own certainty.

'All I know,' I say, 'is that if I trusted my feelings I'd still be living the way I did. Everything in me told me there weren't any options, and there was no reason to move on. I knew my life could always get worse, but it was certainly as bad as I could take. So I changed. I got in my car and I drove here, despite myself. I just put all those feelings on hold.'

'I haven't changed, Carrie. That's *my* problem.' Hannah's eyes flash, trapped and guarded.

'I somehow doubt you'd be the best judge of that' – talking like a caseworker again.

'But if I can't see it, it isn't worth anything, is it?' she asks.

Her question startles me. It is so full of resignation, like a prayer no one should overhear. And yet I know it from inside, a place you can find for yourself where nothing is available. *Perfectly smooth walls mirror-smooth.*

'I guess that's where faith comes in. I mean, there's a reason why the most damaged find comfort in it.'

'Maybe I'm just not damaged enough,' she says. 'It brings me no comfort. But then again, maybe I'm not the best judge of how damaged I am.' She laughs, a brittle, broken sound. Then abruptly turning her body to face me; 'So what's your story? What makes a smart, pretty woman get in her car and drive to the middle of nowhere?'

You don't need to tell your story to get theirs . . .

'I guess I've been running for a long time,' I say, 'looking for a place where there's no emergencies. Everything would just get burned up, so I looked for a place where there wasn't a fire. It's not like I had any great expectations when I came here. My family weren't exactly planners. In fact, my home was one of the first things that just kind of dissolved. I wasn't really a runaway; there was just nothing to go back to. I celebrated my sixteenth birthday in an outreach office for troubled teens. That was like 1976. I hitchhiked to San Francisco and arrived penniless. I didn't know a soul. And I was hungry. Hungry and wet, because it was pouring out. My father was in jail – he still is – and my mother is an addict. So that's how I had my first taste of casework. I wanted a meal, that's all. And I had this counselor who understood me.'

Then there's the story I don't tell, not aloud, not to anyone: Where I took my training from, and where my training took me. I could tell the story if it was, in fact, my past. But I don't have that kind of separation yet. Sitting with Hannah outside the office feels familiar, a repetition. This is, after all, what I did with Victor; I stepped outside the office and outside the roles. It's a common story – not knowing how to live, making the wrong decisions, the same ones, more than once. But how can you tell? If the wrong decisions identified themselves, there wouldn't be any decision, would there? The story I can't tell Hannah is what brings us together now. And when I think of the loneliness that made me call her – how it seemed to invest the walls of my cottage – it seems unreal, and how could I describe it? It's a loneliness you don't forget, like the hunger I felt that day, waiting to see a counselor in San Francisco. It bends you completely around it, distorts you. That kind of loneliness is a sound wall.

My counselor took an interest in me immediately. He was young, but he could convince me of anything. I trusted his authority, that he was looking out for my best interests. Best interests – they were always either mine or his, and somehow locked together from the moment I'd sat at his desk and told him I had no food, no job, no friends. He took me to dinner that night and explained we'd have to be quiet about it. I was prepared to keep secrets. I was determined to survive.

My counselor's name was Bill Avery. He was born on Martha's Vineyard, and he had blue, blue, calm eyes. A shore of regret in those calm eyes, and a mirror there too. When he talked to me, I didn't notice the cafeteria we were eating in, the dead eyes of the women behind the counter, the gray lamb rotating on a skewer, the people in line behind us – many on canes, carrying bottles. The place was close to his job, but also close to where he lived. Just two buildings down, he pointed.

And in his little room, in a gray tower on Eddy Street, for the first time I felt I'd conquered the one-way glass that kept me separated from others all those years.

He asked me why I came to San Francisco. San Francisco was a fluke, a place I'd heard my mother talk about. She said my father gave her the choice when they'd just been married: earthquakes or hurricanes. She chose hurricanes. That's all you're given, sometimes – a choice of disasters. I got up and looked out his window at the strange California sunlight that made the white buildings glisten. Below, I could see people rushing by, lining up for the disbursement of their General Assistance checks; the lights of the porn theaters on the corner, lurid even in daylight when you could see the pigeons roosting between the tubes.

Bill stood behind me, and I felt his hand firmly on my back, rubbing it with a persistence that demanded nothing. I felt safe beside him, rescued. Looking out his window reminded me of my father. I wondered if he had a window in prison to look out of. It's one of those luxuries I don't take for granted, even now. Bill suggested I consider a hotel to stay in. He told me he could help me find a job, get me vouchers for rent. In the meantime, I could stay the night.

What happened between Bill and me never seemed other than

normal. His asking me to stay was an act of generosity. His asking me to keep it quiet, familiar. That night he explored me with his hands, touching me with a peculiar bashfulness. 'Lie on your back,' he suggested. I felt his fingers, butterfly-like along the insides of my legs. 'What are you laughing at?' he asked. He sounded serious, so I held my breath, the laughter moving throughout me, mixing with the shame and the fear. No one had ever touched me so lightly.

The sky turned colors outside the window – dark blue streaked with orange and pink, some kind of magnificent ice cream. He stood up after a while and took his pants off. He wasn't wearing underwear, and I noticed his penis wasn't hard. It was strange then. He'd driven my sexuality to the surface, and now it felt like a layer of nerves exposed over my skin. I felt vulnerable and alone in it, the way I had when I inhaled my father as he slept beside me. I was afraid he'd tell me this couldn't happen, the way Jim had. I always did want to tell Jim: This did happen, and this is happening. But it was too late. Jim had simply taken it all back. I'm still amazed that people can do that.

'I know what you're thinking,' he said.

It had always been my greatest fear – someone reading my thoughts. So many of them seemed impossible to explain or express, or just so fleeting they would die in the light. Mostly there was a big silence in me, and the thoughts that came surprised me too.

'I like it when you just touch me,' I said. But he knew I wanted to know why he wasn't aroused. And maybe he knew I'd be happy with any excuse.

'I take a medicine that doesn't always let me show what I'm feeling.' He got in the bed next to me, and a sense of relief came over me, flooding me with a drug-like calm. I told him I didn't want sex with him. But as he continued to stroke me, his eyes shut and his breathing sounded almost like a low growl. I let my own fingers direct the current in my body he'd located just minutes before.

When the alarm went off the next morning, Bill was already

awake, sitting in a chair by the window, just his socks on. His belt
hung around his arm. 'Damn,' he said. 'Fucking alarm.' I didn't
tell him I'd seen it before. I just kept my head down on the pillow,
followed him with my eyes. 'You might want to look away,' he
said. I didn't. I watched closely as the blood registered startlingly
bright in the syringe.

'There it goes,' he said breathlessly and trailing off, both a
comment on the rush and something he'd let go of.

'I'm sorry, Carrie. I didn't want you to know this about me so
soon.' He began cleaning up around him, putting his glass of water
and spoon in the sink as though it were a coffee mug.

He closed the curtain behind him. A creamy, yellow light came
through it, though it was only 7:30 A.M. 'You sleep,' he said.
'Come visit me at work. And lock the door behind you.'

Soon I would bring his syringes to work. Though I understood
what it meant to be secretive, I didn't take his needs seriously
enough. 'Why were you late?' he'd ask. 'There's nothing to hold
you up when you're bringing this to me. Always consider this an
emergency. No matter how often you do it. The more you do it,
the greater the emergency.'

He gave me stamped letters that enabled me to get clothes from
nuns in dusty church-run shops. The letters said something about
interview clothes, but I'd argue for what I wanted regardless of
whether it looked like something I could wear to a job. Bill didn't
care. He cut me checks for rent that went straight to his own
landlord from my hands. The landlord did junk too, so they
understood each other. Bill set up interviews for jobs he thought
I'd be good at. I went to a few of them; others I'd simply forget. It
wasn't that I didn't appreciate him. While we were together I saw
no reason to work. I had no skills. And though I had no shame
when I walked into a store with a voucher, I felt humiliated asking
someone to pay for my training. What could I possibly bring to
anyone that would be worth paying for? What could I learn? It
was a question I never asked Bill, and maybe one of the reasons he

failed as a job counselor. But he tried. He thought I'd make a good waitress, that I could talk to people.

Watching Bill work filled me with conflicting feelings. I was proud of his ability, the desk he managed and the official paperwork he was always filling out. He seemed to possess a kind of mastery over his own life when he helped others. But I also felt indebted and damaged. I tried to imagine myself doing what Bill did, learning the forms and saying the right things to people. But it seemed like an entirely different world, full of somberness and regret, sometimes punctuated by the joy of somebody finding a job. I never asked Bill about what it required to be a case manager, whether you had to take a class or take an oath. He was taking care of me, and I couldn't upset that balance by asking him how he'd learned to do it.

Janine went with me to look for clothes a few times. I always thought she had a great sense of style, just the way she held herself. She could wear a man's V-neck T-shirt and make it look like she'd spent a lot of money on it. She told me that her mother had a lot of money, and that's why she hated designer clothes. She was already punk, totally fed up with the veneer of money and taste. She got a kick out of the vouchers Bill gave me. It was a challenge to find things at cheap department stores and at church rummage shops.

Bill introduced us, but didn't like us hanging around together that much. She was on his caseload for a little while. I would have been jealous of her if Bill hadn't told me he found her hard to be with. He said she was arrogant, and that she lied. I just thought she knew what she wanted. It certainly wasn't any of the jobs he tried to send her on. She would tell him that she'd gone to an interview, then fall silent when he inquired further.

She did go to interviews with me, though, and I liked her company. She'd sit outside, smoking, listening to her Walkman. 'I hope you didn't get it,' she'd say. 'This place is so depressing – all that fake, optimistic Americana crap makes me sick.' I looked again at the restaurant, with its faux '50s diner decor, its pink and blue neon illuminating pale waiters and waitresses running with heavy trays or listlessly refilling ketchup bottles in its carnival light.

Janine knew right away where we could fit in, and where we couldn't. It seemed to me to be the most essential knowledge to have. And when, five years later, she took me to my first audition as a stripper, I trusted her that this was somewhere we wouldn't have to be anything other than ourselves.

While Bill and I were together, I never told him that Janine was stripping. He believed in earning an honest wage. That included his drug dealer, but not strippers. I thought his opinion about stripping was his way of keeping me close, watching over me.

When Janine asked if I loved Bill, I told her with certainty, yes. I laugh now. The less I knew, the more certain I was. A counselor at the hospital rehab once asked me, 'Did you know that Bill molested you? Did you realize you were sexually abused?' The questions made no sense to me. Had he forgotten who I was, misplaced my chart? Bill did not molest me. And though I was young, I wasn't a child. I was sixteen. I'd seen my household disintegrate, and I forged another. He did the same thing. But later, when I thought about it, I realized that Bill was a thief, an addict – another father to me. It wasn't necessarily a good thing, but it was what we both knew how to do, and there was comfort in that.

And so it made sense when he encouraged me to go visit my mother after her surgery. He could be very firm about family things. 'Loyalty,' he'd say, 'is the most important thing between people.'

I sat at his desk, and he cut me the last check for bus fare to Miami. 'Say good-bye to your history as a client here.' We'd used up whatever state resources were allocated for a single woman on his caseload. He rolled up my folder and discreetly slipped it into his bag. It was that simple then. In that unwieldy bureaucracy in the late '70s, there was little accounted for. Almost seven years later, when I began working in a different division for the same office, there were still easy ways to cover your tracks.

That night I watched him cook up over his shoulder. 'You want to try it?' he asked. It seemed odd at first that he wanted to introduce me to what he both cursed and loved. In retrospect, this may have been his way of continuing to minister to me since I was officially no longer his client.

'Sure,' I said. I had no idea this decision would bring me back to him, again and again.

Look what they've done to my brain, Ma.
Look what they've done to my brain.
Well, they picked it like a chicken bone and I guess I'm half insane, Ma.

When every song was a mirror, we still didn't believe it. We sang it louder, like it was a joke. A mean, vicious joke. It was my mother's brain. A stroke – my father wrote from prison – something serious and no money to pay for it.

My mother was still in the hospital when I arrived in Miami. I took a cab and got there just before the end of visiting hours. I went to the woman at reception. She was pretty, sitting with her head in her hands, bored. She looked me up and down, then pointed me to a set of elevators. I rode up, the ambivalence setting in stronger than at any time during the preparation for the trip. I thought I would tell my mother that I'd made a life for myself in San Francisco. I'd tell her about Bill. Not everything – just that I'd been taken care of. But I felt unsure of what this information would mean to her – did it matter if I was doing well? That I'd found someone? My father insisted it would.

Of course it will, of course it does. But I couldn't take anything for granted. I wasn't sure if I cared about my mother's well-being, whether I wanted to forgive, or be forgiven. I felt strangely unconvincing, nobody's daughter. I looked at my reflection in the streaky metal doors of the elevator, and my body seemed too small to be the person I felt it necessary to be. I was relieved when the doors opened on the fourth floor.

Looking down the clean, white corridor, I thought: Fancy. It was unimaginable my mother would find her way here, a place as sterile as this. Like a good hotel. Outside the rooms were carts with lunch trays, aluminum-covered and stacked one on top of the other. I imagined white foods on each tray, delivered by a nurse in white. I looked into the rooms where other patients were recovering under plastic tents. I imagined what the high of perfectly clean air would be like, and assured myself it would be a light-headed but not a woozy experience, like a space suit where the pressure and toxicity of the environment are siphoned off. Her face had the pallor of a yellow bruise, her eyes closed but fluttering like moths that had landed perfectly over the sunken pits of her eyes.

There was no one else in my mother's room. It felt like a hundred degrees when I entered. There was a large window and a view of the city, barely observable through the blinding-white light that filled the window's frame. A side panel in the glass was slightly cracked. That's how the fly must have come in. It buzzed around my mother's shaved head and landed on the red scar incised in a circle at the top of her skull.

'Mother,' I whispered, wanting to have her hear me, but also hoping not to wake her. 'I've come to visit you. It's me, Carrie.' It was something like a movie, but less satisfying. I didn't believe the characters, not the concerned one I was playing, and not the injured one my mother always played. I sat down in an orange chair next to her bed. I opened my purse and ran my hands through the items I'd carried. I came upon the toothbrush case and looked around the room and at the door to make sure no one was there. I unsnapped the lid and looked closely at the syringe Bill had provided, loaded already with the resin-brown liquid. The closest I would get to perfectly pure air.

There was a small bathroom attached to my mother's hospital room. I went into it and closed down the toilet seat. There were wide beige tiles on the floor, a bathtub with attachments to help a patient move in or out. It looked untouched – a bottle of mouthwash sealed on the sink, two white towels and a facecloth folded neatly. I pulled the belt from my pants, took the syringe from my bag, and settled down on the toilet. The dope was amber. I leaned back and watched my blood rise like a ribbon up the tube, then plunged the contents into my arm. I felt as though I'd been wrapped in gauze and placed in a small box. I thought this must be how my mother was feeling, and the terror of her appearance fell away. Perhaps she would feel like this for some time.

I called Bill from the hospital room, collect. 'I can't stay,' I told him. 'She's under heavy anesthesia. The doctor says she may not wake up for several hours.'

'Are you loaded?' he asked. I thought he sounded angry.

'No,' I said. 'Why?'

'You just sound it.'

That I'd lied, and that the truth was obvious, didn't stop me. That my mother would never emerge as the person I knew, or wanted to know, didn't stop me. 'Can I come back?' I asked, suddenly crying. I promised I'd get work, find some way to be better than I'd been. I'd proven an obligation to my family. I was human now, with real ties to people. That much I'd shown him. I could go back and ask him to hold me, make it all go away. He would make it all go away. And when he needed it, I'd make it all go away for him too.

We lived together for four years before he died of an overdose. There was never any pretense – after that last visit to my mother – of my caring for her one way or the other. Bill was my family. He never asked me to leave him again.

'Ellen's buried in the cemetery where we took our last bike ride, in Burlington. It's beautiful there; rolling hills and so many trees. It's not like a cemetery at all. We weren't morbid; that's not why we used to go there. It's more like a park. I haven't seen her grave, haven't been back since,' Hannah says.

'Probably best not to go. Not right away.'

She leans back against the tractor door and draws her knees up. 'Ellen believed people could change. You believe that, don't you? That people can change?'

'Of course,' I say. 'If they feel they have to. If they let themselves.' *What is she thinking, poor girl? What is she hurting herself with now?*

'Have you ever met people who remind you of someone you've known before? I mean, even the way they talk, or the way they think about things?'

'I think so,' I say, cautious now. I'm not ready to be compared with her dead friend.

'Well,' she says, 'you remind me of her. It's uncanny, but I felt it right away. All the strange things you keep on your desk. Ellen used to cut out paintings too. I don't mean to offend you. In fact, I mean it in a good way, but Ellen just had a hard time fitting in. She could never do an office job like you. She sort of lived in her head.'

'How so?' I ask, thinking: I wish my casework could keep me out of my head, keep the details of others' lives from mixing with my own, muddying the waters.

'She was always making stuff up about her past, about who she was. It was endearing for a while. I don't mean that you do that. You seem more like you withhold. She fabricated. Big difference.'

Yes. And she's dead. You can sum her up however you like. I'm not dead. Remember that.

'Now you're upset,' she says.

'No, I'm not upset.' But I'm thinking: Why should I tell you anything, everything? And the point I reached with Victor: *Now you're not my client. Here are my keys. Take everything, just don't leave.*

She lights a cigarette, then goes on: 'Things happened really fast between us. I think we needed each other. Neither of us felt afraid of the world when we were together. We didn't have to overcome anything to be understood. We took these long walks. We could see Iowa City way off behind us, and we'd be following the railroad tracks out of town, and we weren't bored together, even though we spent a long time not talking, and neither of us asking where we were going or how long before we went back. And she always wore these dresses – dresses and combat boots – and it was funny to see her climbing over fences with them.'

She reaches forward to push King's blanket in my direction,

then pulls her knees up and rests her chin on them. 'I remember how good she was at breaking into buildings. She had an intuition for unlocked windows, and we'd scout out these old manufacturing plants and abandoned schools and stores. It was always the high point of any trips we took, breaking into some place. Taking something with us. We broke into a high school in Sioux City once.

'We drew pictures of each other in chalk on one of the blackboards. I drew her crouched down with a wound on her knee, and she drew me with a slingshot. It sounds silly, but we drew alike, and we could elaborate on each other's drawings the way we could each other's thoughts. And I took a picture of that drawing with one of the Brownie cameras I was collecting before we slipped out the window. We were fearless together; she found an unlocked window in me and she clambered in with those heavy boots.'

She stops here to run her cigarette in the tractor's large, metal ashtray, to bring its burning end to a point. 'There was a lot I didn't tell her, trying to keep things simple between us. We were attempting to live like kids, without responsibility and without concern for consequences. She behaved as though she hadn't grown up, even though she was just three years younger than me. On the other hand, I was trying to recapture something. Something I didn't have originally, because my childhood was never simple. My upbringing wasn't about sharing secrets. It was about keeping alliances. And Ellen couldn't have known that, because I tried to reflect her exuberance, and because I genuinely convinced myself I could see the world the way she did. I was dishonest from the beginning, but I told myself that she was too innocent, or at least unwilling, to imagine it.' She turns to look outside the window just as a star falls, cutting perfectly across the sky like the silver tip of scissors through black crepe.

And then we were high, as high as I thought we'd ever get – and it felt like helicopters landing on my head, this great whirring and gusting that could lift me off my feet and drop me as easily, and my eyes flashed open, blind, white like a surveillance beam from inside – and I asked Victor if it was worth it, the kidnapping and the mayhem and the jewelry she wore.

Victor slapped me so hard I fell from the chair. Oh, well. I'd been crawling for months, it seemed. Crawling.

'Don't start with me now,' he hollered, his face like the masks in the window. My father's friends playing a trick. See if she jumps. But she's down now, possibly for good. 'Did you ask me to fix you, get you high?' he hollered. But I was crying. Crying for her. And then I spit it out, angry at him, 'Of course I asked for it.' And Victor's face then – so human, so horrible – because he knew he could not do to me what he'd done to her. The whole mess was at his feet. And just as I picked myself off the floor, I knew I would have to gather him up too, and never let him know how pervasive the damage was, how desperately he needed me.

Hannah puts her hands on the tractor's large steering wheel, bracing herself, as though controlling this enormous piece of machinery. Her body changes when she clutches the wheel – she assumes a kind of haughty masculinity, as though she were surveying the land, master of it.

Keeping one hand on the wheel and turning toward me, she says, 'She made me so angry once that I just told her the truth. Of course, I later realized there were a lot of things I didn't mention. I shared a small part of the truth. It's not like anyone gets much more than that. Anyway, we were sitting on the edge of my bathtub, and she was wiping the excess hair dye from behind my ears, and I remember feeling really good about her touching me.' I notice Hannah's brief glance at my face, as though she were looking for some kind of response. But I've practiced the impartial listener. I listen like the dead.

'There was always this kind of pressure between us, because we were so close. I can't say it was really about sex, but I think there was a feeling that it could have happened. I had my back turned to her, and she said, "I'm still a virgin." For some reason, I was really angry at her for saying that. It caught me off guard. I'd seen her birth control pills. Her compact fell out of her purse once, and I thought to myself: Well, I wonder who she's fucking?

'So, I told her I'd seen the pills. I knew she wasn't a virgin. She was so furious when I brought it up to her, as though I'd broken a code between us. It was like I wasn't supposed to know she was having sex; it ruined something we'd created together, the possibility of imagining ourselves innocent or without desire. She wanted us to remain free of guilt. I have to say, she wasn't the only one who wanted that. I wanted it too. But I wanted to know why we couldn't be innocent even if we'd done things we weren't proud of, or had sex for the wrong reasons, or with the wrong person. I mean, those were basic things I thought we should be able to own up to.' She looks away from me. I notice how distracted she becomes, thinking about these things.

'But when she was helping me dye my hair, and touching me the way she was, I had the feeling she wanted me to initiate something, that she wanted me to make a move on her. Of course, she would only let it happen if she could remain unsuspecting. It would be something I'd have to take responsibility for. She could maintain being a child if the experience just happened to her. And then she could forget it the way children forget. It would be just another new thing in a succession of first experiences.'

Victor and I stopped having sex after a while. It was so much more intimate to share blood, drugs, despair. Sometimes it felt like we were the last people alive, that the whole city had died in their sleep, but we were up and wired. Sometimes it seemed that we were the only two who'd died, slipped behind some curtain. It seemed like we didn't have to talk for days at a time; thoughts passed between us as though they were there in our blood. Can you pass delusions that way? Can you pass evil? But Janine's not dead, I remind myself, though a part of her must be. Easier to think her not too much alive.

Janine had called it God. God got her clean. Intervened. But what if it wasn't God? What if it were simply the course of despair, ridden out, worn down like anything else in nature? For good or bad, it all has to end. Nothing has an interminable sustain. It breaks. It's like fever. Even misery comes to its end. What if that was the only point of God: to put an end to things? Wouldn't that be good enough? I think that would be grace, and redemption, and the other words we think we know the meanings of.

Hannah reaches inside her pocket and pulls out two caramels, hands me one. There's a part of me that wonders about our eating candy, sitting in this tractor as though we were kids who needed to find a place to go other than home. I wonder if Ellen wasn't the last person she did this with, and whether she felt she was only going along with it, then. But the simple intimacy we acquire by being somewhere we shouldn't, eating candy as though we'd just stolen it, is undeniable. And I see that she's comfortable talking here, that I'll get more from her here than at my desk.

She sticks the cellophane wrapper back in her pocket. 'Ellen decided she had something she wanted to tell me. I guess she felt that one truth deserved another. That's when she mentioned Stefan, her painting teacher. I told her how I watched him sometimes coming and going from his house. I told her of this silly infatuation I had with him, and we'd laughed about it. I took her once to the park across the street from his house, to look out at him while he sprayed his sunflowers.

'Then she told me how Stefan had asked her to model for him. She blushed when she told me she'd agreed to do it, the way she had when he noticed us in the park. And I saw it then – the first time we went to watch him from the park – how she didn't take her eyes away the way I did, but lingered long enough to telegraph to him "I'm watching you," before she followed me down the hill.

'And when she told me that they'd been sleeping together, I was struck by a double pang of jealousy; I had been the one to first point out his features to her, to mention the sleep on his eyelashes that made it seem like he'd always just gotten up. And she'd never appreciated those things until I'd shared them with her. I began to suspect – and I'm sure it was just my own imagination – that she was studying me, taking parts of me into her own life. I know that sounds strange, but I remember looking at the photograph I took of our drawing on the blackboard, and her drawing of me was surprisingly similar to the way I'd drawn her. But I had always drawn that way, and what seemed like this natural affinity suddenly seemed like studied emulation.

'I thought maybe she told me about the two of them because I was unresponsive to her when she said she was a virgin, that maybe she wanted something sexual to happen between us and thought this would make me jealous. I don't know. All these thoughts came at me at once, and I thought all of them might be true, but none of them seemed to bring a revelation, or suggested a way I could respond to her.'

She looks at me with a pleading expression it seems impossible to console, then turns and fixes her expression on King's blanket over my knees. 'That all seems so long ago.' She laughs at the absurdity of her own statement. Nothing has ever been more present for her.

In the distance we can hear what sounds like a group of drunken students, singing intentionally off-key, and I feel a sudden rush of gratefulness to be high up in this tractor, over the frozen gouges.

'C'mon, let's get out of here,' Hannah says, noticing my grogginess. I've adapted myself to the tractor's seat, my head resting against the window.

'Your teeth are chattering,' she says. She wants to drive. She claims she hasn't been in a car since Ellen took Stefan's out for a joyride. 'She took the keys out of his pocket after they'd had sex. She took some money too. The money was given; he preferred her not asking for it. When she told me these things, I went along with it. I thought, She'll fuck it up, and I wanted to be there when she did. I consciously put the fact that I was hurt behind me. I stopped trying to figure out if she had intended to hurt me, or she didn't. And what the hell? Now she wanted to take his car, and I would ride along vicariously. I thought: I'll just watch how this unfolds. "He has money," she told me. This was one of his attributes that she'd noticed. It didn't take my pointing it out to her. The car was an old Buick Park Avenue, sleek black with red pinstripes, black leather interior. That thing was so gorgeous.' She bites her finger for emphasis.

'Ellen picked me up at The Deadwood. We drove out of town so we could show off, but there were nothing but fields and farmhouses and not a single farmer, so we drove back, honking the horn. Finally, we stopped in a gas station just to see someone admire it. This young kid came up to the window, didn't say anything. He had this dirty rag in his hand, and asked if we wanted him to do the windows. I couldn't believe he had nothing to say about the car, it was such a specimen. So finally I called him to the window. I asked him, "You know how we got this car?" He finally looked it over. "Nope," he responded. I said. "We killed some dumb farmer a ways back. We took him out into his field and shot him with his own gun. Now, we've still got that gun, but we don't have a whole lot of cash. May I suggest you let us ride out of here, so we don't have to do anything we don't want to?" That guy was suddenly more observant than he'd probably ever been. He just waved us out of there; I could see him nervously looking at the license plate as we drove off.

'Ellen was amazed, but she'd played along. I looked over and saw her looking stern-faced, straight ahead. She asked me why I did it, and I told her, I can't pull into a gas station without thinking of *In Cold Blood*. I was also thinking of *Bonnie and Clyde*. I've always loved true crime stories. Anyway, we both laughed when we pulled out of the gas station. It was such a rush, totally worth it. But Stefan was so pissed when we got back, and, of course, he didn't even know about the gas station incident.

'Ellen asked me to wait and got out of the car, and I think that's when it turned bad for me, when I saw the way she approached him and how the anger in his face was changing already. It was settling the way mine had when she first told me about the two of them. She had an art for overriding your first instincts. You had to accept her. You had to forgive her. I knew if he hadn't forgiven her just then, he would eventually.'

I remember the state car I borrowed. Of course, it was desperation rather than mischief that motivated me. Perhaps it was more than mischief that motivated Ellen.

I started working for the state of California in 1983, in the same office where Bill worked before he died. I hadn't met Victor yet. Janine and I had been dancing for almost two numb years after Bill overdosed. We were addicted to the money and drugs. And then the numbness started to hurt. Janine got out, and I knew I needed to. Everyone knew me at the office; I lived with Bill for almost six years. Maybe they pitied me after he died, but they moved my application through, and before I knew it I was interviewing before the panel. I told them I had volunteer experience, lies that Bill had tutored me with. I sold them on my sensitivity, high enough to talk about pain without feeling it.

When I started the job, I had less than a week clean, detoxing from heroin. My body was discharging emotion, the stored feelings of a three-month binge, and I could feel tears welling, prompted by the simplest things. When I did cry, it was over foolish things: a television special on young offenders – a fifteen-year-old boy who'd shot and killed his whole family after exhibiting years of bizarre, frustrated behavior. I remember the dramatic re-creation of his driving around the block all night, not really planning the massacre, but letting the voices speak. Then, one early morning before work, the second part of *Sybil* was broadcast, and I wept bitterly when Sally Field asked if she could sit with Joanne Woodward in her big chair. Because I wanted that too. I wanted someone to say, 'You can just be with me,' the way Bill had once said it.

I spent my first week on the state job anxious; my limbs felt heavy and dulled as though blood had stopped coursing through them. At night I would sit wide awake with clothespins clamped to the skin between my fingers, so I could feel them. Everything smelled wrong, tasted wrong. Toothpaste would sicken me. Significance was drained from everything, even the job, though I thought of it as my last chance. Attempting it clean seemed impossible; I was thrown into sharp contrast with the world of non-users, their pinkish, flushed faces and bright eyes – like rabbits blissfully at a carrot. I, on the other hand, a scurvy bird, the blue veins under the scars on my arms, the morning worm I would go at with the needle.

To make matters worse, they sent me on a training out of town during my second week, and I was forced to share a ride and a hotel room with Leslie, a well-dressed and stiffly coifed exercise enthusiast who carried free-weights in her suitcase. It was on my way to training, under a hot white sun like a doctor's lamp, when I felt stricken by the smell of dope, a hallucination engineered by the hungry cells of my body, an amber mirage. I tried to reason it away, telling myself I could crave it without acting on it, wisdom I'd picked up in the jostling line at the methadone clinic. But the charade felt pointless. I would never have anything in common with Leslie. I saw myself like the rotten-toothed junkies I copped with, their faces as empty as the hotel rooms they'd float in and out of, as dirty and lifeless as the makeshift curtains left tacked and hanging in their windows. But people had always commented on how pretty I was, and, after Bill, men had been willing to pay for it, even when my life and my features got ugly.

I put my feet up on the dashboard. Leslie drove the state rental car. Leslie did the driving because I didn't have a license – another thing I couldn't manage. There had always been time and money enough for drugs, but what most people considered necessities eluded me. I always thought myself a functional addict. I'd survived, I'd even come to think myself sharp. But the little things made me reconsider.

The windows were rolled down and a cool wind buffeted the car. The highway rolled out on a thin, finger-like landmass that cut between what seemed like two oceans, but Leslie called the Bay. I had my eyes closed; I was counting days, hours, minutes clean. It would take months of this misery before I'd trust myself, wouldn't fear a strong wind from an opened door that would carry me off. I thought of horror movies I'd seen – *Rosemary's Baby* and *Demon Seed* – and how those women were overtaken by outside forces, impregnated by them, and ultimately became their vehicles. That was heroin. I knew that no amount of psychic fortification could prepare me for the smell of it, the discovery of a balloon they sold it in, the sight of a dealer; any association could leave me hunched around the needle. I looked at the confident profile of my co-worker, feeding plant-like on the sun spread over the hood and glass of the automobile. I pushed my sunglasses up, my pupils making my head throb, gorged with light.

'I hear there's a Nautilus center we can use as residents of the hotel,' Leslie said.

I almost sighed aloud. 'I'm still trying to kick this flu,' I lied. 'I don't think I should exert myself.'

'Maybe you can just steam or sauna. That always helps me.'

It wasn't that I didn't want to do it. It was my arms. There'd be no excuse for them. 'I don't think so,' I said, looking out over the water, deep and full of its own unseen life.

We stayed in what looked like chalets off the highway, each with a peaked roof, loft, living room, and kitchen. I insisted upon the upstairs loft with its own attached bathroom – I thought I'd be more alone that way in case I suffered an anxiety attack, a bout of nausea – but I was almost too exhausted to move my bags upstairs, a small duffel and a larger shoulder bag. I fell heavily on the large bed, its crisp, clean bedding reminding me of my mother's hospital bed. I'd learned from my father she'd come out of the anesthesia with half of her face and body paralyzed. He wrote that she'd panicked, and no one was there beside her.

I wondered if that would be my fate, that aloneness, that panic. Drugs made me superstitious. I was certain my bad fate accumulated around my wrongdoings. I left her in the hospital. I felt the old panic creeping over me. I turned the lamp off and picked up the phone. I didn't know who to call; I'd been isolated for so long. I called Janine. She got clean over a year before and wrote a play that had some success, putting some of her old stripper friends into the roles she'd written, her plots often loosely based on their experiences. They'd called the work 'daring,' but I knew how sedate it was compared with the experiences that informed it.

I remember our last night using together, and I'm pretty sure that had been the decisive night she got clean. We'd finished a shift at the O'Farrell and decided to do a late-night private show at the Kearny Street Holiday Inn. Extra money, we thought, since we'd already spent a good $700 between ourselves that night. The guy had propositioned us at the club, and we'd agreed to meet him after our shift.

When we got to his room, we went directly to the bathroom and locked the door. I pulled out my 'coffin,' the syringe I kept prepared in a toothbrush case. Something I'd picked up from Bill, and I would always think of him when I saw it, until I'd fixed. Then I could forget anyone.

'We're prettying up,' I told the man anxiously turning the knob. 'Just leave us alone for a minute.'

I stood in front of the mirror and looked at my bee-stung arms, my sunken chest, the spots where the makeup was too heavy hiding the places where I'd missed, an abscess on my arm that couldn't be covered. I pulled the belt tightly around the other arm but still had to try several times before finding a vein.

'The light's really good in here,' I told Janine after I found it. She'd already shot up and was throwing up in the toilet.

I braced myself on the countertop. In just a few moments I was able to rinse out the syringe, pull a tube of lipstick from my purse, and draw some color onto my lips.

Janine couldn't leave the bathroom, so I did it alone.

I remember him sweating. He'd been watching videos and free-basing for hours. His lower jaw was swollen from a rotten tooth he was continually grinding and sucking at. I was glad his dick was soft and already rubbed raw. He couldn't take his hand off it, except to replace it with the pipe, or to hold the instruments he put inside me. He'd been up for so long, he lost sight of the whole picture and began micro-managing everything. He was investigative about my cunt, his head between my legs for what felt like forever, not pleasing me, not eating me, but looking, trying to find the kitten trapped in the well.

I had quit smoking, but took a cigarette from his pack beside the bed, staring at the cottage cheese ceiling of this ugly room that felt like a clinic.

When I got Janine home that night, I had to strenuously remove her clothes and shoes. She looked like a traumatized child carried from a refugee center, or led away from a scene of grisly, motiveless violence. She called the next day to tell me she'd decided to take her mother's offer of a private rehab. After six months in the program, I heard she moved in with her mother, a psychotherapist whose home and practice were in Marin, in a gorgeous cottage with Spanish tiles and leather furniture and glass doors that took in an expanse of hillside greenery and the ocean. Janine called it the Summer House after Jane Bowles's play. That's where she finished her own play, recounting her past at a much safer distance than time alone would permit.

I called her from the hotel room in Sacramento. I could hear Leslie unpacking her things downstairs, and cupped the receiver. I suppose I wanted to ask what had happened to Janine on our last night together that had transformed her, what had enabled her to get clean. I wanted to know what kept me from making that same change. I'd heard sobriety was a spiritual thing, and since I'd never had a religious experience when I was younger and more deserving of it, I certainly didn't think it was in my cards. I told her about the job I'd started.

'I'll be working with offenders, helping them find jobs and counseling.'

'Are you clean?' she asked. Smug, bright confidence.

'Yes,' I said. 'Of course.' A part of my mind locked on the idea that I would cop, somehow or another, once I got off the phone with her.

'How long?' she asked.

'It's been a few months,' I answered. I knew the lie was unimpressive to Janine. She'd once said clean time wasn't the same thing as recovery. I guess I wasn't at the point of teasing out those differences. I'd only quit the O'Farrell a week before I started the state job, and I did a lot of drugs that night. A lot.

Janine's recovery, I told myself, could only be a distant inspiration, a curiosity.

'I feel like you've put a curse on me,' I said abruptly.

'What are you talking about?' she asked uncomfortably, as though a part of her anticipated this.

'I saw your play. I knew it was me you were writing about – the girl who can't get clean, who kills herself.'

'It's all a composite,' she said. Rehearsed little bitch.

Now she sounded just like a customer, I thought; all the girls are interchangeable.

'If you're going to condemn someone like that,' I said, choking out the words, 'you might as well be honest about it.'

'I'm sorry you heard it like that,' she said.

I hung up. As long as I'd known her, she would write things down in a pad she kept, phrases, observations, street names, stripper names. I found it irritating, another way that she tried to see herself as separate from the things she did and the people she did them with. Perhaps it was a kind of narcissism that got her clean, a belief that her experience could amount to something, regardless how fractured and pointless it looked while she collected it. In either case, she pieced together the identifiable, exhumed fragments of the girls she ran with, distortions she called drama.

Then my mind raced to plan a trip back to San Francisco so I could see my dealer. My drama. Not worthy of notation. But it was already evening, and the ride was a good three hours. I'd have to come back the same night to make it to the morning training. I wondered if there was some way to get the rental car from Leslie.

I hated Janine. I hated everyone who talked about me as though I didn't have the language down. Talk over your head, that's what they did.

Leslie's radio played downstairs. I felt nervous confronting her for the keys, but I was so determined I didn't bother to construct a good reason for needing them. She came out of her bathroom with a jogging suit on, and patted the edge of the bed where she wanted me to sit. She drew matching pink sweatbands over her wrists.

'I need the keys to the state car,' I said.

'You don't have a license, Carrie.' She sounded exasperated.

'Yes, I do,' I said grimly. I was preparing myself for further interrogation, to be asked to show the damned thing.

'You told me you didn't have one. That's why I drove up here. That's why the car is in my name. I can't let you take it.'

'I'm just going to get some groceries.'

'Well, Luis is getting groceries later. Why not ride with him?'

I wanted to punch her. I wanted to scream, *Can't you see I'm falling apart. I'm sweating and I'm freezing and I'm so anxious I'd cut my own throat just to get some feeling back in my body!*

'Never mind,' I said. 'It's not that important.' After she went out to the gym, I searched her room and grabbed the keys from the top drawer of her nightstand. I found where she'd parked the car, then I got in and started the drive back to the city.

I clenched the wheel, accelerated. I left Sacramento. I left a job, a chance, the painful resolve to get clean and live with myself. I cried as I drove. They were the same meaningless tears that welled from nowhere. I could hear Leslie talking with the others, anxious about the car she signed for, perhaps calling the San Francisco office. My mind was so cluttered with irrational thoughts, I imagined driving to another state, another life. I rolled down the window and momentarily felt an inexplicable freedom, and the tears rolled from my cheeks. It was a freedom so circumscribed, it allowed no fear. It was the simple choices allotted an addict making her way from point A to point B. I'd have to stop to cop, and get gas, and then, maybe then, I could keep driving.

I remembered the documentary on young offenders, the boy who drove around the block before entering his family's home and killing them all. The rage he must have felt. For a moment, I saw my parents behind the life I was living. I would never escape them, no matter how fast I drove, no matter how much heroin I could afford. The quiet tragedy and excruciating effort of my mother to navigate the world, the cell my father cleaned up in. I could feel their mistakes replicating in me – a fate of bad genes, sick blood, memory.

Bill said we were like a family – all the people we'd see outside his hotel window – selling syringes for a dollar a pop, selling dope, our bodies. We treated each other just like the families we'd come from, carelessly, with as few words as possible. A meeting of needs. He thought junkies were better than that; that their weakness should make them more compassionate. He had a great, naive heart. But I think he first learned how to love by counting on me. And wasn't it our desperation that made our love genuine and stronger than both of us? Wasn't our wish to make life bearable for one another a true thing?

I remembered my father holding my mother, their bedroom door open and light falling over them like dust. Sick light. Canal light. I saw them from the kitchen; I was standing underneath the fly strips and a fluorescent ring. 'Don't worry,' he intoned, more tender than I'd ever seen him. I wasn't sure if it was my awkwardness or his that I was feeling. I knew my jealousy, though. I hoped my mother was dying, but that seemed impossible. I took her life for granted the way she had. Who cares what she needed? She manufactured need. It was the milk she weaned me on, laced with drugs.

I thought of Josephine, my dealer. I'd seen her last Christmas, the only person on the gauntlet, the strip of Mission Street from 16th to 21st where I'd cop. I almost gave up until I saw her – recognized her gait – the way she moved on her cane. I saw her emerge through the fog, an apparition, death on bad legs. She invited me to her hotel room, something she hadn't done before. But she was alone, and she could tell I'd take her up on it. She offered a bag of spice drops. 'Hard on my teeth,' she said, revealing mostly gums. 'But I can't resist them.' Of course not.

'This time of year I always think of my children,' she said. She used the small lid from a bottle to cook her dope and used the wax from her ear to keep the syringe plunger from sticking. She laughed at the appalled look I gave her.

'They took my little girls away. They were so smart.' She moved one hand down to the height of her bed. 'They were only this tall. They were like tiny ladies. They didn't even cry when they got taken.'

Whenever Josephine sold me drugs on the street, she crossed herself. She was superstitious, like most helpless people. When she'd cross herself, it always made me feel looked after too. I remember once when I told her I was getting clean, and not to call me, and not to expect me. 'That's really good, Carrie,' she said. And she meant it, though she had probably witnessed it a thousand times before, had probably said the same things herself, though not recently. On Christmas night, I stayed with her until 4 A.M. The door was busted and a few people from the hotel came in throughout the night, either not acknowledging the holiday or making the best effort at cheer. Josephine, like her little girls, didn't let on that anything was out of the ordinary, that a huge part of her had been torn out.

Please be home, Josephine, I thought, and before me the carnival lights of the Bay Bridge rose up over a black mirror of water. The lights were like tracks on the darkness, illuminating the narrow way. I felt suddenly convulsive, my body responding to the thought of drugs with an anxious nausea, and I clenched the wheel, heaving, my eyes tearing. Then suicide, like a second strand of lights, a shadow strand, rose up in me with the irresistible pull of my drug thoughts. I could go over the edge of the bridge so easily. And it would be black and silent for the Poison Girl.

The traffic was moving rapidly, but I'd have to drive more quickly to crash the barriers. And as I looked out, my mind engrossed in the calculations, the wheels cut along the edge of the walk zone and I momentarily lost the wheel. And then instinct, and not will at all, pulled the car back into control. Blind instinct. Heart, lungs, adrenaline – the parts of me I had no control over – had kept me alive, countered the chemicals I'd used to slow them, submerge them, kill them. The mechanism, and not the will, survived and saved me.

Hannah and I lie head to head on the rug, both of us stroking King. I am not lonely, but calm. Hannah rolls onto her back. She plays with the pulls in her light blue sweater.

'I guess I always wonder what's a fair amount to ask to be forgiven for.' Her voice sounds very far away, but still clear.

'Always ask for more than you need,' I say.

She's quiet for a moment. She measures her confession. She's a smart girl.

'Ellen stood there, and I don't think she was explaining why she'd taken the car – that wasn't her way – but I think she told him where we'd taken it. And I thought of how *I* would tell about the excursion, about the young boy at the gas station, and how he'd assumed we were capable of anything. It was a great prank. That boy had such fear in his eyes. But Stefan led Ellen into his house, looking skeptically over his shoulder at me. I guess he figured it was my doing, that it was my decision to take his keys and go out driving. It was easier to hate me. The funny thing was, I also wanted his forgiveness.' She rolled over again and looked at me. 'I wished I'd never felt that. If I had just walked away, without jealousy – that's what it was – then Ellen might have had what she wanted. That perfect life she wanted.'

'Wasn't he married?' I ask.

'She would have had him; the marriage wouldn't have stopped him. But later, she started really pursuing him – crazily – and he felt threatened by her. He was the kind of guy that always wanted to be the aggressor. He was a womanizer. He liked that control. And she was a skillful little girl, the perfect match for him.' She looked up at me angrily. 'I didn't kill her, Carrie. But I wanted to hurt her. When I got out of the car and walked away from his house, I knew she'd let him hate me. I knew she'd let him blame me. I shouldn't have cared what he thought, but I did.'

I imagine myself sitting in that theater south of Market Street in San Francisco. And Janine's play. What was it called? *Saved*? It ran for a week, but the reviews were good. Of course, she hadn't invited me. She'd relied on the assumption that I wouldn't pick up a weekly, see it advertised or reviewed, or that I'd died. My death was probably easier and more satisfying an assumption. I was high at the show because directly after I had to dance, and that was impossible to do clean. But from the moment the lights went up, it felt as though a spotlight were trained on me; I felt more naked and exposed than I'd ever felt on the tables of the O'Farrell. When I danced, I was clothed in persona. I knew what I was showing. You want to see my teeth, here's my teeth. Don't look at the arms, look at the eyes. The eyes, so stupid and small. A pigeon's eyes.

The girl on stage staggered and spoke with a rasp. She was one of many girls on the stage, all of them with story lines as heavy and artificial as their makeup. Janine built their characters from glitches and derailments. They dumbly follow a course of errors, perpetually startled or numbed by the outcomes. They're conscious only of themselves as fringe-dwellers – because they're strippers, addicts, low-lives – and they dress the part. They never come offstage. They expire slowly. The spectacle they present is hypnotic but not compelling. Bad actresses, bad idea. Good girls playing bad. Janine should've played the role. Perhaps by then it would have been acting to her. But her story is always in her eyes. That's the part being clean doesn't change.

When I walked out of the theater, I pulled my coat around me. I was so angry at first. Then I couldn't stop laughing. I was laughing even when I walked into the O'Farrell. 'It's art,' I thought. 'She really made something of herself.'

I get up and offer Hannah tea. I go to the kitchen to make it. I have a light blue teapot, and when I add the water to the tea the smell of bergamot settles me. I call her in to look at the teacups. While she turns one in her hand, I tell her, 'I love the things you can find here. In San Francisco, you could never find things like this in the thrift shops. Everything was picked over.'

It reminds me of the cookie box she made for me. It's fragile like that. And for a few moments we talk about the things that could content us, and how they're rare things, from a different time.

II

Owls

4

Everything that has been put together decays and disintegrates, everything that has been united dissolves, everything created disappears.

Severo Sarduy

'Janine forgot where she came from. And she needs to remember that walking away isn't as easy as she thinks.' Did I say that? And what had Victor planned? And what part of the plan went so wrong? You see, you're always alone. And that's how people get in trouble: They don't think alike, but they think they do.

The office is dead. I feel Frances's hand on my shoulder. Not her hand – her nails. They are long and thickly painted. When she holds a cigarette to her mouth, the nails extend across her cheek like deep, red cuts. 'Let's go outside,' she says.

We stand out by the parking lot and she looks at me for a long time without talking. 'You seem distracted today,' she says carefully. 'Are you distracted?'

'This winter's hard for me. I think it's the winter.' Snow is falling again, and now it seems it will never clear.

'That's Iowa,' she says dispassionately. 'Is that all that's on your mind?'

I stop myself. 'It's not important.'

'I'm not stupid,' Frances says. 'I've spent a lot of years here, and

[89]

I know when something's the matter. But I'm not saying you have to tell me. I just know.'

'My client missed her appointment.'

'They always do,' she said. 'Nothing strange about that.'

'But I care about this one.'

'Not good.' She shakes her head. 'You've got to watch yourself. That's the kind of person you are. You mean the best, but you get too deep.'

She goes back to that point. She doesn't think there's a difference between depths. Deep is deep. Stay afloat. She doesn't know about loneliness. She is already out of here, setting up a new home with a man she trusts. She is on the phone all the time. Her voice is always full of interest. People interest her, at a distance. *Don't get dark on me. Don't tell me about winter. I've seen winter.*

Victor wasn't a good client. I remember when he'd first come into the office. He was mandated by furlough, and his attitude was as thick as his arms. 'Nice-looking lady,' he said – or something like that – as though he were talking to someone in his wolf pack. But he was alone and looked sort of nervous and self-conscious in the chair.

Hernandez-Lopez, Victor. Served seven years, assault, possession with intent to sell. And on and on.

He conveyed his story either with indifference or as a boast. I looked at his face and I could see his mother, still in Cuba. Her eyes were pistachio green, and her cheekbones high and delicate. These he had. He had his father's scar, just below the eye; his father's broken nose that looked flat, like a boxer's. He had the distance between his estranged parents in his eyes. Light eyes, black hair. And his chin where he stored his pride, and his neck where the rage rose to the surface. But it was his lips that could talk of love and vengeance with the same whispered intensity.

'What are you going to do for me?' he asked.

'If you keep your appointments, then I won't notify parole. If you don't, you'll be visiting your old cell.' I knew it was best to start by breaking things down into simple components: action

equals consequence in this relationship. There was nothing I had
to do; he, however, was mandated to see me.

He should have known I would keep that leverage. He could
not take that from me. I had earned my place at the desk. I'd seen
clients – one after the other – stay out or go back in, and my case
report was an important component of that decision. I'd started
early. It was probably just those few words that I'd exchanged with
a police officer in my backyard that had years ago helped them
apprehend my father. That was the first, but not the last time I
would introduce the men I loved to corrections.

'I'm from Miami,' he answered when I asked his birthplace.

I held up the alligator and told him of this first thing we shared
in common.

'I grew up in Sweetwater,' I said.

'I know where that is. I used to pass it on my way to the
Everglades. I've seen a lot of bigger 'gators than this.' He took my
hand in his as though to extricate the alligator from my grasp, but
he didn't take it, just let his hand settle on mine until I drew away.

He said, 'My father had an air boat we used to go out in. He
had a lot of money, my father. He married another woman in
Miami, and she just used it all up. Suddenly they had this big
house, and all this security. She hated me, so my father asked me
not to come around. I used to just look at that house through the
gates. Once I saw her come out the front door. She saw my car
and she went back inside right away. And I thought: She better
not come out of there again. She was like a prisoner of her
expensive house. She was afraid of me because she knew she tore
my father and me apart.'

The threat of him. Was it authentic? Should the words 'assault'
and 'possession' make the threat of him authentic? But his charm
is tied to his threat. For girls like me.

There are extra locks on my cottage door. First paycheck in Iowa:
security. But you can't buy that feeling, and the locks remind you.

I call Hannah at the end of the day. 'You didn't come in,' I say. 'I
was worried. You didn't call.'

'I left a message at your house this morning. I just thought—' and she is thinking now, measuring '—since we're friends now, maybe we don't need to see each other in the office.'

'You're right,' I say stiffly. 'I'll close your case.' But I close off the structure and open the inevitable. Close the structure, open the inevitable.

'Anyway, I called to invite you over,' she says. 'If you're not doing anything after work.'

When I leave the office, Frances turns in her rolling chair. 'No good-bye?' she asks.

'Good-bye,' and I waver there, knowing if I shared any of this with her, she would surely be disappointed and alarmed.

There is a carpeted stairway up to her apartment on the third floor. My footsteps sink into it, silenced. She is standing, welcoming in the doorway. 'Come in,' she says. The apartment is dim and cluttered. I sit on a wooden chair, but it's comfortable. And her oven door is open, giving more heat. She is sitting, facing me.

'Well, this is it.'

'It's nice,' I say. 'You have so much in here.'

'You want to see?' She stands up and points to a painting, high on a wall, boxes underneath. 'This one's Ellen's.' There's a girl in bed, blankets pulled up to her chin, the ominous shadow of scissors stretching over the wall.

'Creepy. When did she paint that?'

'Later. It's creepy unless you know the story. You notice her braid? It's the dread of a haircut that's being conveyed, but in a very Gothic way. Or maybe a Freudian way. But that's what the painting's about – at least, that's what she said.

'Here's one of mine.' She points to a lurid, thickly painted canvas that looks like a doll's body with a smeary head, as though the face were in motion or agony. And the chest is flat, the background falling into pitch.

A feeling closes me off – a sense of dread in realizing that I don't know her – having brought this stranger into my life. I recognize a dangerous willingness in myself that I thought I'd lost. A dangerous trust. Like most, I guess. But I think: It's not so creepy when you know the back story, when you're familiar with its depths.

'This one's pretty dark, I guess.'

'But it's good,' I say, looking closer. 'They're both really good.'

'Do you paint, Carrie?'

'No. I used to draw a lot. And I've always looked at paintings. I always felt I could appreciate them without being able to really talk about them. It's like music. You don't have to know about music to like it, but people think different about something in a frame.'

There are records in boxes. Hundreds of them. 'I have a lot of music,' she says. 'Listen to this.'

She pulls out Pere Ubu, Tuxedomoon, Suicide. I sit on the edge of her bed looking at the covers, and the music comes on with ferocity. 'Non-Alignment Pact,' she says, and begins dancing. *I wanna make a deal with you, girl. Get it signed by the heads of state . . .*

'Dance with me,' she says, and it is like my mother, her movements slower than the beat suggests. At first I'm self-conscious dancing with her, but she brings me out. We lift our shoes higher off the carpet so we can hear our feet connect to the floor. We adopt similar steps, both of us jerking our arms, glancing at each other only for instants at a time. She becomes frenetic, smeary. And when the song ends, she grabs my hands and laughs. Her eyes are bright and magnificent. We're both flushed, breathing heavy. But she puts on another record, and away we go.

After that, I throw myself on her bed, winded. She drops beside me. Still smiling, she says, 'I'm on acid, you know.'

'No, I didn't.'

'It's really good. You want some?' She is already going to the refrigerator where she keeps it. 'I know the guy who makes it.' She takes it out of the saran wrap and drops three hits of black blotter on my lap.

'No,' I say. 'I don't do drugs any more.' I say it tenderly, carefully. Not to upset her.

'But it's acid,' she says. 'It's really good.' She says it coaxing, and so innocent. Turn on a dime. Inevitability.

I sit rigidly, silent. And the old mechanisms turn on, a cold machine that instantly grows hot. This isn't heroin or cocaine. Acid isn't addictive. And the loudest thought: don't be alone now. 'Oh, all right.' And I put the blotter under my tongue until I can taste it, and it almost makes me gag. I swallow the rest.

'Here's some orange juice,' she says. 'It's easier with juice.'

We sit listening to the music, and the room is like a messy painting, the sound infusing it with color and shadow. 'Doesn't that sound great?' she asks, lying beside me, and her voice is very far away but clear. This is a cathedral and a train station, somewhere dark and underground, now bright as a tree house. Our bodies swim over the ceiling, and the room turns and changes.

'God, I love this,' I say, my voice thick and foreign.

She's laughing, and I crawl up to touch her arm, find out what she's laughing about. I bring my eyes to her lips and whisper into her neck, 'What are you—'

I feel her hands on my face; they are my face, my contours, tears. Like tiny ladies. I feel like I'm a tiny lady walking away from my mother's care. I see myself walking into pitch, but I'm not crying. Or am I? Into her hands . . .

And the quilt on Hannah's bed is hand-stitched. A woman with time, sitting very still in her body, making this for warm sleep, to wrap another in. When you're sitting very alone and still in your own body you can make these gifts, and you need not give them away. And the music has that density and warmth, and you can burrow into it and lose yourself at its center. I don't know how long we stay there, or if I'm crying. But her body tells me it doesn't matter.

'Do you want to go outside?' she asks after some time.

'What time is it?' I ask.

'I think after eleven. It should be pretty quiet out, and I know a good walk.'

We begin the slow process of putting on coats and mufflers and gloves. We are completely concentrated on locating and figuring out our items of clothing. It's not an anxious concentration, but languorous and personal, as though each of us were preparing for an intimate date with winter.

Outside, everything has a crisp, fresh look about it. I can feel both of us entering a new dream where our energy doesn't threaten to wake us but enables us to navigate the vivid dark. We both watch as a plastic bag is kicked up by the wind and carried down the street like an airborne jellyfish. Under the last street-light, she turns toward me and gathers my scarf around my neck. 'Do you like it?' she asks.

And though I'm unsure of what she's asking specifically, I say, 'yes.'

We make our way up a quiet street with just a house light here or there, and finally come upon an expanse of snow with no houses nearby. We lie in it, feeling it for the first time, knowing if we pushed our hands under it we could pull them out transformed. We have to float on the snow, and the feeling of its movement beneath us makes us both laugh. And then I go very deep into myself, leaving her laughter like a safety rope I can rejoin later, and begin to recognize the perfect reflection I see in the branches of a barren tree, strong in its nakedness, but awaiting its cover of leaves. When I sit up, I notice she's gone.

I spend a long time standing and waiting, until the question 'What are you doing here?' gets too loud in my head, and I begin to walk. And as I walk, my mind finds its way to Victor. And again, I cannot shut it out. Because this is one of the first nights I've found myself walking alone late at night. Since Victor, I've carefully monitored myself, devising well-lit paths to follow, even planning variations on each path so my comings and goings wouldn't fall into the inevitable patterns. Staying home in the evenings happened naturally. I think I displaced the fears of my personal darkness on the night. Now, night intimidates me with its ambiguities, its suggestions. So I start walking, fearful of shadows, not as strong as that tree. And it occurs to me I might not be able to speak if I were to run into somebody. I might not be able to run if I see Victor. But of course he can't come here, unless he's been released. And that is always possible, even probable. Because there is just not enough space to house them. Too many prisoners. Too many predators. And I wonder if Janine imagined she would ever be harmed in the Summer House, each day one day further from the past. Now, fear crowds at the corner of my journey and remorse follows it, spreads uncontrollably through my stomach and rises to my heart. The remorse asks: 'Now you have done this acid, what else will you do? How long before you're on the wheel again? How long before you have a needle in your arm? And will you die this time, running the wheel?'

But I must stay calm. If I appear calm, if I keep walking toward the streetlights, no one will ask where I'm going. No one will say a word to me. And I'll see Hannah, and she'll make this a good experience if I don't let it get out of control. I mustn't let this get out of control. So I begin breathing, and the cold outside has frozen my thoughts. And by the time I approach the bakeshop, every thought has died in the cold.

I go up the stairs and I am quiet on them, gliding light as a person with all their thoughts dead. I arrive at her door. I knock on it, but no one responds. No one hears the dead knocking. It is too solemn.

She does not answer, but I know I can't drive home. I must wait for her, so I sit in front of her door, and after a while I close my eyes.

There's a coldness around my heart, and it feels as if it were being squeezed. But I cannot open my eyes. If I open my eyes, I will see the figure reaching through my skin and I'll know its face. I do not want to see that face.

'Carrie?' Comforting, kind voice, I open my eyes. 'Where have you been?' Hannah asks.

'Where did you go?' I get up and notice a neighbor's head sliding back behind a door.

'I'm sorry,' she says. 'I went for a walk, and when I came back you were gone.' We go into her apartment. Safety and confusion. But safety wins out. I sit on the hard chair in front of the oven. The light bulbs are blue and red in the two small lamps she turns on; the room is ocean deep in their harmony. She sits down in front of me, smiling.

'How long have you been here?' she asks.

'I don't know,' I say. 'I have no idea.' We both laugh; it is too abstract. Clock hands are fear and relief. They sweep over us.

'I went to his studio. We weren't far from it.' She's still smiling, but her eyes are implicating. I look away from her.

'What did you do there?' I ask.

'I can get in there. I've gone in there a few times since Ellen—' She reaches into her pocket. 'That whole place was cleared out, all the paintings and things. Another teacher's in there now.'

'Let's not talk about it.' I say it suddenly, my heart cold again.

'But it was so weird,' she goes on. 'It was like I was drawn there, and I knew exactly where to look. I felt like I was Ellen, and I was really scared and upset, but I had to go in and look. So I broke in just the way Ellen once showed me she could, and I just felt guided. I walked over to the desk and opened the drawer and it was full of this other teacher's stuff, but I put my hand all the way back into the drawer, and caught up inside the desk I found this.' She shows me a photograph folded up like an accordion. She flattens it on her knee.

'It's them,' she says, handing it to me. 'Standing in front of the cemetery gates in Burlington.'

'It's too creepy,' I say, unable to keep my gaze off the picture. She is thin and clever-looking with large eyes and two long braids. She is wearing a turtleneck and a short, plain skirt. Her hands are stiffly by her side, and she is looking intensely at the camera, and I know instantly she has considered this expression for posterity. She's staring us down, will not be forgotten.

He is a big man with an almost boxy physique. His hand, grasping her shoulder, looks very large. The other is tucked into a jacket pocket. He is wearing glasses with a simple wire frame, and his hair is thick and wavy and black, his beard with whorls of gray. He does not seem capable of controlling her; her eyes have something too hungry in them, too ravenous. Next to her, he seems like a slow and defenseless animal.

'It was so strange,' Hannah whispers, 'how I knew just where to look. I went straight to it.'

'Let's not look at it anymore,' I say, laying it face down on the carpet. 'I really don't want to look at it anymore.'

Because I saw Janine's face, what Victor had done to it. They described how they found her, and how her throat had been cut. That's the kind of danger you learn to live with when you're out there. It was something she and I had to be concerned about before we did a private show in a stranger's hotel room. Or every time we copped with some dealer who wanted more from us than we wanted to give. But I don't remember us talking about it, working out some kind of plan in case someone tried something, did something crazy. That was before the dark possibilities had outlines, shape. Now I see them everywhere.

We knew we could be discovered like any of the women you hear about and forget. Women who hand themselves over to fate, to malice. Still, the unreality and inevitability of his violence stays with me, some dull disbelief I can't shake off. And I wonder if that's because she had already stopped dancing, and changed her life, when Victor entered it.

And the picture reminds me of Victor and me, how we looked standing beside each other. Never an easy intimacy between us, only a proximity, a defiance of odds. Never an easy intimacy. Someone must have taken a picture of us together, someone who'd passed through our lives for a night, sharing the drugs, and the hustle it took to get them. Someone must have had a camera. Victor would have told them to shoot. He would have posed. He said I looked like an angel when the drugs drained my color.

We spend the last part of the evening sitting on the floor in front of the large mirror on the back of her closet door. The acid ebbs and builds again, like light. We sit very close to each other, staring at our reflection. 'Now,' she says, 'I'm going to concentrate on your reflection in the mirror, and I'm going to make one half of your face disappear.' I watch my face and see the ear and the eye go. And then she says, 'Now do it to me. Make me disappear.'

I drive home when the acid is just pulsing, almost burned up, and my thoughts are very even and quiet. The colors are still magnificently vivid. Now there is an aloneness, a starkness shared by every tree and house and every person behind their walls, as though nature were about differentiation, about the austerity of our separateness and individuality and its particular ache.

King gets into bed and calms down quickly, giving me just what I need. He is close and soft. I keep my eyes open, looking at the ceiling and the shadows crossing it, how they move. And then there is the fear again, the fear of the wheel. For months after I'd thrown out my syringes I dreamed of myself with the belt around my arm. Sometimes I'd be doing it at my father's feet, sometimes in the office. Always with shame. I would wake up with my heart racing, the terror of thinking I had actually done it, couldn't or didn't stop myself. And then seeing I hadn't done it, I would feel a sense of peace that made that day seem a triumph. But the acid was real. I could not consign it to a dream regardless of how dream-like it felt. And this made me fearful again – that I might go back to the needle. Turn on a dime. An accident of reason.

The needle draws time out of the blood. It plants you solidly in a place where there is no memory of anything that came before, no hope of after. Time exists between shots, and each shot starts the clock over again. You can use for many years and have no sense of the years going. But one day of not using feels like lifetimes. The rise and fall of each day is so subtle, so immeasurable unless your blood is the baseline of its measure. Then time flies away from you, blows past you like a breeze. And I don't want to lose this year that separates me from the past. Now I want to hold on to every sober day that felt like a lifetime. I measured each of those days with remorse and anger and solitude and sleep. I want what I worked for, what I endured.

I'll tell Hannah about my drug history and why I have to guard myself. She can understand thinking right about something and still doing the wrong thing. *Oh, God, please don't let me wake up tomorrow to discover I've done something I didn't want to do.* It's a prayer, but my fists are clenched. I fall asleep just before the sunrise – a stone outside my window.

It is Saturday, and I wake in time to see the mailman walking carefully away from the cottage. I am also walking carefully, as though the environment has shifted while I slept, grown denser. There's a bill, and there's a letter postmarked from Florida. I open it on the couch.

Your mom passed away on December 6. Your grandmother is handling all the arrangements, and you should be hearing from her soon. I'm sorry, baby. They did everything they could for her, but she had two more strokes after the first operation. This last year has not been good for her. I hope it's better now.

I'm still in general population, but I may have to be moved. The other guys say I've got dirty blood, and they harass me a lot. But I keep pretty much to myself, and I've proven myself to most of them.

I'm so proud of my little girl! Please go to your grandmother if you can. I'd hate for your mother to be alone.

Your Daddy.

5

I remember her hair, the way it fell out over the pillow when I put her makeup on, her eyes closed and her breathing so light. And when she wanted to talk to me she'd grasp my hand without opening her eyes. 'I want it to look good,' she'd say. And I got to where I could always make it look good, until the drugs made her stop caring. Her head on the pillow and her face like a mask, the eyes blank but the expression grim. As though there were a war going on in a deeper part of her she could not affect. Always the war on her face, but nothing in the eyes to disclose its particulars, if such wars have particulars.

That's what I'm thinking when my grandmother calls. The last time I talked to her I was ten years old.

'I know your father wrote,' she says. 'I thought you should hear from him and not some old lady you've never met.'

'I hope we can meet.'

'I do too.' Her voice sounds tired, but not old. 'I'll be spreading your mother's ashes next week. I know it's last minute, but I can help you if you need some money to come down.'

'No,' I say. 'I have money.' There's a moment of silence before I ask, 'You cremated her?'

'I didn't know how to reach you. I had to wait on your father receiving my letter and writing me back. I didn't know what else to do.' She informs me of these facts with what sounds like an edge of disgust or disappointment. I'm not sure which.

The family – not just the death – has its complications. She's pursued a tangle of paths to contact me. I'd warned my father, over the phone, that no one could know my whereabouts. He asked no questions. This was familiar to him. He had anticipated his daughter's hiding out, this flowering of his blood.

She tells me where she's staying in Miami and asks me to meet her at her apartment, a converted hotel for seniors. 'You can stay with me,' she says. 'I'd like us to have a chance to talk. I've always wondered about you.'

'I've wondered about you too.' I say the word 'wondered' back to her so she can hear how odd it sounds. But perhaps it isn't odd to her. It was all my mother allowed.

'Your mother never wrote a will,' she says. 'Not that she had anything.' She says this with a kind of sadness in her voice – it is not a condemnation of her daughter, nor is it meant as a discouragement to me – she wants me to know what to expect, the simple, barren facts. The facts as they have always been.

When I hang up the phone, I remind myself I can do this. I'll get a ticket, stay in Florida for a few days. Easy enough. But I feel my heart racing, a strange panic that I decide is grief. I know it was my mother's hand on my heart; cold, squeezing it. That's who I felt waiting at Hannah's door. And that is why I couldn't open my eyes to see her face, because the war had ended, but her face had fossilized its horrors. Even death can bring no peace to some – those who crave it selfishly, who think they can practice death by endlessly killing pain. For them, death is just a prolonged denial of rest.

And I'm grateful to not have to see her face, but something more elemental, the ember of her needs. Ashes. My mother once said: Ghosts are forgotten people. That was her mother, and me after I'd left home. She never sought us out. We were harmless ghosts. We betrayed her, some dim ache. But my mother could not remember herself, either. She had no memories of herself when she wasn't bereft, betrayed. She had no memories of a world that wasn't only ghosts, the cold sense of them passing through and beyond her.

Gina reminds me to pack lightly. She's on the floor with King. She's agreed to walk him and to keep him company while I'm gone.

I do what she says.

'I think you should give your grandmother a picture of yourself, so she has something to keep.' She and King are in a tug-of-war with a sock puppet.

'I don't have many.' I reach up for the one above the fireplace and hand it to her. 'Can I give her this?' I ask. 'Or is it too crazy?'

'She might like it,' she says doubtfully. She's crossed her legs and is rocking slightly at the waist. She looks at it a moment longer. 'What a strange picture. You look like you're praying.'

I take it from her hands and notice the pupils, soul closed up. Victor took it. I'm high in it, slightly out of focus.

I pack it just in case she asks for a picture, but I don't expect much of this meeting.

'What do you wear to scatter ashes?' I ask.

'Where are you scattering them?'

And I can think of no place suitable, except the doorsteps of the men who sold her drugs. Or the doctors' offices where her pills were prescribed. 'I don't know,' I say, looking up from shirts I've folded and put aside. 'I don't think there was a place she felt comfortable. I don't know what places held any meaning for her. I think she was wary of everything, equally. I hope my grandmother doesn't want to take her out to the ocean or something. She hated the outdoors.'

'Let your grandmother do what she wants,' Gina says abruptly. 'When my father died, I had him buried next to my mother. He'd divorced her. He never had a good word to say about her. If he'd had his choice of burial, he might have chosen the bottom of a bottle of tequila. But it was my choice, and I wanted to have something I never had growing up. I wanted them together, and if it took death to resolve their differences, so be it.' She looks as if she's about to say more, then turns her head and looks over at King.

'What else is on your list?' she asks. She calls it mine, but she's written it. She's thorough, and there's comfort in looking over the tasks she's numbered for me.

Throughout the entire preparation – which is no more than a couple of hours – Gina sits quietly, patiently guiding me. Once the bags are packed and Gina has my spare key, I tell her, 'You're so *capable*. Here I am packed and ready to go two days before my flight. That never happens. My family certainly never organized like this; my mother should have taken lessons from you.'

'Nah,' she says, standing up and going to the door. 'If your mother wanted to get her shit together, she would have taken lessons from you.'

Late that night I call Hannah and tell her what's happened. She suggests we meet at Dave's bar. I hang up the phone, take King out, and watch him run. There's a faint pink glow on the horizon that makes me feel ineffably sad, as though it were the last pleadings of light. For a moment it reminds me of how I often felt in San Francisco, everything bleeding through, no separation between myself and the city. I couldn't see an old person without feeling a morose pity. In my neighborhood, they were always alone, on walkers or canes, their skin and bones like glass. They had either lost anyone who could support them or were too headstrong to recognize the danger that seethed around them at every corner. They were alone, period. At least my mother didn't have to see old age in that kind of impoverishment.

I let King in the back door, then get in my car and drive into town. When I arrive at Dave's, the place is still pretty empty. Two guys are playing pool, one lanky and pockmarked with a striped tie that looks like a barber's pole. The other is older, silver-haired and burly, with wire-rimmed glasses at the bulb of his nose. He leers at me from the moment I walk in. I smile at him, and catch him off guard. He quickly looks sheepish.

Hannah is leaning over the bar. I squeeze her arm and she smiles at me, asks me what I want. 'Go sit down,' she says.

She joins me a few moments later.

'How long are you leaving for?' she asks, sliding into the tight wooden booth. Her scarf is pale blue and has gold metallic thread running through it; it looks old and from another country. It brings out her features, softens them.

'Just a few days. I'm leaving the day after tomorrow and coming back on Thursday.'

'I'm glad it's only a short time.' She grabs my hand over the table. 'So, how are you doing?'

'Just numb, I guess. The last time I saw my mother was right after she had her first brain surgery. I was using then; I couldn't feel much for her. Even now, though, without dope, I still feel mostly unaffected by her death. I didn't have any relationship with her in the last ten years. Longer than that. And the funny thing is, I didn't hate her when I left home. I was angry at her. Sorry for her too. I feel like she cheated me out of a regular childhood. But sometimes I think it was destined to come out the way it did.

'My father used to write and ask me to visit her, but I never did. He got out of jail a few years after her first operation and took care of her before he screwed up again. Now he's back in prison, and he wants me to go to scatter her ashes. For years at a time he'd leave her alone while he was serving his sentences. Then he'd come out of prison stronger and she'd be whittled down from the drugs and what it took to get them. And then they'd start using together, like he had to catch up with her. I always knew she'd die first. I stopped charting her progress once I left home.'

She lifts her beer, and I take a sip of my soda. 'Who could blame you for distancing yourself? You saw what was happening and you knew you couldn't change the outcome.'

We sit quietly looking at each other. *Now make me disappear.*

'Did you get home OK?'

'Yeah,' I say. 'I really had to concentrate on my driving. I was higher than I thought.' My stomach turns a little – I really did that, swallowed the blotter, took those risks. I'm drawing my nail over the frost on the glass when I tell her, 'Don't let me do it again. You know, acid. I've never made good decisions, so I need you to help me. I need you to look out for me.'

'OK,' she answers, and I think she is a little ashamed; her concern is immediate and grim.

'I'm sure I felt my mother while I was waiting in front of your door. I just felt this coldness around my heart. And then today, the letter came. All day I felt very slow and methodical, as though I'd prepared for it.'

I don't tell her I deserve this. When I get high, people die.

'That's like my experience with the photograph.' She leans against the dark wood, names scratched in with keys and knives. She puts her feet up on the seat. 'That's the thing about acid. Things become very coincidental on it.

'You know, I came in here and I saw Ellen and Stefan drinking one night. This was a little while after she took his car. And Ellen called me over, but the two of them had been drinking, and it wasn't good when he drank. Anyway, I remember Stefan asked me to sit down, which I did, and he kept staring at me. I felt really nervous about it, but Ellen didn't seem to notice. I forget what she was talking about, but all along I felt his foot – he'd slipped it out of his loafer – traveling up and down my calf. I just sat there, pretending to listen to her and not look at him. Then out of the blue, Stefan leans over and says to me, "Hannah, why do you always dress like a man? You could be pretty if you did something with yourself. Maybe if you dressed more like Ellen." I sat there stunned for a second. When I got up to leave, I couldn't hear anything. I had to steady myself walking out.'

She looks down at the napkin she's been shredding. 'You think I'm pretty, Carrie, don't you?'

I remember the story Gina told me about Hannah's short stint in a sorority house. The knife. The threat she'd made to her body. Could that have been true? Is that what drinking does to young college girls? But Hannah's unlike anyone else. You can look at her deep wounds that are slow to heal, and you wouldn't think of telling her how others walk away from the things that hurt them.

She doesn't understand that. She understands the wound too well. 'I think you're beautiful.' I say it quickly, without consideration. I say it as though it were simple.

'I went after him, Carrie. After that. I humiliated myself. I can see myself doing it, walking up to his studio in a dress. I never wear dresses. And going behind that door, and behind Ellen's back. That's what started everything.'

I look over and notice the older man at the bar, his stare more pressing now. He lifts his beer bottle in my direction.

'You'll make me lose my job,' I tell Victor. He's unimpressed. He knows about my taking the state car; I told him that part of the story. Not the humiliation of my returning with it, how I stood weeping in the doorway, answering to Leslie.

'You went through my things,' she kept reminding me. Her bafflement made me continue stammering out my story, something close to the facts, but less ugly. I had a knack for lies that could work again later. Lies that were always just at the edge of the truth. I told her I was detoxing from antidepressants. I was unreasonable, out of control. I couldn't explain why I needed to get away, but I was suffocating in my skin.

I could see how she wanted to believe me. She wanted to help. I told her I didn't know what I'd do if someone went through my purse, took my car. I know I screwed up, I told her. I'd made it impossible for her to trust me. But I wasn't myself.

Victor didn't care what it took for me to appear conciliatory. He didn't know what *acting* it took to build Leslie's and my other co-workers' confidence after that. He knew his own needs – didn't consider their deferral. I kept the job for three years, until living with Victor started to bleed through. Even, and perhaps most acutely, my clients began to notice. Sick all the time. All the sick days, depleted. And Leslie, who had said nothing to our supervisor about my taking the car, began to show the resentment of someone whose goodwill was betrayed. But for Victor, that was the way to respond to someone else's gullibility. If someone opened a door to him, they might as well take it off the hinges. He'd be back for it.

'Your friend's got money,' he said. He was always going on about her, especially then, when he must have sensed I wouldn't be working long. I should have never shown him and his friend Bobby her house. They liked circling up the mountain. 'So quiet here,' I said, as though I could make a car full of sick junkies appreciate the environment, the golden facade of wealthy people's lives.

'Filthy rich,' Bobby said. And there it was, a home for the sun, sitting on stilts plunged into the ragged cliff. It catches all the light of the day, until the ocean sucks it back.

The Summer House. That's where you retire from ugliness. Where you can walk out over the abyss and the battering depths, and find the whole thing energizing and natural and like it was the beginning of something, and not like the end.

'It started right here,' she says. 'After he insulted me.'

I look around, consciously diverting my eyes from the man at the bar, trying to imagine this as the place where a girl's murder might find its genesis. I settle my attention back on Hannah. It's not places that make these things happen, not the dirty hotel rooms or the fine homes that are supposed to deliver you from them. It's the rooms inside us, how we manage their emptiness.

'I didn't want to lose my relationship with Ellen. I'd ask about Stefan, but she stopped talking about him with me. She did say that I shouldn't take Stefan's comments to heart. She was sure he liked me. But I knew her sentiments weren't with me; she was protecting him, her image of him. If I said his comment about my dressing like a man was abusive, she'd insist I had put a spin on it.'

While Victor was away, I curled up in bed feeling the cold blood coursing through me, knowing that soon my limbs would go numb – dying parts – the rest of me anxious, hyper-aware. Like a story where frostbite takes you out silently. But I was not silent. I choked out prayers and promises to God. *Vicious Bastard, please don't kick me while I'm down and I promise to get up again. I'll get up and I'll get on the wheel. You've made me what I am, and once I'm not sick I'll get up and start running it again.*

And then Victor came in with Bobby, and they had money, but they also had blood on them. None of us wanted to mention anything until we'd copped. Victor called the beeper number. Fucking beeper numbers, after you've done almost anything to get the money together. Because there's no trusting anyone, even though the man hugs Victor like a brother. A brother you make from something terrible and shared. Jail time. Sells him any quantity, except lately he says we order too small. Not worth the time, not worth the risk. You want to buy from babies on the street? Go ahead, buy from babies on the street. You want them to cut it for you, jack up the price, sell you less at night than they do in the day, go ahead. Flaco's happy to do business with you. Flaco has no teeth in his smile. Flaco is just some urchin – one step above you – who sells a couple of tampered bags to get one for himself.

That night we had money. We could buy like we used to. If he called back. It was like him to let us know where we'd settled on the list. Victor's source wasn't like Josephine. No. Josephine you worry about when you get clean. You think she needs your business. You think that's why she crosses herself. Not this guy. He's no Flaco. He had a crew of cab drivers delivering for him. He had two drooling girlfriends trying each batch, but he never touched the stuff. 'They are happy girls, They've got the one cock they care about,' he said, holding up a syringe, 'and they don't mind mine.'

While we were waiting for the goods, I thought I should ask about the blood. I'd ask flatly, as though I wasn't alarmed. There wasn't a lot of it, so it couldn't have been too bad. But they were awfully nervous, and it wasn't just that we were dope sick. I couldn't concentrate on anything until I was well again, so I didn't ask. I'm like my mother; I think about asking. I'm almost interested, almost concerned, that something is terribly wrong. That there's been a terrible wrong, but you can't ask about it until you know you can handle it.

'Janine was home,' Victor said suddenly. He stripped off his shirt and I noticed how thin he was; it seemed to make him look more threatening, his fists seemed larger. He was so beautiful when I met him. Incarceration had been good for him. Dragons-layer, his buddies called him. But his dragons were alive again.

'We had her take us around the place. She packed one of the boxes. Then we drove her to a bank machine. Then we dumped her.'

The sound of the machine. It is the only sound that has meaning.

Bobby was just sitting there looking at his hands. He saw the little half-moons where she'd fought, marked him, but not permanently. He was willing them away by concentrating on them, like the half of my face Hannah removed from the surface of the mirror. I wanted to make him and Victor invisible, but I couldn't.

'Where is she?' I asked Victor.

'Don't ask,' he said, walking the length of our battered couch. I was sitting on it, a hand in front of my mouth, and he walked back and forth like a rope swinging. We would have sold this couch if he hadn't come up with this plan. He and Bobby. We couldn't have gotten shit for it. It's so worn out, it's like sitting on a fence.

'She's dead,' he said.

I started to ask what happened, and Bobby's hand came up. He wasn't worried about my getting anyone's attention. People were always raising their voices down the hall. Long halls of identical lives. My voice was just an annoyance; his instincts were alive to quiet it. I didn't bite his hand when he pushed me down onto the couch and sat on my chest, but I felt my eyes tearing. I wasn't asking for her, after all. Hungry cells buzzed in my ears. My ears had buzzed for hours. Her screaming was buried beneath the buzz.

'Don't fucking say anything. Not a thing,' Bobby advises.

I wanted to count her money. I wanted to get so high, and so far the hell out of there. Victor was no pro. He was too desperate. He'd kill to get us high that night. He'd kill for the promise of money or dope when he started to come down. That's how much he hated pain.

'Where's her money?' I asked when Bobby got off my chest and I was quiet and sick and restored. And he pulled some of it out to calm me. The money meant we were close to drugs. The money affects physiology. 'We got jewelry too,' he said. 'A lot of money in jewelry.'

The call came, and Victor practically raced out the door. 'It looks like you made out,' I told Bobby after Victor left, a little fear in my voice. I never felt comfortable looking at him.

'Lot more than that,' he said, without much interest. He stared at the carpet. His attention moved from burn to burn.

Who was Bobby, and how did we get involved with him? But you don't ask those things, and suddenly the involvement is deep. We sat there, not looking at each other, permeated by each other's presence, our shared desperation and mutual secrets.

When Victor returned, I gave myself a big shot and nodded for the first time in weeks. My mind slid back along grooved passages.

A boy moved to Sweetwater when I was eleven years old. His name was Patrick, and I remember he had a sparse blond mustache that made him seem much older than he was. He said his parents were never home. I would visit him, and the house was always empty. We went through their drawers. He said I could take a bottle of his mother's perfume. It had a long, gold tassel. He had his father's dirty magazines; he would push them under his pillow when I sat with him on his bed. One day he invited me to see what he'd made. He pointed out a mound of dirt in the backyard. 'A graveyard,' he said, 'for the ducks.' He proceeded to dig them up, first the mother duck, eyes speckled with sand, but still alive. Then the baby ducks, all of them dead, powder-soft in my palm. I wanted to run, and I remember I cried with my face turned away from him, unwilling to let him see how he'd disturbed me. Because something in his sharing this with me made me feel for him. Perhaps I knew instinctively that he would never connect with people. He had adapted to a life where his parents never watched him. He was making sure that people would continue to turn away from him for the rest of his life. Someone else would have to teach him shame, and then he'd just keep his experiments to himself.

When Victor kissed me, I thought of how hard it was to look at him. Maybe he thought he could get away with this, that he had no place in the minds of others.

'Let's go back to your place, Carrie.' She puts five dollars on the table and starts to slide out.

The man with the glasses and white hair moves from the bar toward the table with the seriousness of an assassin. I smile at him, at the predictability of it, the awkward amassing of courage he's left undisguised.

'My name's Joel,' he says, reaching for my hand.

I notice Hannah's expression, the sudden rigidity of her mouth. 'Go away, Joel,' she says, not looking at him, but speaking firmly, as though she, too, has prepared for this.

For a moment I think she knows him. He asks her, 'Was I talking to you?'

'I said get out of here. Can't you see we're talking?' She will not look at him, as though her provocation were directed at any phantom.

'I see you're leaving. I'd like to speak to your friend before you go.' He's flustered, and I feel badly for him, all that pointless inflation.

'It's OK,' I assure Hannah. 'If you want, I'll meet you outside.' Her eyes are full of rage. I stare at her for a moment, watching her slowly reason out that this is different from what happened between her and Ellen. She turns her face from mine. 'It's cold, Carrie. I don't want to stand outside for long.'

'I upset your friend,' he says, watching her leave.

'I think you did. But it wasn't your fault. I'm Carrie,' I tell him, offering my hand again. I feel I owe him this much for the trouble he's gone to.

'Is she always that possessive?' he asks. I can see that he's still reeling from her harshness.

'I think she just really wanted some time alone with me.'

'I understand *that*,' he says. 'Do you have a few minutes?'

'I really shouldn't keep her waiting.'

'Can I give you my number?' he asks, extending his card. 'Maybe I can buy you a drink sometime.'

I take his card. Joel Case MD PhD, Department of Psychiatry. I laugh, putting it in my purse.

'What's so funny?' he asks.

'I'm not really sure,' I say, putting my gloves on. 'I guess I was just thinking that meeting me and my friend – well, that we might have seemed a little unstable.'

He smiles at me, though there's something apologetic about it, as though he's recognized something unfortunate now that he's close up. I excuse myself, suddenly concerned by what he sees, and by what I might have missed.

Hannah is standing by the car, smoking. I should have given her the keys, I think.

'Is everything all right?' I ask.

She stands still for a moment, not responding. 'I hope you're not going to ask me to explain myself. I didn't mean to get so angry.'

I unlock her door. 'Get in,' I say. I walk around the car, watching her reluctantly sit down, close the door after her.

'I hope I didn't ruin that for you,' she says as I warm the engine. 'I just hate it when a guy immediately assumes he can interrupt and be welcomed.'

'Well, I think you ended that assumption, for him at least.'

'You're really angry at me?' She asks me as though I'm persisting in this, not letting it drop.

I decide not to answer her. Telling her I'm angry might make her think I was interested in the guy. She'd find a way to confirm her fantasy. I turn on the tape recorder. We sit there quietly listening to Laura Nyro singing *Stoney End*, finding our way back to the familiarity between us. There's a bruised quiet between us neither one of us wants to touch. After we've passed the last convenience store, the houses begin to thin out, the stars appear more dense.

'It's beautiful, isn't it?' I ask, leaning forward to take in as much of the sky as I can.

'It seems like a big empty dome with a billion lights. You can almost imagine it echoing with voices, people who have never been heard.' The snow has been falling steadily for the past week. The new cover is glinting innocently under the moon.

'I can't believe you've never met your grandmother,' she ventures. 'You have no other family?'

'We were cut off,' I say. 'It was something my parents wanted, but I think it sort of got out of control. They could have used my grandmother's help, but they were too proud.' I laugh at the word.

I remember my mother saying of her mother, 'Too much water under the bridge.' The water doesn't move; it is mirror-still.

We pull up to the cottage and begin to crunch our way up the path.

'Do you need me to take care of King while you're gone?' she asks, as we shake our boots off on the porch. 'I'm good with dogs.'

'No,' I say. 'My friend Gina's going to do it.'

'Gina who?'

'The one you know. Or she knows you, at least.'

She looks into my eyes as she passes me in the doorway. 'Did she tell you I worked for her?' she asks, handing her coat to me.

'I don't remember. I don't think so.' I hang them, use the chance to look away from her.

'I did it for a little while. It wasn't really sex. But it wasn't really massage either.'

'Listen, Hannah.' I turn on the lamp and remove some of the files from my couch. 'You really don't have to explain it to me because I've been there. I did all that shit in San Francisco. I don't have an opinion about it one way or the other.'

But I do. I hate it, and she hears it. 'I wouldn't do it now,' I say. 'I don't have it in me' – the desperation, the numb body.

She sits down heavily on the couch. 'I've thought of going back to it,' she says. 'It wasn't so bad.' She picks up an unwashed teacup, looks it over. The way you look at things when you're not thinking.

I wonder if she says this to upset me, or because she wants me to convince her of her faulty memory. She asked me not to treat her as a client, so I won't tell her how confused she sounds to me. I imagine her holding that knife to her breast, but I won't tell her how crazy it sounds. Things happen when you're drunk. Isn't that how Gina looks at it? I would have thought the same – less – just a few years ago. I would have stepped over a dead body to get a fix. I would have bent down and taken the jewelry to sell.

Funny how you come about caring. I think I started feeling in the dark – a few brief flashes fixed in my memory: My father carrying my mother to bed. Or Bill, when he sat on the edge of the window, watching me nod off. At night the lights were red and pink from the theaters in the Tenderloin. They'd flash for just a moment, then return to darkness. And there's a desire to imagine these moments sustained – these surprising and comforting feelings – to watch them played out or extended indefinitely, but the darkness is the other side of our character, and the light is always resolved in it.

'I finally seduced him. I went to his studio, dressed the way he had suggested, more like Ellen. I told him I wanted the three of us to get along, because Ellen was my closest friend, and she obviously cared about him.

'I knew I looked gangly in that dress, and I'm sure my self-consciousness and my awkwardness – not that I looked more sexy or feminine – are what aroused him. He invited me in, and he lavished attention on me that I wasn't stupid enough to trust, but that I liked anyway. I remembered how he'd run his foot up and down my calf, so I felt it would work if I saw him alone. I thought he wanted to hurt Ellen, and I didn't mind if he used me for that. I wanted to hurt her too. That's how it started out – that touching him was a way of hurting her, and it didn't matter whether she knew or not. Do you think some actions have an effect on the universe? At first it seemed like a small wrong, an irrational decision I made – but now it seems almost malignant, evil, what Stefan and I did.

'I wanted to hurt her, but I didn't want to lose her. I would say to her: I don't think Stefan likes me. That was true, even after we'd had sex. And I'd tell her: I feel pushed out of your life, a third wheel. That's why I think she invited me to Burlington with the both of them. To prove she cared about me; that she and Stefan and I could resolve our differences and get along. Also, she could take the pressure off introducing him to her parents. She knew she'd have a hard time calling him a friend. After all, there was undeniable sexual tension between them. He looked like a man who was cheating on his wife, and he was.'

Hannah and I are standing in the frame of the front window. I notice an owl perched in the tree, its head winding back and forth like a nervous watchman. I point him out to her. She stands admiring him with her face pressed against the glass, the long curtain tacked behind her shoulder. And though she's interested, I know she is less comforted by his presence than I am.

'I don't think I'm going to stay,' she says after a while. 'In Iowa City.'

'Where will you go?' I ask.

'Maybe Madison,' she says. 'I need to get out of here. I've just made life hell for myself. You've no idea.'

'Leaving won't stop you from making bad decisions. Trust me,' I say, more alarmed than I intended. 'I'm always battling a part of myself that would rather bury everything and forget.'

She walks away from the window, back to the couch. She looks at me strangely, and I recognize the look as unwillingness. She is not interested in my warnings. She doesn't want the wisdom I dispense at my job. If I'm truly with her, I shouldn't be too unlike her.

'I didn't mean to interrupt,' I say, following her onto the couch. 'What happened when you went to Burlington?'

'Well, you saw the picture.' She puts both feet up, locks her hands around her knees.

'You took that?' I remember her holding it out to me, and the faces of Ellen and Stefan – a severity to their expressions, a stiffness that can come with fear, or with unexpressed rage, the features of people doomed to stay together until something intervenes.

'Have you been to Burlington?' she asks. When I tell her I haven't been outside Iowa City, except for Cedar Rapids, she insists we should go. 'I still love it there,' she says.

'Of course, Ellen's house wasn't how she'd described it. She made it sound like this stately mansion, and I just imagined her parents were tremendously successful. I was shocked when I went up there the first time.

'The house was run-down, painted a dull yellow. I guess it was pretty in a simple, understated way. They rented it, which of course Ellen neglected to mention.

'Her mother welcomed us from the front steps, wearing an apron. She had just what you'd imagine of an Iowa face; it was open and unadorned. She was beautiful in the same way that Ellen was beautiful. But she seemed tired, and I'm sure she'd been arguing with Ellen's father. I could imagine how his belligerence must have worn her down over the years. God, the man was everything to Ellen. She talked him up as a genius – the man who'd brought the Burlington newspaper back to life with his vital, politically savvy editorials. I don't know what I expected – some Marxist, intellectual journalist type. But the first time I met him, I saw a moody, opinionated man at the dinner table who seemed to take umbrage at every affectionate gesture his daughter made toward him. And that saddened me, to watch her try so hard. She could never reconcile her hopes for him with the person he was. You could see he was completely unsettled by her, by her pretense of innocence, her sort of dreamy idolatry of him. "Why don't you grow up?" he'd ask her. You could hear the accumulation of bitterness in it – as though he'd been asking the same thing of her year after year. And of course it was something all of us had wanted to say to her. But he was so mean about it, you couldn't help but feel sorry for her.

'The newspaper he worked on went belly-up, and it was never anything, a few free sheets of Republican jabber they circulated at the bars and stores. He'd been unemployed for years. Nothing was good enough for him, nothing Burlington could offer. And the truth is, he never had much to offer Burlington. Not much to offer his family, either.

'And Ellen's mom would try to defend her. She'd say, "You know, I was just like her when I was her age." And you knew – if it was true – that the man she married had single-handedly wrung it out of her.

'That night at dinner he asked Stefan, without looking at him, "So what's really going on between you and my daughter?"

'Ellen tried to jump in, but her father told her to go upstairs. We just got silent, even Ellen's mother. Then Stefan said, "I think your daughter has a lot of talent." That's when Ellen excused herself from the table. The whole thing was just so strange; I couldn't imagine that she would actually do what she was told. But it had an even stranger undertone to it, as though she were allowing a conference between her father and her suitor – straight out of Henry James. I also left the table, but I didn't follow her. I went out the front door and sat in the car smoking.'

I laugh out loud. 'Did he really say, "I think your daughter is talented"? That's too funny.'

She looks at me closely. 'I like talking to you,' she says. It is an intimacy I'm both certain and uncertain of. I wonder if she loved Ellen, and how much that love scared her.

Did I envy Janine? Did I love her?

She got clean, and she possessed it; it was like a skill she could show off. She could step over the Poison Girl, torso lodged in algae, wearing a garland of seaweed. Janine was somehow able to convert dirty water into air. Perfectly clean air, the toxins siphoned off. But did I envy her after I got clean? I got clean – the first time – after the training I did for the state; and I could sense that everyone, Leslie especially, was waiting to see if I could keep it up. I walked back from the office to my hotel room during lunch hours. I sat at the window, watching the lines of people cashing their General Assistance checks. I never felt better than them. Never kidded myself about how close I was to standing in that line. Sometimes it was only the window glass that kept us apart, the fact that I'd paid for the week. The room was mine. Small, dirty, cramped, mine.

And Janine wouldn't think much of my efforts, but why should she? Rule of the survivor: some don't. Don't reach out to someone struggling. They'll drag you out, drown you. Don't ask yourself: 'Why did I make it, and why can't they do the same?' Especially not when you smell the ocean from your window, like she did. I couldn't open my window – the pigeon shit and soot were like a hard glue. I could smell the Indian food in the Patels' hotel – five dollars for each guest who visits after 8 P.M. – and the constant squabbling at the gate, voices calling up to the windows at all hours. But I didn't envy her, because I'd always wanted a *real* life, and that meant something precarious and painful. The rest was wonderland. Janine had been removed from the hotels and dealers. She had the choice to forget. It was human to want to. Human and unwise.

The room I ended up in reminded me of the one I shared with Bill. Possibly it was the same, but now it was my responsibility to pay the rent on it. I sat behind the desk and counseled 'hard-to-place' clients during the day in order to keep it. I felt as uncomfortable in that office as they did. I wanted to walk out with them, give up trying to stay clean and get back to the life I was familiar with. But I just bit my lip, waited it out. Then I'd return to my room down the airless, dim hall. Behind every door were the people I counseled, their rooms paid for by benefits I authorized. But there's some imperceptible quality that separates the hopeful from the hopeless, the survivor from the one who doesn't. So subtle it's no wonder most people don't experience it. If I can just stay clean, I'd tell myself, something might change. You believe you can convert your experience, learn something from your own struggle. You believe you might be able to use it somehow, but you don't know why. You're a closed system awaiting the paradox of hope. There's some faint sense that you're larger than your trials, and that you'll live past them.

'I could break your father out. It's not impossible if you have some money.'

'Yeah, right.' I looked out over my body, floating like a pale piece of balsa wood, notches on the insides of my arms. Like a lamp I'd seen in one of the hotels, balsa like a collapsed skeleton, notches painted black and blue.

'I know people all over, Carrie. I know all about how they run a prison. I could break him out.' Vic talked crazy after he hit himself. Big ideas.

I reached for the syringe on the ledge of the tub. Now we were just using coke, saving the heroin for the last hit of the night. I shot up in the bathtub, everything open, everything receptive. And the coke kicked my gut; I heaved forward.

'Man, look at you,' he said when I stood up, asking for a towel. 'You're so pale.'

The abscesses happened despite my cleanliness, as though the skin retaliated – would spite itself – when I pressed the point to it. The skin rebelled by dying.

'Don't,' I said. 'Don't look at me.'

He kissed me. 'You're so pale,' he repeated, this time whispering. 'You're like a ghost.'

We didn't have sex. We fought and made up over the framed picture we cut the drugs on. We cut coke on the one picture I had of my dad, on the glass that sometimes held the glare like a halo around his face. I felt a little guilty doing that. Every day I'm creating my fate, I told myself. An affirmation turned sour.

'You're just fucking with me. You can't get him out.' Disgusted, because I wanted to believe him. I imagined us as outlaws, but our life lacked even the heroics of cab driving.

'Yes, I can,' Vic said. 'All we need is a little money.' And I sat there staring down into my dad's face, practically nothing left of the lines we'd cut.

'Ellen suspected something between Stefan and me. After dinner, her father called her downstairs for a talk. Stefan and I were standing in her room, still decorated like a little girl's room. I never had that kind of a childhood. My parents didn't encourage my playing. When I was young, my father had a car accident that crippled him. He was drinking, taking my mother home from a party, and he wrapped the car around a tree. His side of the car folded in and trapped his torso and legs, and he never could walk again, never had control of his body functions. So I was like a young nurse growing up. And when I wasn't nursing my father's injuries, I was trying to heal their relationship. Because my mother hated him after that. You could feel it. And when they argued, they'd send me outside the room, and I'd just listen from outside the door. She felt stuck with him. And he didn't stop drinking right away, either. He drank to antagonize her and to forget that he couldn't do much else for her. But that's another story. Except that when Stefan mentioned that I could be pretty if I were only more girlish, I thought of how hard I'd worked to compensate for my father, for his weaknesses. And that's what made Ellen so alien and fascinating to me; she had an entirely different set of options to pursue.

'But I also knew how futile it was for me to try to engage the same fantasies she had. Her bedroom was proof of that. I'd somehow managed to pull Stefan from her world of playacting into mine. And mine was always about consequences. I was looking at her shelves and he was close behind me. We were both whispering, as though we were thieves or something. I reached up and put my finger underneath the skirt of one of Ellen's dolls, pretending I was arranging it and acting like I wasn't noticing him doing the same to me. I liked the idea of defiling that room. That's when she walked in. She found us both startled, and she knew what was going on.

'But she'd been crying already. Her father wanted us to leave the next day. He didn't like Stefan. Stefan was only a few years younger than him. Ellen's dad was a curmudgeon but not a fool. So we never even unpacked the suitcases. We left early the following morning, and Stefan slept on the couch downstairs. When Ellen and I were alone in her room, she didn't ask why Stefan and I were so nervous when she walked in, or why he was touching me. And I started to think – at least, I wanted to believe – that she hadn't noticed.

'But I remember sleeping with her that night, and how stiff she got when our bodies brushed accidentally. We were talking about her dad, and I had told her that sometimes we can't win the love or approval of our parents, no matter how hard we try. But this horrible feeling came over me while we were pretending to sleep – this horrible revelation – that she'd love Stefan with the persistence with which she loved her father, regardless of his cruelty. And that's just what happened.

'I knew that I'd betrayed her, and yet I couldn't ask her to forgive me. And I think then, the whole need to connect with others seemed confusing and futile. I didn't have the honesty for it. All the things my mother warned me about – the cruelties of other people – were inside me. I couldn't help but act out of these feelings of exclusion I'd been raised with. And I wondered if I were pregnant. Ellen had something that all of us wanted – we thought it was innocence, but I realize now that it was loyalty. It was innate to her, and foreign to Stefan and me.'

Hannah and I find our way to the floor and stretch out on the brown, fake fur rug that has a brittle softness to it. I've lit the fire, and there's a comfort between us amid these confidences that would chill anybody else. Hannah rolls over on her back, locks her hands together on her stomach.

'The next day we went to the cemetery. We got up really early, before Ellen's father woke up, and went out for breakfast. We were prepared to go to the cemetery and then drive back to Iowa City. "We'll have fun anyway," I said. "Why don't we just drive and check out thrift shops?"

' "I'm not going," Ellen said. "You guys can go." And at that point Stefan and I were pretty certain she knew what we were up to. But I still can't figure out why she stayed in Burlington. She said she was seeing a therapist there. That's what she later told Stefan. But we never believed she actually saw one, because she came back to Iowa City and broke into his studio, and then wrote these lengthy letters about how she missed him and wanted him back.

'Anyway, we stood there sort of stunned by her decision not to return with us. We both took stabs at what was wrong. She answered with a disgust we couldn't figure out even in that brightness, even in the glare of our own guilt, our own knowledge of what we'd done to her. Stefan kept asking, "Are you sure you're all right?" and she answered, "I need to spend some time on my own." She turned to him and started rummaging in her purse for a few dollars. "This is for gas," she said, and you could see how humiliated he was. He'd rather have her picking coins out of his pocket while he was still sleeping.

'Then she asked me to take the picture of them. We started walking silently. She said she wanted to find this one stone angel that she loved. The cemetery there is huge, it seemed like forever before we arrived at it. It was like this interminable punishment she was putting us through. None of us was talking. Stefan had glanced once, briefly, at me. It was almost desperate the way he looked. But I found myself walking apart from both of them. It was partially guilt, but maybe a sense of the real dynamic between them; it was too intimidating. I could see how affected he was by her decision – how well she operated. She was surprisingly cool. But I guess it was obvious that Stefan and I were miserable. We were both chastened. You could see it in her expression in the picture – how open her eyes are – how she was daring me. I think she was daring him too.'

'Do you want to stay over?' I ask when she sits up and takes the last sip of tea.

'No, I've got to go soon,' she says, rattling the cup on the saucer as she begins to lift herself. 'I can't believe how late it's getting.'

She turns the watch on her wrist. Just then I hear a car outside. I think nothing of it at first, though it's unusual for someone to chance on this place.

'They must be really lost.' And it sounds like a door closing. It's not a slam, but a firm push of the car door that I hear, and I rise to my feet instinctively. I go cautiously to the window, not wanting to concern Hannah and so walking casually – or what I think to be casual – and of course she asks me what I'm looking for. I put my eye to the peephole and my lips touch the door. There's a dark car idling about a hundred feet from the house, and I strain my eye trying to make it out. Do I recognize it? And then I see the owl lift from his perch, its massive figure swooping low to the ground, effortless as the stretch of a shadow. Shadow of a stone angel with no power to ascend. I reach over and flick on the porch lights, and notice the figure by the car. It's unmoving, and though it wears a ski mask I'm certain its eyes are trained on the peephole, watching the watcher, waiting it out. As Hannah comes to the window, the figure reenters the vehicle and drives off. I feel I can't move from the aperture in the door, and feel my hand instinctively reaching for the chain.

'Are you all right?' Hannah asks, and when I tell her I'm just a little concerned, my voice sounds weak with hesitations, breath I can't catch.

'Can you please stay?' I ask her, without taking my eye from the door. 'That's the only way I'll sleep tonight.'

'All right,' she says. And I feel her arm around me, tentative only at first.

She stands talking to me in the bedroom while I make up the bed.

'King's being exiled tonight,' I say, pushing him off. I throw up the new sheet like a tent. I always think about things like bedding and soft towels and plush slippers. Comforts. My education in comfort comes from magazines, and it always feels slightly staged when I do something good for myself. I pat the down comforter and wonder what she knows of comfort, how she learned it. While she's in the bathroom, I return to the door and recheck the locks. I look out again and wonder about the hazy perimeter of the porch light, a line of security I've drawn that ends indistinctly where the darkness amasses and fortifies itself. I step away from the peephole, expecting the masks to lunge forward, contorted and terrifying. I quickly leave the room, overcome by the feeling of panic.

I pull a large knife from the block, then another, and another. I carry the three of them, blades down in one hand, and walk back out to the front door. I look for places to put them where Hannah won't see them and where King won't get at them. Finally, I slide one into the deep pocket of my coat hanging in the entryway. I hear the water running in the bathroom, and quickly run into the hall and stick another on the top of my bookshelf. But I save the largest knife for the bedroom. I go to the side of the bed and lift the mattress, and that's when Hannah reenters the room, a perplexed expression on her face, the water still running in the basin.

'Carrie, what are you doing?' She remains in the doorway, and I see she's afraid of me, of my desperateness and my secrets.

'Take those off.' Victor was lying on the bed, wrapped in a blanket, shivering despite the heat.

'They have to look like they're mine,' I said, fingering the necklace and looking at myself, 'or they'll be suspicious.' This is how my mother must have felt dressing for my father's court appearances. I was suddenly a respectable woman about to go out into the sunlight, talk to real people, people who work, and have families, and who fence off depravity with a set of skills I never learned. There was a lot of jewelry in front of me, expensive pieces. And I had to sell them, which meant selling myself. And that's what I told Victor, who wanted it done yesterday and didn't care about how much we made as long as he got his next hit. He didn't care that we risked getting caught if we were too quick. I think he believed that sooner or later this would all have to stop and that someone else would have to put an end to it. It was the kind of thinking you see in people who've been out there for too long, who can't sustain the energy it takes to run the treadmill of copping and detoxing. But then he'd always been reckless; if he'd been a success I wouldn't have met him.

God, my face was so worn and the bright diamond looked stolen on me no matter what expression I tried. My smile looked forced and nervous, and my attempt at a poker-faced expression just made me look tired. I unclasped the necklace and put it with the other jewelry in its case. Even the case looked expensive, and I remembered my cigar box. But these were memories, someone else's memories. I snapped the case shut.

'I once did something,' I say, laying the knife down beside the lamp. 'I did something and it hasn't gone away.' I turn and look at her and see she's tense. I know I have to warn her about who I'm afraid of and who I am. Because once Victor did what he did to Janine, fear became second nature to me. She knows I'm not responding appropriately; I should be more alarmed. But I'm dulled by the forgetting and the running.

'I got involved with a client of mine a few years ago, and in the beginning I thought I could exert an influence over him. But it worked out differently . . .'

I sat still at the mirror. I can carry this off, I assured myself. I can do this without thinking of Janine. If she rises to the surface, I'll push her down with dope. I opened the small box with the big ring. Put it on. I smeared some base on the top of my hand to rub out the marks, the endless jabber of needlesticks on my flesh. But the color didn't match my skin tone. What name would they call that sickly color? The hands were uncontrollably shaking in my lap. No one's going to look at my hands.

Victor was trying to cop again. Money brought him to life. The promise of more money made him anxious. He had a kind of nerve damage that made the walls of our room feel like cards. His edginess made the light vibrate. The resources were always running out, and he was bird-like, moving from branch to branch, forgetting the pleasure, the capacity for flight.

I went to the Shreve Building in San Francisco. A woman entered the elevator and we rode up silently, listening to the muted bell announcing each floor. The woman had shoes pointed like the tough, dull beaks of birds. She clutched her handbag, its stone clasp at her heart. She looked at me with a wavering smile, as though she were staving off tears. When we reached her floor, she slipped a pair of dark glasses on and left with a sudden confidence, her expression locked in place.

I felt a dull panic thudding away at the dope. Why shouldn't I sell these? Victor's capable of any violence if I don't sell them. I heard the bell, and watched the doors slide open on a place where the word 'precious' had a meaning and wasn't just a dancer's name. I walked in carefully, the way I walked out on stage the first few times. But I intended to reveal nothing. I wore the one pair of heels – too high, too provocative – I'd worn for stripping. *I could dance in these.*

One foot before the other, handbag to heart. The man behind the counter was wiping the surface of a long glass cabinet. His teeth were white as stones, his mustache black. 'Good afternoon,' I heard him say, with an English accent. He wore a small eyeglass on a chain around his neck, his collar buttoned to the top. He was Indian, I thought.

'I'd like you to look at my stones,' I said. 'I haven't had them appraised, but perhaps you can provide an estimate.'

'Certainly,' he said, eyeing me. The dress was too low. He looked at me expectantly, his eyes chipping away at my composure. I reached into the handbag and pulled out a small box, handed it to him.

'Beautiful,' he said, after flipping open the top and eyeing it closely. I could hear the real admiration in his voice; he spoke as though to himself.

'The stone is over two carats; looks like a nice yellow marquise.

About sixteen quarter carats along the side.' I began fidgeting with the necklace, suddenly tight on my neck.

'Is this for insurance purposes?' the man inquired. 'You can leave the ring with us and we charge three percent of its value for the appraisal.'

'I'm interested in selling the ring.' I felt I'd said this too hastily, too firmly.

He looked at me with a smile I found unreadable. I thought: This is the theme of the day. Everybody complicit, smiling at me. They divine my plan before I do.

He put his eye to the loupe. 'An old piece like this, I'd have to find the right buyer. And that takes work, and time. Not every woman would feel comfortable in this ring. It's a rather bold statement. What are you hoping to get for it?'

'Listen,' I said, suddenly desperate to get out of there. 'I really can't wait. I have an important situation, or I wouldn't think of selling a family heirloom. It's a good piece, you said so yourself.'

'Would you wait here, please?' He took it to the back. I felt myself perspiring, and turned from the counter. The cameras were mounted on both sides of the door. I turned back around and stared straight ahead. I wondered if I'd have to sell all the jewelry, but I thought I'd wait to hear the quote on the ring first.

When he returned, he looked at me reluctantly. I was certain then that this would go very poorly.

'I can offer you $4,000 for the ring. That's quite high for us, but it's clearly a unique piece. Of course, we'll need to see your papers on it.'

I was being very careful not to appear too enthusiastic. I'd never had that much money at one time in my life. I answered him as though I were unmoved, even a little disappointed.

'I don't suppose there's any value in haggling over it? I never received papers for it. When my grandmother died, the jewelry went to my sister. Years later, while she was in the hospital with terminal cancer, she asked me to take it from the safety deposit box. I never thought I'd sell it.'

Who is this sister who turns up so readily when the truth

is unspeakable? Perhaps it's Janine: convenient and inconvenient sister.

'Do you have identification?' the man asked.

'Of course. And here's where I work. I work for the state.' There was no end date on that piece of identification, and I was used to flashing it whenever I needed to build confidence. It had an undeniable air of officialdom, the state seal. Though by then I'd been asked not to appear on the premises. Policy for terminated employees. They'd had some tragedies with fired employees coming back to the workplace with guns and grudges. I'd never return. I had enough shame to keep my grudges in check.

He gave the identifications a cursory look, then passed some papers over the counter for me to sign. I knew I was leaving a paper trail, but Victor had no idea where I'd gone to sell the jewelry. He suggested a pawnshop. But it was Janine who had taken me to the Shreve Building the first time. She'd once sold a piece of her own jewelry here. It was a small pendant her mother had given her. I'll never wear it, she said. She was at her lowest then. And here I was, learning my best moves from her most desperate ones.

The other jewelry, I thought, I'll keep. If I'm ever asked, I'll claim Victor had given me the necklace and told me it was his mother's. To dump it all right then would have been hasty. And then it occurred to me that I would eventually have to sell it all if I stayed with Victor. We'd be through that money faster than we could imagine. And of course the question of what would come next was unfathomable to either of us. We were well beyond the realm of losing jobs or apartments. Now the prospects really opened up, seemingly bottomless.

But I could leave him. The thought was like seeing a curtain of fire over the ocean, conflicting and alarming. The thought of leaving him had a terrifying vastness to it, an elemental threat. It didn't seem possible it could come from my head. Perhaps it came from Janine's. The thought persisted, demanded consideration.

I could take the check for $4,000 and live on it for a couple of months. Disappear before her body turned up. And I thought: Janine would have wanted it to go this way. I owe it to her to use the money to get free of Victor. But of course it was too late to owe her.

Victor would be waiting for me. I began to tick off what I would have to leave behind in order to get out from under him.

I signed the papers and passed them to the man behind the counter. He went to the back to write the check. I imagined my clothes, a few furnishings. Did Victor believe these things would keep me with him? Of course not. He believed I loved him, that I'd go back for him despite the murder and all that led up to it. Maybe he thought Janine's blood was a kind of covenant between us – that scary, ritual thinking of his.

I would have to have a car, and I'd have to cash the check. My mind quickly shifted from what I'd leave behind to what I would need to take. I could deposit this check and have a car and some cash by the weekend, I thought. But first I'd need to cop. I couldn't call our dealer. I'd have to go buy on the street. But I would quit this fucking habit if it killed me. I'd detox in some hotel room. I'd turn the 'Do Not Disturb' sign on the door and toss and turn for three days. I'd lie in the bathtub and rub vitamin E on my track marks. I'd drink water until it sickened me. The thought of those cups wrapped in paper made me smile, a bed with the sheets changed every day. I could afford this holiday, this new beginning everyone assured me I'd never have. I'd take a vacation from sickness. Sick of sick.

Hannah is expecting more from me, but I've put a lock on these events. I'm a door that opens inward; I take on the stories of others, and never let mine pass. Frances would be proud of me. You don't need to tell your story to get theirs. I tell Hannah simply, 'I worry he might be after me.' Now it's another story of an abusive relationship, blurry as the heads – confused and raging – she paints on the girls of her canvases.

'Did you lock the doors?' she asks. She leaves the room to

check them. I wander out behind her, feeling weightless as I move through the hall, and find her looking out the window.

'No one's there,' she says. 'I think whoever pulled up was lost.' She feels better saying it. But she stands at the window for a long time. I remember what my mother used to tell me: A person who's waited on never comes.

I spent the first couple of nights with Josephine, interrupted from sleep when she'd arrive at the room with a trick. It had come to this, for her, and she would nudge me with her cane to wake me, and I'd sit in the hall while she earned. She seemed grateful for the company, and the quarter gram I bought her, and she didn't talk about her daughters, or any other accommodation she'd made to take her pain away.

I left the hotel in the morning and walked briskly to the used car lot on Valencia Street. I tried to remain as inconspicuous as possible. I knew he was looking for me, and he would get to this neighborhood if he weren't here already. I craved that car like an armature. And when I'd finally purchased it and drove it off the lot, I felt my life coalescing, as though I were suddenly moving forward. The car felt like I'd grafted it on; its insularity calmed me immediately.

I knew I'd need to get high or I'd never get out of town, and bought my drugs on Mission Street from the car. A Mexican boy on a bicycle sold me a gram, first peering into the window and looking at my eyes, the pupils rebounding to vast, hungering tanks. 'Let me see your tracks,' he said. I unbuttoned my sleeve staring into his eyes. There's no end to the humiliations of this life. No end.

I was ready to drive off when I saw the newspaper headline in a rack across the street. 'My Night of Torture,' and there was Janine's picture beneath it. I pulled over and grabbed one and dropped it on the front seat, determined to read it later, once the city and Victor were behind me. But my mind kept crying, she's alive, which suddenly seemed more terrible than if she were dead.

'I'm not going to tell you there's nothing to worry about. I'm pretty scared myself right now. If you want to go, I'll understand. Though I do think we're safe. Victor's been in prison for some time. Not long enough, of course. But I'd really be surprised if they let him out,' I tell Hannah. In my mind I'm spelling out the words 'attempted murder,' jotting them into a case file, then passing that file into another person's hands. This passing goes on and on. And then someone drops it.

'What did he do?' she asks apprehensively.

'Assault, robbery. You name it. He had a record before I ever met him, but I thought he'd change.' I laugh out loud. When you say these things – see them for the first time – how can you justify them?

'Drugs made him wild. He really was someone else when he used. So was I. I was easily deceived. Willfully and gladly deceived.'

'Why do you think he'd come after you?'

'Because I took his money.' I notice her look over her shoulder at the large window in the living room, but the drapes are closed.

'Shouldn't we call the police?' she asks.

'I took the money,' I say sharply, walking toward the bedroom. 'And besides that, I already talked to the police.' I remember calling the police station, an anonymous tip. I know Janine and I know who did that to her.

I looked at her picture on the front page of the paper. I don't know where they found a picture of her, so much hope in her eyes. But I knew they hadn't pulled it from a yearbook, despite how young she looked. She always looked young; it was the only way she possessed a childhood, in her features. She left home when she was fourteen. She couldn't get along with her mother, so she lived with punks and pimps. For a while, Bill and I let her sleep in our tiny room, but she never liked to stay somewhere for too long. The moment someone got close to her, she would imagine she was unwelcome. So she split. I used to ask her why she didn't just call her mom and get off the streets, but any prolonged visit meant she'd have to see herself through another's eyes. She preferred the distorting glass of being alone.

The picture must have been taken after she got clean. Perhaps her mother took it, capturing an image she hoped would be permanent. A clean daughter. Daughter with a chance in hell. I could suddenly put Janine's chirpy voice – the one I'd heard in Sacramento – with this face. Not the face of the girl cowering in a hotel bathroom, telling me she was too high to jerk off the man waiting outside the door. No, that was the other face. This face had come together like a fresco, its broken pieces holding so that you could not imagine them disordered. They did not publish the pictures that were in the crime report. Anyone would have been convinced she was dead. Though I could have told Victor she'd hang on. It was her instinct.

If the police pursued me, I would say I left fearing Victor's temper, his retribution. Though it was leaving him that first made me fear him. The leaving, and the strange appearance of hope in Janine's picture; it scared me to think I'd never seen it in her before.

Hannah undresses in the bathroom. She emerges in a long flannel nightgown I've let her borrow. She looks pale against its black and gray checks. I'm already in bed, looking at my hands under the light. I have a book opened on my lap, but I can't retain the words; they are many voices whispering. And my eyes shift to the window with its curtains tightly shut, but there is a thin seam of moonlight between them. I wait there, watching and listening to the water in the basin, and thinking of my father's friends and the masks they wore to frighten me, and how they'd taken them off when they saw me step back, my eyes filling with tears. And I know that Victor would never be moved by tears. Not when it mattered.

When Hannah settles in beside me, I try avoiding the subject. 'So, Ellen stayed in Burlington?' She lies there staring at the ceiling. She is upset about Victor. I can see that. She has never slept with a knife under the mattress. But when she begins talking,

I realize she is more concerned with the events she cannot defend herself from. It's Ellen and Stefan who preoccupy her. If she can end it, finally, once and for all, by telling it, she'll end it tonight. But words won't affect them. They're deaf to her. I often think memories precede our lives; they lie in wait for us.

'She stayed there for a couple of months and I heard nothing from her. Stefan, in the meantime, returned none of my calls. I didn't want to see him, but I wanted to know if he'd heard from her. I started asking myself what we'd done, how it happened. I was racked with guilt. I was perplexed by my own actions, led by them. And the silence from the two of them echoed in me; I was that empty. I'd walk around feeling nothing. I can't honestly say I've gotten the feelings back, either. I just sort of mimic people with feelings. That's how I get by most of the time.

'I thought: Maybe I did it out of jealousy; then I thought it was malice. I couldn't decide; they both made me sick with myself. When I wasn't totally hating myself, I'd convince myself that I'd had sex with Stefan as a desperate measure to bring Ellen back to me; now we would both know the depths of Stefan's deceit, now that we'd both been wronged by him. And I'd let myself live with the fantasy: that Ellen would call and we'd both agree that he should have never come between us.

'So when she did call, I think I expected that she'd come to the same conclusion. She was back in Iowa City, but her voice sounded very far off, and she was whispering as though someone might overhear her. And I asked if I could see her. She told me, "No," very firmly. I could see there was no point in trying to change her mind. I consoled myself with the thought that she'd called me and that eventually she would come around. After a long silence, she asked if I wanted to apologize, and I admit I was taken off guard. I never expected her to confront me directly, and I was surprised she took the burden from me. I didn't want to bring it up, but when she asked I said, "Yes, I do want to apologize. I'm sorry I let this happen." I knew I could never tell her I was pregnant, but I could feel the baby in my sobbing; I cried with complete abandon, overtaken by it.'

Hannah looks over at me then, and the seam of light seems to separate her face, though both sides possess the same contraction of shadows. I can see in those shadows the pain of final decisions, of termination. 'And then she hung up, and that was the last I heard from her.'

On the trip to Sacramento, during the training for the state, I called Janine for an apology. I wanted her to apologize for leaving me, for getting clean and leaving me to pretend I'd made a decision to keep using. Instead, I asked her to apologize for the play she'd written. And when she hung up on me, I realized I would never be able to ask her what I really needed to know. I needed her to tell me how she had skipped over the locked groove of addiction. I wanted to know what made her rush to her mother's care, the absolution she would find in expensive facilities and dark church basements, where her story could mean something, and the door could swing both ways at last.

And I knew that I would use drugs again – even that evening – assuring myself it was the only way I could sit through the training seminar, where I was learning case management and where I'd heard the words 'ethical distance' for the first time. I knew exactly why Bill had made an exception of me, had kept no distance, followed none of the simple rules of his profession. Bill sought the absolution of likenesses; he saw in the damaged people he counseled some shared burden, and if it was not absolution, it was at least absolute. I've sought this comfort, and not just in Hannah, but in Victor too. I've sought the identification that comes not in the similarities of our stories, but how we hold them and don't let them go.

Hannah turns toward me and asks if she should turn out the light on the nightstand. I tell her it's fine, relieved by the bathroom light still illuminating the bedroom doorway.

She turns toward me and props herself on the pillow. 'After Ellen's call, I started to work with Gina and Rachel. I thought I could make some money quickly and that I'd take care of the baby and eventually I could move out of town, maybe go back to Sioux City. I knew I could never tell Ellen about any of it. I knew on the deepest level I never wanted the baby. Of course, Ellen would have thought me a monster if I told her how I felt. I felt humiliated by the pregnancy, disgusted by it. I couldn't tell Stefan about it, either. I didn't imagine I'd hear from them again, and sometimes I would go up into the tractor and just think about the irony of it: how I'd interposed myself between the two of them, and how this child was really theirs. And I would get so tired, replaying the whole thing in my mind and thinking about how this baby was just one of the many secrets I carried, and how maybe I could take the baby somewhere and there would be no consequences, because that's what *we* were – the consequences.

'Sometimes my mind would go back to them when I was working at Gina's, and I wondered if they would get back together, and whether Ellen would have a baby too, and whether he'd divorce his wife. Because I thought: Even if I disappear, they'll have their own things to work out. Though, at that time, I somehow imagined that they would make it work. They seemed destined for each other. That's why I felt it was fated to turn out so bad for me. I tried to stop the inevitable. I didn't imagine what would happen to them. Or that I'd be the lucky one.' She laughs weakly, then puts her hands over her face.

6

For years I would wake up with the chalkiness of the stones I carried still on my fingertips. I took them from the rough embankment of the canal and scraped them along the sidewalk in front of our house, and they were powdery stones as though they'd been pulverized and reconstructed. And for years they were the strongest memory I carried from my childhood, and even now I feel them, after a dream, on the tips of my fingers.

When Gina calls, I've just woken from the dream, its disturbing residue. Hannah practically jumps from the bed; it's just before 8 A.M., but I can see she's anxious to get dressed and get out. Neither of us slept well. Even King seemed uneasy, moving around the living room.

'I'm going to shower real quick,' she announces, and heads toward the bathroom. Gina simultaneously says, 'Don't forget to confirm your flight tomorrow.' She sounds oddly cheerful, as though she were sending me off to camp.

I keep myself from asking, Why am I going to Florida? The trip is suddenly ill-timed. Or perhaps perfectly timed. I was up all night in a state of dread. I feel like I've been given a choice of tragedies, obsessing over Victor or collecting my mother's remains. And I'm still angry at her; I wonder why her ashes can't wait. I try to keep my resentment from showing; I'll do what

Hannah does – mimic appropriate responses and feelings. After all, my mother is dead. There's no point in anger now.

'Hannah's in the shower,' I tell Gina after she asks about the other voice she's just heard.

'She stayed over?' I notice the tinge of slyness in her inquiry. Gina is always entertaining the thought that I'm keeping my lesbianism from her, that the moment I'm alone with another woman we tear each other's clothes off and make up for lost time. I tell her about the car in the driveway and realize it's not hard to make it sound sinister even without mentioning Victor. 'That's why I asked her to stay,' I say informatively.

'Is she away from the phone? Can I tell you something?'

'She's in the shower.'

I expect something lewd. Gina's full of coarse revelations.

'I know you've gotten really close to her, but I think you should know that she's maybe more troubled than you think.' I'm surprised by how seriously she says this. It's a seriousness I rarely hear in her, and I wonder if she's priming me for a joke.

'I know how troubled she is. We had to have something in common.'

She dismisses my comment. 'Did she tell you she was pregnant?'

'Yes,' I say. 'And this is beginning to feel distinctly like gossip.'

'Did she tell you what she did?'

'She had an abortion. I know you're not going to condemn her for that.'

'Did she tell you she had an abortion?'

'I can't talk about this. Yes, I think so.'

'She had the baby, Carrie. By the way, it's not gossip. This is your job, isn't it? I thought you talked about these things.' She resents my being a case manager. I want to remind her that it's not clinical psychology. It's government service, food stamps for the soul.

'She's not my client anymore. Anyway, what happened after she had the baby?'

'Your guess is as good as mine. But Rachel and I noticed she didn't have the baby when she checked herself into the psych hospital. I wonder if you shouldn't find out what she did with him?'

'How do you know she even had the baby?'

'Well, now I really get to impress you. She had him here. She wouldn't let us call a doctor. She insisted we not say a word to anyone about it. So you see, I feel partially responsible. When you've taken someone's baby head first out of their body, you don't just suddenly forget they had one.'

'What are you trying to say, then?'

'I think the worst.'

'You think she killed him?'

She's silent for a moment. 'I think so.'

'That's too strange,' I say. I hear my own train of thought die out. It dawns on me that it might not be strange, however awful. And I begin to wonder if it's the baby and not Ellen that she can't forget.

'Listen,' Gina says. 'She'll probably tell you, anyway. She probably needs to talk to someone about it. But if she tells you, I need you to let me know. Promise you'll tell me. Promise.'

When Hannah comes out of the shower, I hand her a large, fresh towel. When I hand it to her, I wonder if I'm not asking her to cover up. On some level, it's too much to know about her, too much to presume. I feel pity and an odd sense of betrayal. I wonder if she simply hasn't gotten around to this part of the story; maybe it comes after Ellen's death. Maybe there's something she hasn't told me about that too. It's funny when you find a breach in someone's character; a missing detail can become their strongest feature.

I take King out behind the cottage while Hannah dries her hair. I'm tired of living in fear, I think as I unbolt the door. Tired of precaution. She asked if I want to go out for breakfast with her, and since Gina's helped with all the packing there's really nothing for me to do before tomorrow's flight. I sense Hannah's asked me because she doesn't want me to stay here alone. She doesn't want to be here either. I don't blame her. Perhaps there couldn't be a better time to scatter my mother's ashes. Leave an empty house for Vic.

After the snowfall, the pond is virtually indiscernible. I stand close to the back door, fearful in a way that's both familiar and new. The fear is compounded by the fact that I no longer know Victor, or rather that he no longer knows me. I suspect he's the same. That's why he's come. But I fear I have no sway over him now. I wouldn't know how to fake the love I once felt for him, can hardly imagine what I called love in those days. There'd be no talking him down, now. He's learned he doesn't need me and cannot trust me. There'd be no recognition. He'd put me down like a dog that turns against its master.

I call King inside and lock the back door. It's Sunday and usually quiet downtown, a good day to look in the windows without buying. That's what I'll do today, look into the windows. I'll scan the reflections in case anyone's standing behind me. I won't be surprised by the surfacing of masks in the glass. I know I can't ask Hannah to stay with me; I've already pushed her too far. I worry she might be angry with me about last night, suddenly asked to be my protector. I sit down on the couch, waiting for her to gather her things.

'I'll be right there,' she hollers from the bathroom.

Once she comes out, we drive into town and park. We discuss breakfast unenthusiastically. 'Do you mind if I say good-bye to you here?' she asks. 'I feel antsy, like I need to get home.'

'That's fine,' I tell her. 'I'm sorry about last night. I got paranoid, and I think I made it impossible for you not to stay over. But I'm really grateful for the company. I needed it.'

'I think you should stay with me tonight,' she says. 'Don't stay there alone.'

'It's my home, Hannah. I can't let my fears get the best of me. Someone pulled up and drove off. It's more likely that it was just someone who got lost. No one knows where I live.' I reach over and grab her hand. 'There's nothing to worry about. If I get spooked, I'll head over to your place tonight.'

She gives me a hard look. 'I hope you've convinced yourself

that there's nothing to worry about. You haven't convinced me.' She looks away from me for a moment. 'I'm sure your trip will be good for you. Remember to call me as soon as you get back. If anything happens out of the ordinary, just come over.' She hugs me and steps out of the car.

I begin to amble my way toward the cluster of streets that constitute the main shopping area, thinking that I'll maybe pick up a frame for the photograph I plan on giving my grandmother. I notice a figure sitting alone on one of the benches, his hands brushing his arms to keep warm. It's the newspaper boy who is rumored to be retarded as a result of his family's incest. This could be lies. No one I know has ever spoken to him. He sits there silently rocking in the cold, his tongue involuntarily appearing from the side of his mouth. I want to ask him why he's sitting there, and if he needs a coat.

I think of how often I saw people in need in San Francisco, how walking past them made me feel I had a toughened skin around my heart. To consider helping someone beyond offering them a couple of coins would be a kind of madness. You learn your limits, don't pick up strays. You might be killed, robbed. Most likely, you'll encounter the disappointment inherent in those situations: the unshakable habits and patterns of someone acclimated to a life of begging, destitution. Don't try to alter the unalterable. Life is terrible. Most people never see above despair. But the boy is engaged in his rocking. He seems transported by the rhythm of his bobbing torso, the sounds of his hands running over his windbreaker.

I stop, standing far enough away so he doesn't notice me, and pretend to be looking elsewhere. I wonder if he'll be offended if I offer to buy him a coat. This is crazy, I tell myself. I can't fix him, can't fix anyone. I pull my hat down around my ears. It's too cold for him to be here alone. I start to advance toward him. What if I scare him? What if his parents are nearby and think I'm abducting him. He's probably eighteen, though he looks like a child. Or at least I see him as a child.

'What's your name?' I ask him.

He looks up, doesn't respond. He goes back to rocking, but faster this time.

'What's your name?' I ask again. No pressure behind it.

'Robert,' he says. It's hard to understand him at first.

'You seem cold,' I say. 'Do you have a warm coat?' This is ridiculous, I hear myself saying. Stick to case management. This is embarrassing. 'Are you cold?'

'It's cold,' he says. 'I'm waiting for the store to open.' He's rubbing his arms. His rocking has slowed, as though his body were a vehicle slowing up, allowing me to get inside.

'You have another hour before it opens. Are you going to the drugstore?' I ask.

'I'm going to the drugstore,' he says, his answer offered seemingly independent of my question.

'I'm Carrie,' I say. 'Can I sit next to you?'

The boy's face is thin and long; a sparse black mustache and individual, coarse black hairs pepper his cheek and chin. His nose is leaking. His eyelashes are soft and long; he looks like an El Greco saint, a kind of modesty to his abstracted expression. I want to push my arm through his, to warm the poor child. I push the snow off the bench and sit close enough to him to see the flakes of dandruff in his black, wavy hair, the pattern of sleep flattened in the hair above his ear.

'I've seen you delivering newspapers,' I say to him.

He turns his head in my direction but avoids looking at me. 'I carry newspapers,' he says. 'To downtown stores.' His speech is difficult, his tongue softening every word. I allow myself to feel a tenderness for him I've only sometimes expressed with King. Acceptable pity. Pity for animals is all right but one learns that it's condescension to feel pity for the retarded, the poor, the elderly. It undercuts their integrity, their potential, their resolve. Pity is no rescuer; it's selfish. And of course I can't hug him the way I do King. I feel a sudden ache, as though he were some part of me I'd abandoned, something I hadn't learned to love until now.

It gets increasingly cold sitting still beside him, and I ask him if he wants to walk to the Mennonite store. I've already determined that I will return with a coat whether he goes with me or not. If he's no longer here when I return, I'll simply ask someone at The Deadwood to hold it in the back, and the next time I see him delivering papers there, I'll get it for him.

'What is the Mennonite store?' he asks, a little agitated. 'I deliver papers to downtown stores.'

'The Mennonite store sells coats. It's not downtown, but it's only a twenty-minute walk from here. We can walk together.'

He nods his head.

'Do you want to walk with me?'

'Yes,' he says. 'Mennonite store.'

I practically have to pull him from the bench; he seems almost frozen in place. He takes his first steps laboriously, then loses some of the stiffness in his gait except for the heaviness in his right foot which I've noticed before when I've seen him delivering papers with his canvas bag. He holds onto my arm, not saying anything at first but looking over his shoulder at the bench.

I wonder whose child this is, and how often he's alone. I feel strangely insulated walking with him, as though the two of us were figures in a snow dome, the environment shifting around us while we remain still. He holds steadfastly to my arm, repeating the name of the Mennonite store and laughing each time he says it. I imagine him thrilled with the excitement of another store, one he's unfamiliar with. Someplace where he might deliver papers, find a connection or routine.

His delight does not keep me from my own disturbing voices, urging me to see in my gesture an attraction to doomed and stunted things. Victor and even Hannah are drawn into this circle. They all have a damaged beauty about them; I'm drawn to them sexually, even this boy whose trust momentarily shames me. Perhaps it was Jim who'd set this pattern into existence. He came to me wounded, and I'd brought a girl's fantasy to the war he'd witnessed. I thought my loving him could make him whole. But I was attracted to people I couldn't save long before him, long before the Poison Girl grew up in me, unable to resist the colorful things that could kill her.

The chimes on the door of the store fascinate Robert. He pulls it open and closes it again. I take his hand, nodding quietly to the Mennonite woman behind the old-fashioned cash register.

'Hello,' she says, more to Robert than myself. 'Is there anything I can help you with?'

Robert is pulling me along now, past the crowded racks of dresses.

'I'm just here to get him a coat. I know they're in the back.'

She nods, and goes back to reading through a large magnifying glass. I wonder if she thinks I'm his mother. I would be proud of this beautiful boy. I'd discover the things he loves and make sure he had them. I'd find a way to bury the bones of my past, to put my failures behind me. I'd let him teach me; abandon all my lessons of life and its limits.

The whole store smells like a winter trunk. In the back of the store the racks run at waist and eye level completely around the walls. They're jammed with coats. I reach up and grab a blue down jacket. I help Robert on with it. His eyes are wide and expectant. When I pull up the zipper of the coat, he falls toward me, pushing his face into my breasts. I allow myself to pat his head, then take him by the shoulders and hold him away from me, looking at the fit of the coat. A little small, I think. I find an orange one with a hood. It looks larger, and I begin to help him with it when he pushes himself to my breasts and grabs at them.

'No,' I say, holding him away from me.

'I'm sorry,' he says. I can see in his eyes a gentle, beatified confusion. The jacket fits him perfectly. When I zip him up this time, he looks away as though his interest has alighted on something else in the other room.

'Do you like it?' I ask him.

He nods his head. I pull the tag from the sleeve and leave him wearing the coat. By the register I notice some shelves with frames of varying sizes. I pick up a couple of small frames. One is made of wood and painted pale blue; the other is covered in brown leather.

I decide on the wood frame and pay for it and the jacket. I call Robert out of the store. We walk back to town with him holding my hand. I banish my doubts about my motivations. The bright, orange coat will not only keep him warm, I think, but safe too. You can see him from a block away.

In San Francisco I passed a black man almost every morning on my way to work handing out the homeless paper for donations. He stood in front of the coffee shop not far from the Employment Development Department. I liked the way he spoke to me, his consistency. One day I asked him what kind of work he'd do if someone offered him a job. He didn't have to think about it.

'I'd go back to plumbing,' he said. 'I'm a trained plumber. I had a drug problem. I went to jail. I served my time. I just haven't had an employer willing to give me a chance since.'

I handed him my card. I thought this was an improvement. In the past I might have urged him to come to work with me. I left it to his discretion. If he wanted help finding work, I'd assist him. We weren't supposed to recruit, but our services weren't advertised either. Other social service groups referred us clients. He seemed startled by the offer and took my hand in both of his. I worried he might kiss it, but he just shook it gratefully.

The next morning I didn't see him hawking the *Street Sheet*. I bought my coffee and walked into the office. He was sitting in the waiting room and stood up when I entered. He had a maroon tie on and a dress shirt. I led him to my desk, though it wasn't yet 8 A.M. I started to take his narrative. He lived two buildings away from me with his girlfriend, who was an unemployed legal secretary.

'I haven't used since I got out of prison a year ago.'

'How long were you in?'

'Four years.'

I knew it would be tough with him at least five years out of work. But I thought I could pitch him, vouch for him. He'd worked for some major plumbing outfits. I called and got confirmations, even a recommendation. I was ambitious. I hadn't met

Victor. I was clean, transitioning back into the world of whole people. I opened a Yellow Pages and looked up plumbing companies, tried to find someone smaller, independent. There were tax incentives I could offer. We could arrange to match the employers' salary for the first three months.

I cold called and found someone willing to listen to my pitch. I set up an interview. I created a résumé for Cal. He sat at my desk, stunned. I made the world seem easy to navigate. Incentive was everything.

'Remember,' I advised him, 'you deserve this. You can do this. This is your field. These are your skills.'

He came in two days later, after his interview. 'I start this weekend,' he said, beaming. I had to follow up with the employer every three weeks.

'Cal's working out great,' he said. 'He's my right-hand man.' He was making more money than he ever had, working sometimes sixty hours a week. Sometimes he slept on a cot at the shop. He called to ask me if I'd see his girlfriend, Dianne. She needed work too.

Dianne was a tall, thin, red-haired woman. Her bangs fell into her eyes, the rest fell almost to her waist. She looked Irish. She had freckles, and deep crow's-feet around her eyes. She used Cal's last name.

'I guess you haven't worked in a while,' I said, thinking her hair was a problem. It was red but going gray. It was clean but functioned like a ratty frame. Her face was washed out, revealing a hard, grooved shell.

'Cal's gone all the time,' she said, 'We barely have any time together.' She talked to me like I was responsible for this and could put an end to it.

I put my pen down, looked at her. 'It's good that he's working, isn't it?'

'I miss him,' she said. She thought for a moment of how this must sound. 'I just need to get back to work. I used to work as a legal secretary.' Her lips played nervously over bad teeth. I thought the hair and the snaggletooth were going to work against her in a law office.

'When was your last job?' I asked her.

'Over ten years ago.' I hear in her voice that she doesn't believe I can help her. Her presence suddenly exhausts me. I don't even want to begin a case for her. Her hair falls slack like my mother's. Her eyes show a dull, obligatory attentiveness. She's been sleeping for the past ten years; now she's suddenly bored by sleep.

'What happened to you?' I asked. No need for me to be gentle in my inquiry. Something was wrong with her; she couldn't pretend otherwise. Ten years of unemployment is never just bad luck.

'I drink sometimes,' she said. 'I have a problem with it. But since Cal came back, neither of us have used anything.'

She answered no to the other questions I asked her:

Do you know any computer applications?

Do you have any references we can contact?

Any paralegal skills?

Lawyers don't want their new hires to be tax exemptions from the state. They don't build offices in enterprise zones. I couldn't imagine how to pitch her. I felt helpless, enervated looking at her. I'd heard of people who used helplessness as a defense mechanism. They forced people to give up on them.

'I can call around,' I said. 'But I'm not really sure if I can place you. You may want to start at a community college, get some computer skills.'

She only said, 'I hope you'll ask Cal to come home more often, when you speak to him.'

About nine months later, everything had changed. I'd met Victor. I was using, and I was under scrutiny at the job. It was almost Christmas. I arrived late one morning to find Cal standing in the lobby, a particularly battered chrysanthemum in his hands.

'Hi, Carrie,' he said. 'I wanted to wish you a good holiday, and to give you this. I thought maybe I could talk to you if you have a minute.' He held the potted flower out to me.

'Thank you, Cal.' I was flustered. There were other clients in the lobby, clients I was late for. We weren't supposed to take gifts either. 'I have just a couple of minutes,' I informed him, speaking loud enough for the other two clients to hear.

I brought him back to my desk, hoping he wouldn't notice my pinned eyes, raspy voice.

'This is quite a surprise,' I commented, shuffling some papers, looking down.

He said suddenly, 'Dianne's dead.'

'What?' I was shaken. She'd called about a month before to see if anything looked promising. I'd never done anything on her behalf. Nothing looked promising.

'I tried to stop her. I was holding her wrist, but she got free and jumped out of our window. I tried to hold her back.' He was weeping, both hands spread over his face.

'Oh, Cal. I'm so sorry.'

'I loved her so much,' he sobbed. He brought his face low to his knees. 'She was depressed and drinking. I tried to hold her back, but she jumped.'

'When did this happen, Cal?'

'Three weeks ago,' he said. 'I've lost everything.'

He straightened up and looked at me. I saw his eyes then.

'You used over it,' I said to him. I wasn't condemning. I was in no position.

'There's no point to anything without her,' he said. 'I lost my job and my apartment. I couldn't hold on to her, and I lost everything.'

I saw in his reduced pupils the full horror of resignation, the pulverizing force of life on the weak. We weren't allowed to work with active users. But I was using. I'd break the rules for him.

'Cal, we've got to get you working,' I said. 'How can I help you?'

'No, Carrie,' he said, shaking his head. 'I don't want anything anymore. I'm through trying. It's over now. I came to tell you about Dianne, and to thank you for being there for me. I'll never forget it.' He stood up and left abruptly.

Over the next two years I saw him about three times on the

street. The first time he was arguing with a white woman, standing at a bus shelter in the rain. The last time, I'd lost my job and was out copping dope. 'Carrie,' he called. I turned and saw him on the corner where I'd sometimes bought syringes.

'Cal,' I said, glad to see him and walking over to him.

'What are you doing here?' he asked.

'The same thing you are,' I answered, and we looked at each other knowingly, smiling as though it were good fortune that brought us together.

I leave Robert downtown, eyeing the orange coat as I make my way across the street from him. He continues waving for a long time after I say good-bye. I stop turning around, prolonging my departure. I feel good knowing he'll be warm, but my sadness for him is more acute. It doesn't make a difference if that sadness is appropriate. Caring about people is wounding. That's why so many people are reluctant to care. It hurts.

I go for lunch and return to The Deadwood for coffee. I think maybe I'll run into Gina here, or Hannah. It's central. We all come here. I like the buzz of the students; a few of them seem genuinely interesting. I sit close to a boy who seems to hold court here. His hair is a recently dyed, blue-black mop top. He has a thin, expressive face and abnormally long fingers, always moving at the sides of his head when he's reading or talking, as though he were constructing a cat's cradle. He carries a mailbag filled with books, magazines, and records. He puts these items out on the table as though he were setting up an exhibit. He engages for hours while friends come and go, maintaining an astonishing ability to keep them laughing and interested.

I find myself staring at him. He's sitting alone, completely confident in his aloneness, as though he's certain that people will seek him out. He appears not to wait on them, doesn't look up to consult a clock or check the door. I imagine the luxury of his downtime, untroubled by his own thoughts and unafraid of who might visit him.

I stir my coffee, my eyes jumping from him to the window of

The Deadwood. Unconscious jumping, scanning. My anger, it occurs to me, never rises up with menace the way it should. My anger doesn't protect me. But here it is, a kind of paralyzing hyper-observation. I'd just begun to put fear in its box, and now I see the box torched, a paper house. I managed to live here in Iowa City without asking myself if I liked living here. I gathered slipcases, a duvet, throw rugs, unmatched pieces of china to create something that's mine, and now that it's threatened I can see how hollow it is. Other people can create with certainty; they don't work within ever-shortening parameters. I see how Victor's made these choices for me, and before him it was all the others. A choice of tragedies.

By 4 P.M. it's dark outside, and by 6 I feel myself growing roots. The energy changes, shifting focus to the crowd at the bar. They respond to a small mounted television set. I don't even bother to trace the source of their excitement. Some kind of game, no doubt. People want to be excited. I like to imagine a permanent frozen silence, a block of ice holding the earth still while the sun recedes like a rock thrown in reverse.

The boy beside me begins packing his traveling show into his mailbag. I pay my bill, leaving a large tip. We both recognize the change in the bar; it's suddenly a hostile environment, a dangerous sporting event. I want to speak to him as we make our way to the door, but I've had my share of strangers today. Talking to another person would tip the balance somehow. I might have to ask myself if I weren't looking for allies, last-minute circumstances that might change my fate.

We part ways at the door. I'm at first reluctant to walk alone to my car. There's no choice. I remember this condition; people without choices take the next step. I take it quickly, as though I'm late for something. I berate myself for leaving The Deadwood after the sun has gone down; I should be home already with the doors bolted and a knife in my hand. I can't even laugh at the thought. And when a street lamp flashes on, I find myself stalled beneath it. It seems to illuminate my dread, catching me almost running.

7

The plane touches down. Men with flags move hurriedly over the hot asphalt, and I can imagine the humidity already, watching one of them wipe his brow with the short sleeve of his shirt. I gather up the music I've taken along with me, and put the tapes and the Walkman into my purse. Gina's pared me down to only carryon bags, and as I pass the line of people at the baggage claim, I'm grateful she's done it. I quickly pass a family, all of them squat and seemingly missing the same teeth, staring down at an unmoving carousel. I'll glide through the whole experience, I tell myself. I've come to finalize a separation I made when I was sixteen. No need to make myself too comfortable, or bring back souvenirs.

My grandmother is staying on Miami Beach, and I drive the rental car slowly along the strip of pleasantly dilapidated and ostentatiously revamped hotels, noting the perplexing mix of models and retirees. I approach her hotel, looking over the tan, thin legs of the seniors sitting on their folding chairs, reading the paper and watching the waves behind their white, creamed noses. I try to imagine which one will rise and wave when I pull into the drive.

I remember my father taking me to the beach on one of our many excursions. We'd walk from lobby to lobby, buying post-cards, bags of shells, or pouring quarters into the hot molding machines that delivered sky-blue, plastic dolphins. The beach was all Jewish at the time, something we seemed oddly unobservant of, considering our neighbors' vigilantism and the influential though hardly organized presence of backwater racists in nearby towns. It's odd to me now that we were unaffected by those attitudes. Perhaps it was a tolerance my grandmother instilled. Or we sensed ourselves similarly marked, not by religious observance, but by the possibility of damnation.

My father stood me before a panel in one of these hotel lobbies. The panel was covered by pink glitter. Mounted to the wall was a chandelier sheared in half, faintly illuminated by sputtering orange, electric flames. He took a picture – blurred and dark – and the arms of the chandelier looked like flower-tipped antlers, and me like something smudged out on the wall. He placed it on the truck dashboard, and in days the sun had bleached the image until it seemed that image was of another time entirely, one we'd never lived through.

I wend my way up the driveway of the small, three-floor hotel with yellow walls and a large veranda. The glass doors read, in frosty white script, the Columbus. I pull in, take my bags from the backseat, and stand for a moment squinting up at the small screened windows and listening to the surf crashing behind me.

'Carrie? Is that you?' A woman has emerged from the glass doors, her voice like a small bell announcing my arrival. 'Do you need help with those?'

'That's all right,' I say, walking toward her. She embraces me, and I immediately recognize the strength of her grip. She holds me away from her and looks me over. 'My God,' she says, 'we finally meet.' And I can smell the violet on her, and recognize that smile, which is almost a wince.

'Do you think we look alike?' she asks. 'Of course, you don't think you look like this old lady, but I can see a resemblance.' She does not mention the link between us. She is clearly my mother's mother; these genes are tenacious, struggling toward some sublime articulation.

'I think we do,' I say, noting how her eyes search my face more curiously at my acceptance of this bond. She is younger than I imagined, in her sixties. Her youthfulness registers as a surprise because of my mother's features and what they betrayed, how old she seemed.

'Well, come on up,' she says, turning in her silver sandals. Her hair is white with a blue tint to it, and she's wearing a white T-shirt and shorts. There are a few elderly residents in the lobby, iced tea and egg sandwiches on the glass-topped tables. An older man, much less preserved than her, asks, 'So, May, is this your grand-daughter?'

She introduces me to Herbie, who painstakingly lifts himself from the seat to shake my hand, then immediately sits down. 'You're a lovely girl,' he says, catching his breath. 'May's told me a lot about you.' A lie, I know, but it's kind of him.

'I think we're both looking forward to this,' I say.

Herbie appears to have stopped listening. May grasps my arm and guides me up the stairs and down a carpeted corridor. At the end of the hall I can see the whitecaps rising and the wild swaying of a palm. Her room is small but clean, the light stretched wall to wall over the swirling blues of the carpet.

'Have a seat,' she offers, pulling an orange Eames chair from the kitchen. She sits across from me on the sofa beneath the window.

'I've made us a salad. Are you hungry now?'

'No, I ate on the plane. Thank you.'

'Thank you for coming.' Her face grows more serious, and she glances over to the pictures positioned on a small bookshelf. 'I suppose I have more questions for you than you have for me,' she says, turning now to look closely in my eyes. She drops both thin hands on the couch beside her and stands up abruptly. 'Your mother and I spoke very little.' She begins walking toward the kitchen, as though she needs an excuse to turn away from me. 'I don't really know what kind of a person she was.'

I listen to the spoon on the inside of the pitcher, then hear her pouring a drink into glasses. After a moment I say, 'She was unhappy, I think.'

She places the iced tea before me, and keeps one glass in her hand. 'Yes. I gathered that. She probably never told you why she refused to see me.'

'No,' I say. 'Too much water under the bridge is how she explained it, nothing more pointed than that.'

'Well,' she says, sitting again before me, 'I tried to get custody of you when you were five years old. I can't claim to be ignorant of what was happening in that home,' and I hear in her voice, in the way she articulates *that home*, the disgust – the judgment – my mother must have reacted to. I hear my mother's voice too: *She cared about you more than she did me, and only because she couldn't stand what I'd become. She wanted the chance to do it over again, and you would have turned out just the same, maybe worse. Even she couldn't protect you from yourself.*

May's voice has softened, and she leans toward me as if to gather my attention back. 'I didn't ask you here to dwell on these things. I lost my daughter many years ago. It's just that I—' her voice falters slightly under the accumulation of this loss '—It's just that I learned to love my daughter at a distance, and I didn't see the need to continue that with you. I didn't want you to think you had no family.'

'My father has made an effort to keep us together,' I say, looking past her, but not at the ocean. A hardcover book, *Christian Science*, sits on an end table, a framed picture of my mother beside it.

'Please don't think I'm trying to diminish your mother and father in any way, dear. I worried it might be too early to bring this up.' And she sounds genuinely saddened by where we've arrived, so quickly, in our meeting. 'I'd be perfectly content to put aside all this talk if I could encourage you to smile like you did when I saw you downstairs.'

I feel I owe her this much, and look at her with an ease I find not difficult to settle into now that she's asked for it.

I say, 'Let's not be afraid to talk about these things.'

The woman kicking stones around the driveway doesn't turn to look in my window. And I'm glad of this, because it's very late, and she'd holler for me to go to bed, to shut my eyes at least. 'Shut your eyes,' she says. 'I never seem to sleep anymore, even when I take sleeping pills, but all the body needs is a few moments with your eyes closed. Then you'll feel refreshed and like new.' She is always outsmarting the body, jump-starting it, fasting it, dulling its responses. My father's friends continue to pull up, drive out. Though soon it will be light. She walks between their motorcycles, gently running her hand over the leather seats. In the other hand she holds a can of beer. She barely acknowledges my father's friends, but some approach her and drape an arm around her, or honk and wave after they've turned over their engines.

She appears to be looking for something, and burying it with her foot at the same time. She appears to be walking off, and also fearful of going too far. Or perhaps she has arrived at the end; this shifting of gravel is her response to finding another precipice, another potential fall, an unspectacular view. I press my face to the window screen and the mesh itself has a smell, as though it has trapped the scent of the lawn and the hibiscus flowers, and it's always cooler than the muggy Florida nights. The mesh stays imprinted on my cheek, but fades sooner than the sadness of seeing my mother, aimless and drinking as the sun comes up. I watch for too long, but give up on her before she comes inside.

When I leave home I pack my own bag the way my mother once packed for me. I roll everything – the shirts, pants, and windbreaker. She is in the living room, her arm tied off, a sulfur blemish on her knee. She needs this to confront me, to convey the part of her that is still concerned with being a mother, to put up a last fight for the vague companionship she worries she might miss. She needs this shot, or she will be too obsessed with the changes in her body to concentrate on anything outside it. She is more and more preoccupied with the coldness of her blood, the splintering ache in her bones, the anxiety that makes all phenomena outside her body spectral.

Already, I know where I'm going and I have no illusions about it. A choice of disasters, and I'll choose one of my own making. She lifts herself from the couch and moves slowly toward me. I put my backpack down to embrace her; her fatigue and distress are convincing, as though she walks with lead chains and lifts her arms with lead chains.

'Don't go,' she says simply, clutching me, her body over-whelmed by a paroxysm of sobbing. Floodgates. I imagine her whole world vanished, first my father and now me. I don't say anything, and she holds me tighter. 'I need you. Please don't go.' I pull myself away from her, lifting her fingers from my arms. Her fingers have an inhuman, bruising strength. She is slumped forward and looking at her feet. She gives up. 'You have to do what's right for you,' she reasons, as though it could ever be right, this decision to leave her here and to step out into the world of decisions, none of which I'm prepared to make.

After dinner, I ask May to see the ashes. I ask simply, as though it were a contract I'd come to sign. She has put the tall, heavy box of my mother's remains at the foot of her closet. It is especially cumbersome in the context of most things here; all the appoint-ments have a card table, snap-to simplicity. Her dishes are bright plastics and infinitely stackable; even the TV is small enough to sit on the edge of the table. She puts this box down between us, and we both look at it awkwardly for a moment. It is like a gray pillar – Lot's wife – the result of a compulsive looking back. I remember looking back at the front of our house when I left it, and knowing I would not see my mother come out on the doorstep or appear behind the window. I knew I'd left her in that stillness which had been her aspiration, the stillness of someone who accepts life as an eroding force, nothing more. I reach out for the box with what I imagine to be an appropriate reverence, and pull it closer. May lights a cigarette, which puts me at some ease, and I open the top and see the ash and ground bone fragments in a heavy plastic bag. I consider opening it, but refrain. 'Where do you want to scatter these?' I ask, looking up at her.

'There's a place she once took me when she first came to Florida. Your father was still in the trucking business, and she was pregnant with you. She had a few dreams, then, and she wanted to let me know that she'd made the right decisions and that her life was going to be a lot smoother. It was out in the Everglades, and I remember it was so hot, and I didn't want to walk any further. We sat down under a tree there, and we drank some lemonade from a thermos. And I think it was the last time we both believed things might work out. I remember that spot, anyway.'

It is not so much the words, but the distant expression, the hard effort of conjuring this memory, that brings my mother back for a moment. I imagine her in May's kitchen, plucked briefly from the squalor of her fate and deposited here, living out some last, simple days, no longer reeling from a thousand half-forgotten indignities.

'I haven't shed a tear,' she says suddenly, putting her cigarette out. 'I'd like to think I'm past the point of being angry with her. I suppose it's a more general anger now. Angry at the waste of it.'

I don't try to console her. She feels something, at least. And I would be ashamed to comment on my envying her anger. 'We'll go to the Everglades, then,' I say. I think of what Gina has advised me: let her have the end of her choosing. I, for one, have no faith that my mother will ever rest, or that I'll remember or forget her sufficiently.

The hotel I've chosen is up-scale, further up the beach, with deco appointments and a high price tag. I drop my bags in the room's entryway and open the curtains. The moon has risen pale yellow over the ocean. I can make out its mottled surface, ascendant, scarred. I feel good about paying for this room – to not have a memory of cheaper rooms. I sit on the edge of the bed and listen. Nothing but a faint buzz from the ice machine down the hall. I know how the ice can burn, can be punishment. I look at my palms; they are not the lines of an old soul that I once thought they were. They're the lines of someone who tried to cheat time, to make it stand still.

There's fresh fruit in a basket on the desk beside the bed. The hotel room encourages an indulgence I'm unfamiliar with. It urges me to forget. I take my shoes off and walk around the room, which shows itself like a prize, a reprieve I've given myself. And it does not matter that other guests who arrive here – two nights from now – will give themselves this same gift; in fact, it's better to be part of this procession, to enter this place that does not keep its memories. It seems impossible to dream here; these walls guard against the faces of Victor and Janine, or my mother's face, reconfigured from the ash.

But I do dream – of Hannah. And she is anxiously guiding me around the cottage. It's snowing outside, and the cottage emits a strange low hum like the ice machine. She is holding my hand and it's too warm, too warm to be a dream. And she is asking me to hide, and I don't know if this is a game, but I wake up with my heart racing and a memory of her hot hand clutching mine.

May insists on driving. 'I tell myself, when this body can't drive, it's time to retire it. But I still have some good years left. I'm determined to outlive this car.' She drives a white Honda. The sun seems to rush the windshield between patches of shade. 'Turn on the radio if you'd like.'

'I'd rather we talk,' I say.

She leans forward, watching the road like a scientist. 'Well, that's fine.'

'How long are you planning to stay on the beach?'

'I've lived here for the past twenty-eight years. I don't see myself leaving too quick.'

'You lived this close to us all the time.' I wonder if she hears the privation in my voice. I feel the fingers of the Indian woman on my braid, and wonder what it would have been like to have been raised on the beach and not some miles away on the canal. These bodies of water seem suddenly indicative; the canal, like something starved, a slow vein.

'Your mother wouldn't let me visit or talk with you, so I would sometimes drive by the house and not stop.' Her words are edged with regret. 'The lights were always on.'

I wonder if I'd seen her moving down our street, my face pressed to the screen. The world was so much greater than the one-way glass allowed; a world of helpless spectators, suspended interventions. But my mother was probably right; I would have turned out just the same. I would have found this old woman's kindness too sad, the compulsion to look back too strong. And I recognize now how any vestige of normalcy, of adjustment, had to be forfeited by the woman beside me; how driving by her daughter's home at night is nothing she'd tell Herbie or the other residents of her hotel. She would have had her secrets too – her adaptations – and I would have found it too difficult to pretend these did not exist. I would have been susceptible to them. Now I recognize how they give her profile strength; I smile at her, but she's watching the traffic.

'I moved here to be with her and your father. I got a job on the beach as a waitress and decided to live there. When I moved into the Columbus, they hired me to do the cooking. I've known some of those residents over twenty years. That's how I got through. I made them my family. I still cook for them, know every one of their favorite desserts.'

We drive down 8th Street, remarkably transformed into Little Havana, its Cuban groceries and fruit stands crowding the streets. I remember nothing but trees here, the sound of my father's truck as we drove – the rattletrap rhythms I could feel in my teeth – when there were only a few barbershops and dime stores. And I remember the old cowboy Rudi walking his horse alongside the road, and how he'd wave to us. And once we'd stopped, and that horse stuck his head through my opened window. My father poured a packet of sugar in my hand, grasped it, and held it under the horse's tongue. I was terrified, but he and Rudi were laughing at me.

'All of this has changed,' she says, aware of my silence. 'Your mother sold the house to pay for medical bills. It would probably have some real value now. She moved in with a friend of hers. I'm not sure where they were staying. When I last saw her, she was in the hospital. I would have asked her to live here with me but she couldn't leave; the strokes made it impossible.' And now I see the houses of Sweetwater through the trees, multiplied like a real neighborhood and not just like abandoned lots, a stragglers' community. Still, the homes seem depressed with their clotheslines and junk cars, though the streets are newly paved.

We start to make our way into the Everglades, its dense mangroves bleeding into marsh water, still and thick with light-green, almost luminous algae. There are flocks of birds wheeling overhead, and the air is heavy and damp. We pull up behind a bus full of children on a science expedition. A group of kids stand outside the bus before a man with a brimmed hat and a bullhorn. He is calling their attention to a snail in his palm. 'You'll see lots of these, mostly on leaves,' he says.

May is holding the box of ashes in front of her. She walks briskly ahead of me, and I notice the children watching us, their attention drawn from the man with the snail. These are my mother's ashes, I imagine telling them from his bullhorn. That's today's lesson. The dead become something else, something science doesn't reveal to us.

We slip from view down a dirt trail. I try to imagine my mother walking here along this thin trail, the sounds of children and cars subsumed by the low buzz of insects.

May stops abruptly. 'It was around here,' she says, as though afraid to go any further. She looks around anxiously; the ground is soft beneath our shoes. 'Shall we have our ceremony?' she asks. I want to slow her down, to look around this place, but she is out of breath as though the encroaching environment were hands around her neck.

She holds the box and I open the bag inside, take a handful of ashes and begin to drop them at the tangled roots of a tree. There is no wind here, and we have to make some effort at scattering them. I imagine children hiding behind these trunks, or May and I like children, leaving this gray trail to find our way back. I go much further into the trees, where they have grown almost together, warding off intruders who would come between them.

May is weeping, standing in the shade with one hand pressed to her temple. I feel awkward going over to stand beside her. It's enough that I'm here, I think. My presence gives her the chance to feel this grief, diminishes her sense of loss at the same time. I turn from her and hold myself close to one of the trees, closing my eyes.

'Come inside, Carrie.' My mother stands behind me. I'm sitting on the sidewalk in front of our house. I've scratched the word *Fuck* onto the sidewalk. She opens my hand and takes the rock from my clenched fingers. I'm angry at her.

'Why are you sick all the time?' I say, standing up and turning around to her.

She doesn't answer, just takes my arm. I want to say: You can't protect me from anything. You can't protect me from the way I've come to see you, see the world through you. You're a terrible revelation. And though she's wrested the stone from my hand, I feel like I'm still squeezing it, my hand bunched like cables inside of hers.

'You can't be angry at me forever,' she says.

'Yes, I can.'

May's sobbing makes me turn back to her. 'It's good that we came out here,' I say, standing a couple of feet away, ash clinging to the sweat on my palms. I wipe my hands nervously along the rough bark of a tree.

After a while, she gathers my hands into hers. 'Yes. I'm glad we did. For some reason, I keep remembering her as a child. I think she was happy then.'

We have dinner not far from her hotel, and she embraces me for a long while before we separate. We agree to meet for breakfast before I fly back to Iowa. The breeze over the ocean is very strong, and she holds her hair in place with one hand. 'Your mother asked me to give you something,' she says. 'I'll make sure to bring it tomorrow.'

'Thank you,' I say. We look at each other warmly, and for a moment I begin to imagine visiting her again, wanting to do that.

'I'll walk to my hotel,' I say, kissing her cheek.

I cross the street to the beachside, where there are bonfires, silhouettes gathered around them. There are swimmers too, dark figures cast about by the waves. The hypnotic play of oncoming car beams and the intermittent rush of sound from their open windows momentarily makes me forget I'm walking. I feel strangely elevated, one element of the night with no more identity than any of the shadows joining on the waves. I imagine the perfect hiding place where everyone abandons their identities for shadows, sharing equally in the anonymity of ocean and heaven.

From a short distance I notice the cerulean glow of my hotel casting a cool shell of light over the sidewalk. Its glass doors slide open, and it's like being bowed to, like being acknowledged by someone silent, waiting.

I lie in bed still carrying a feeling of elation that makes my limbs seem heavy, drugged. The renovations are recent; the room feels like a showroom. I prop some pillows by the headboard. I decide to call Gina, just to make sure King is all right without me. When she answers, I lie back on the pillows, staring at the empty screen of the large television set and the fruit behind yellow cellophane on the nearby desk.

'How was it?' she asks.

'Easier than I thought it would be. But I'm exhausted, now. We scattered her ashes today. In the Everglades. I'm sure it was illegal.'

Gina tells me about the bad weather, terrible icy conditions. 'I've got King here with me,' she says. 'I let him run behind your house, then put him in Rachel's car and took him back here. The weather sucks so bad, I just thought it was better not to be driving back and forth. Anyway, he's happy with the extra attention.'

I hear Rachel call out behind her. 'He's getting all the love he needs.' She sounds like she's got her arms around him, playing with him, and I think how glad I am to have the two of them as friends.

'Do I need to pick him up?' I ask.

'No,' Gina says. 'I'll have him back at your place tomorrow. He'll be waiting for you when you arrive.'

'Let me talk to him,' I say. She puts the phone to his ear and I call his name. He barks, an anxious recognition that thrills us both.

The next morning, I take a booth at Wolfies. There's a clattering of silverware all around, making the place seem more bustling than it actually is. I pull the photograph from my purse, and the frame I'd intended for it. I know instantly I won't give her the picture. Let her remember me as someone sensible, sober. I don't want this memory carried or memorialized. I tear it in small pieces. When the waitress brings coffee, I ask her to throw out the bits of photo in my hand. 'I do that with my bad pictures too,' she says without smiling.

May arrives flushed and with two packages under her arm. They are wrapped in bright pink paper. I know my mother didn't wrap them, and, sure enough, she apologizes for having done it.

'One's from me, and the other from your mother. When I wrapped one, I couldn't resist doing the other. Have you ordered?'

'Just coffee,' I say, suddenly taking her hand in mine. 'You shouldn't have brought me a gift.'

'I thought you should have something to remember me by. Let me give it to you first. Here.'

I unwrap the box and there's a small note she's written. *Dear Carrie, So you always sleep with warm thoughts. Love, May.* Inside is a throw she's knitted. Before I can respond, she asks, 'Do you know how long ago I made that for you? I made that when I first moved here, long before you ever left home. It might be a little small for your bed, now.' She reaches over and lifts it, still folded, from the box. 'Use it if you can.'

I put it to my face. *The generosity of someone sitting very quietly in their body.* 'Thank you. It's beautiful. I would have cherished this as a child. I appreciate it even more now.'

'This is what your mother wanted me to give you.'

I unwrap it, knowing what it is by its lightness. The cigar box brings me to tears even before I've opened it. I don't know where these tears come from. The ochre judges have faded; the box looks battered, the seam of the lid slightly torn. Inside are yellowed papers, early letters from my father, and the perfectly preserved bar of violet soap my mother used to initiate the box.

There are other things: a photograph of the Wallaces' horse, and a picture of me in our backyard. Behind me, you can see the tarred stump of our orange tree, a motorcycle my father never fixed. It would have been mine if I'd graduated or he hadn't gone to jail. I think my father's friend Ernie took the picture, and I seem happy in it though I must have known it would all come apart. I must have recognized the desolation, like a child who plays on the burned beams of a lost house. I look closer at the picture; it's odd to see myself managing that knowledge.

May's hand touches my cheek and shocks me from my rumination.

'I hope you don't find this too upsetting,' she says.

'No,' I answer. My eyes return to my younger self in the square-format picture, its muted colors suggesting the vagueness of those years, the sad, bleeding colors of those Florida afternoons. 'I had a photo I intended to give you, but I think this one is better.' I fish the frame back out of my bag and slide the old picture in, arrange it so it's at least sitting evenly behind the glass.

'You're always welcome to come back,' she says, taking the frame from me and looking closely over the photograph. 'You haven't lost your courage, Carrie. I can see you've always had it, even way back then.'

8

What would you do if you bit down and your teeth raised blood from an apple? Flesh from an apple? What would you do? Flesh and blood from an apple. What would you do with the apple? How would you feel?

Gayl Jones, *Eva's Man*

The airport parking lot is like a wasteland; it's edged in gray light leached from a featureless sky. Rows of cars are iced over. I pass their strange shapes, imagining each one as an impermeable shelter. I find my Valiant, open the trunk, take the ice scraper and begin to clear the windows. I pull out the heavy parka I left behind, zipper it up to my chin. Again I remember how foreign winter is; how Gina had to introduce me to tire chains, to the dangers of black ice. You leave it for three days and return to find it more entrenched and brutal. A fortified enemy. A bad omen, I think, finally getting the engine to turn over.

Then again, returning has never felt like a homecoming for me, not here or anywhere else. I imagine the gratitude I'm supposed to feel on returning. Despite my apprehensions, I'm looking forward to seeing King and Hannah and Gina. But some people feel connected to the place where they laid down roots, for the local bar where people know them, or even where no one knows them. That's as close as I get to home: a local bar where no one knows me. I've made a home of Iowa City, but returning feels odd, as though the plane might have landed anywhere. That's how I arrived here, searching for an anywhere.

I know these thoughts – these feelings of displacement – recognize them for what they are and where they lead. Victor is behind these thoughts, in the restlessness and anxiety they inspire. I think of how pervasive he is, how he's part of my thinking now.

And it's Victor who occupies me on the drive home – not my mother's death, or the kindness of my grandmother. I tell myself that thinking about him might diminish his threat. *A person waited on never comes.* But Victor came before I knew what to ask for. I'd been waiting on something in that office in San Francisco, something to direct me once I'd lost Bill to drugs. I thought at first my job could save me, but I was unprepared for the regularity of the office. The normalcy of it was too much at odds with me. It demanded a constancy I didn't have. The drug addicts I knew – like some tribe with their needle-induced scarifications, their language, and superstitions – seemed more comprehensible to me.

Victor knows my story long before I venture to tell it; he can smell the vestiges of dope in my cells. He knows how it makes each day precarious, undermines whatever semblance of authority I have. He senses it in my compassion, my show of confidence, the way I fight to maintain the upper hand while I'm writing his case notes. I know it's all clear to him, but I persist. Tough interlocutor. This toughness he's seen in the places he doesn't recognize as ugly. This one negotiates, compromises, risks, he thinks. This one never got anything for nothing. She won't stay clean; she wants this kind of life – a job where her past gives her leverage, expertise – but she knows it isn't her. I can remind her of who she is. I can give her back to herself.

He whittles away my resources. I know they're diminishing, but I willfully imagine them in reserve. I've lived with the feeling that everything is used up too quick, that there isn't enough to go around. I want to believe I have this control of my life, that I've worked for it, and that it's abundant. I can play up to him and not give up to him. And if I whisper to him at the desk, if I tell him my story to get his, nothing is compromised so long as no one hears.

And he whispers too, because he knows that these are confidences and we are close to sharing blood. What we share is a current between us, not an intention. We surrender to our similarities. I can do my job better if he lets me know him, and he can learn from me if I let him know me. And on and on. I am in the dizzying world of desire and justification. I'm so busy sweeping over my tracks I no longer know where I'm going. And he persists, from appointment to appointment, a formal suitor obeying the conventions of the state. Two more weeks of furlough and then the long parole, which doesn't mean anything, doesn't mean he can't embrace the new life we're establishing.

I issue a check for $300 for interview clothes. He comes in wearing the suit, modeling it for me. It embarrasses me, the way he stands at my desk, flexing his muscles in a business suit. My co-workers look away, flushed. They're charmed by him too.

'He's something, isn't he?' Leslie asks in the break room. She offers that look that says, 'Yes, I can imagine it.' But she'd rather not; she plays at being naughty the way Victor models the suit – without the slightest intention of carrying anything out. We have both gone through the same training; we can joke about temptation. I joke about it less than the others. It makes me uneasy.

I notice myself anxious about his appointments, but he always comes. He is always late, though, and I begin to wonder if he stands outside smoking, knowing I can get nothing done while I wait. And it goes on like this, until he whispers he'd like to kiss me, and I imagine the smoke on his breath. I imagine myself being carried away on it, something burned up and released. He smiles while he gives me excuses for missing job interviews. He gets away with this, promises to make it up to me with the kind of smile that makes me nervous. Sometimes I think he must have this kind of power over everyone, and then I remember he was locked up. You can't melt the bars or charm the guards. But my sternness is staged, and my professionalism is staged, and the whole damned office is like a worn-out drama, eight hours a day.

When he leaves I go into the little closet with its reclining couch. We call it the headache room. It's dim and stocked with Xerox paper boxes. I drape my arm over my forehead, like a woman in a painting or a movie. And this is temporarily comforting; to feel the unreality of everything even in my gestures, to make a storeroom a fainting room. It's all so dreary, I say under my breath; everything here is dreary. I'm the English lady who walks through the gutter. I convince myself I'm a woman who will make a bad choice simply because I've only made good ones up to now. And then the voice of my supervisor breaks the spell – though the fantasy couldn't last much longer – and I'm back to my desk.

Victor suggests we go to lunch. He wants to do something nice for me, despite the fact that I haven't found him work. He tells me he can look for work on his own, but having lunch alone, that's a different matter. I meet him at a Thai restaurant where every meal is new to him. He makes jokes about the names of the dishes. Chu chee pla is at first perplexing, then something he says again and again, imitating our waitress, not with malice, but trying to amuse me. It's so silly, it brings me to tears. And later, when I think about it, I imagine how he enjoyed those words on his tongue.

I tell him it's not ethical. I can't see him after work, though I already have. He suggests I close out his case. Easy enough, and after all I'm getting nowhere with him. He sees the hotel I live in and wonders why I don't have an apartment. Nothing crosses his mind that doesn't cross his lips.

'I'm living paycheck to paycheck,' I tell him. It's a first lie, and not even necessary. I'm afraid of things like electric bills and phone bills. I'm afraid of making something and losing it. The logic is simple, if it's logic.

'We've got to get you out of this,' he says. And for a moment I imagine him as capable as Bill – strong enough to look at the holes in my life and love me anyway.

I drive home slowly. No wonder Gina didn't want to make the trip. At several points the car feels like it's about to slide completely out of control. Closer to my house, the roads are empty; then it's simply a case of trying not to slide or brake too quickly on the ice. Ten minutes away from my house and I begin to think: People don't come here by accident. They don't get lost here. I consciously try to keep my adrenaline from racing; I know how it works on me. It doesn't focus me. It confuses me, makes me jumpy. When I pull up to the house, I feel almost pinned down by waves of apprehension. I scan the outside. Everything looks fine, the way I left it. Everything's fine. Maybe Gina's inside.

I carry the ice scraper up the walkway, try the door handle, then put the key in the lock. I turn on the lights and call out to King. Nothing. The place looks all right. Gina's gathered the mail and put it on the couch. Everything is fine, but she hasn't brought the dog back. I walk through the rooms; they appear intact. I can't live with this fear buzzing in my head like bad wiring. I go back out to the car and bring my bags inside. I call Gina but no one's there. I leave her a message: I'm home. I'll pick up King. Just let me know when you get back. Then I call Hannah. The thought of unpacking – of taking off my coat – never occurs to me. I turn up the thermostat, though. The place is freezing.

We meet at the Sheep's Head. The light outside is diffuse, almost completely obliterated at 4:30 in the afternoon. Hannah has a beer. I drink the coffee I've ruined with too much sugar. She wants to know about my grandmother. She has never met hers, either.

'Exterminated.' She says the word bitterly, washes it down with beer. 'I have pictures of her. My family have a thing about pictures. Anyway—' she turns her head, not interested in pursuing this line of thought '—did you like your grandmother?'

'I'd think about moving closer to her,' I say. 'I think she'd like to have me around.' I wonder if I'd really consider this; the thought is insubstantial, a smokescreen. I talk to Hannah about May but find myself confused by the feelings. May commented on how my mother had stopped making choices until the idea of choice never entered her mind. It seemed to throw Iowa City into question for me; it made me wonder if I'd ever chosen to live here, and whether I could choose to live here now.

Hannah talks about the film she saw at the Bijou while I was gone, *Celine and Julie Go Boating*. She describes its images, its hypnotic, inexorable repetitions. 'I'm astonished by the conservatism of film now,' she says. 'The '60s and '70s were so much more morally ambiguous.' She's painting too. 'Just small things,' she says, and I recognize how modesty is her way of not jinxing this troubled start.

'Gina was supposed to bring King back today. But she didn't. I can't reach her.' I don't mention that I'm troubled by the cottage, that something felt wrong. But perhaps it really was that I'd expected King and so it had a strange abandoned feeling about it.

'The electricity went out briefly yesterday. The weather's been horrible. Don't worry about it. Why don't you just come over to my place?'

I tell myself I'll check my messages from there. Then decide to drive by Gina's before I go to Hannah's. I don't want to bring Hannah to Gina's or to my place; it would be too awkward. I realize I'm still embarrassed about the other night, potentially endangering her by asking her to stay with me. Plus, I just want to get King home while it's early. I can visit Hannah later tonight. I tell her my plan, and she says that's fine. Then she leans back.

'Do you think it wasn't him we saw the other night?'

Her question makes me angry, but I'm unsure of why it does, and I try not to show it. 'I don't know who that was. I can't do everything under the assumption he's here. You saw the car as well as I did. Are *you* certain?'

She sits silently, looking at me until I'm uncomfortable. 'I don't think you should doubt yourself. I think that's more dangerous than trusting your instincts.'

'I don't have instincts. I have fears. They're not the same.'

'In your case they may be.' She leans forward, whispering. 'I believe in planning. Most people don't have the benefit of planning for the worst. There's no reason we have to take things as they come.'

I look at her, perplexed by her suggesting there's some benefit to my situation. She's drunk, I think. And it's only just after five.

'I'll keep that in mind,' I say, standing up and gathering my coat.

When Victor's on a 'job,' it's something he doesn't want me inquiring about. I try to go about my business without noticing, making it on time to the office, eating dinner alone, waiting for him to show up, usually in the middle of the night. We get a studio apartment in a building where he knows the manager. Same neighborhood as my old hotel, but it feels like progress. I don't like the manager; he sticks his head in the door too often. 'Just making sure you're up to no good,' he says. Victor asks him in, and then they leave together after their conversation has become inaudible, distracted, coded.

Victor's passionate when he makes money, also when he's high. He doesn't think I notice these changes in him. He doesn't want me to know how much he's made, how much drugs he has at his disposal. He likes withholding, holding these things over me. It's obvious. His lies are obvious. It makes him seem like a kid, but it's not endearing. He wants me to act like I don't know what he's been up to, so he can surprise me, or so he won't disappoint me. And from the beginning I play wife, girlfriend, whatever uninterested, undemanding thing I'm supposed to be. For a few months, anyway. For a few months I let him determine how much I'll use, when I'll use it. I don't tell him about Bill; that I've already had a boyfriend who introduced me to the world of dependencies, tended to my needs.

I wait for him to fix me for the first few months. Days that move like sludge. It's like waiting for things to degrade, to change their shape. But I'm edgy, less inclined to make it to my job if he gets home late. Now I want the fruits of his stolen TVs, stolen sides of beef, stolen computers, motorcycles, credit cards. I don't want to sit in the apartment while he goes out all night, selling coke for heroin and cutting a little bit here and there so he can stay high while he does it.

Victor knew what he was looking at when he saw me. I'm

every bit as desperate as he is. I'm not new to this. Janine knew this when she hung up on me: even if she's clean, this can't last; it's an aberration. She knew I hadn't had the experience yet, the one that changes who you are essentially, the one that purifies, turns your blood to harp strings. People make decisions to get clean all the time. It doesn't mean they don't have the wrong motives. She thinks I let go of drugs, of the lifestyle, only so I wouldn't burn my hands on the rungs going down. In her eyes I was still falling.

And when I first asked Victor to fix me, I meant it in every way possible. But he knew only the one way. He was reluctant. 'This could change us,' he said, though he wasn't concerned with what we'd become, just that we wouldn't continue being what we were. 'It will bring us together,' I assured him. Now I'll do it myself, thank you. Now I don't even trust him to destroy me. He doesn't attend to it quick enough. And I decide that I'm willing to do whatever I have to do to keep up with him.

We will both be on this wheel together. I see it narrowing, and we're suspended on it like empty buckets. The wheel is celestial; its rotations include heaven and hell, the highs and then the unbearable lows. And with the first shot, my mind drifts off over the past few months, and I think: I'm still a good person when I'm high. I'm still a person who would stop at harming someone else. The words – not even spoken – have a drift of their own and are carried off, weightless.

No one answers the door, so I walk to the back of Gina's house and look into the windows. There's lights on, but no one downstairs, no way to climb up and check if someone's in the upstairs bedroom. I think she's probably at my place, dropping off King, writing me a note of apology. I decide to drive home and wait for her. No point in bothering Hannah when I just told her I would be going over there later. But I'm nervous about going back to my place, a little less so each time I make the trip. I had a little scare a few nights ago, but there's no point in dwelling on it. I wonder what Hannah meant by planning, though. If there weren't some

way I'm missing an opportunity to turn this around. I hate drunkenness. Though now it seems less likely she was drunk.

The Valiant takes forever to warm up. I sit there revving the
engine, staring blankly at Gina's house. Could he have come here,
posed as someone looking for a massage, then done something to
her and to King? Why didn't I tell her about him? I put it out of
my mind. She doesn't need to be privy to my phantoms. Besides
that, talking about him might make him materialize. You learn
that as a junkie; dealers arrive on empty streets, a magical presence
responding to your needs, announcing themselves with the
tapping of canes or whistling from mouths full of aching teeth.
The only thing an addict can't conjure is money.

On the ride to my cottage I listen to Hannah's tape of Blondie's
Plastic Letters. I almost laugh at the irony of the lyrics:

Something in my consciousness told me you'd appear.
Now I'm always touched by your presence, dear.

I take the roads slowly, carefully. As I make my way out of
downtown, I notice a car turn around in the parking lot of a
long-empty restaurant, a place where I'd noted amusing graffiti, a
painting of a woman's outsized silhouette, a teacup balanced on
her exaggerated buttocks. The car turns out and follows at least a
couple of hundred feet behind me. I note it in my rearview
mirror. It's not the same car I saw pull up at my place, and the
driver appears to be keeping his distance. It's dark outside, and
people are leaving work. The darkness may as well be their collec-
tive misery. Tomorrow I'll have to return to work. Frances will be
leaving soon to start setting up her new home; she's quietly trying
to sign off on as many of our cases as she can. I'm sure she'll
inquire about Hannah, ask me why I closed her case early. 'We
chose friendship' will not go over well. I'll simply note that she
never returned. Bureaucracies welcome disappearances; these
people would be invisible if it weren't for us, anyway.

I take the long flat empty road that curves like a tossed rope
through snow-covered cornfields. When I make this left, I leave

all the cars behind me; this ten minutes of driving is like a private entryway to my place. A minute or so on it and I notice that car again, turning after me. The road's treacherous; the city road crews treat it like a private drive, not their jurisdiction. I drive it at twenty miles per hour, still gripping the wheel. The car behind me flashes its lights. 'What do you want from me, you idiot?' I holler, looking in the rearview mirror. What does he think I'm going to do, stop and offer directions? The ice is shadowy, impossible to navigate.

His car glides side to side like a heavy black cradle. His flashing blinds me, so I stop looking in the mirrors. I sense him up on my car, now. No one would try intimidation on this road; he'll get us both killed. But I speed up, anyway. Is it Gina or Rachel in someone else's car? Could they have asked someone else to drop King off for them? I look again in the rearview mirror and can vaguely make out the features of a man behind the wheel, obliterated almost immediately by the flashing of his high beams. I step on the gas, hearing my own breath catch, trying to identify those features. There's a hill on the road, and I remember I need to prepare for it, slow down, but I lose control before I can. My car slides out and smashes into an embankment. There's only a moment before an eerie ice-blue light descends with the impossible, muffled silence of a burial. I hold the wheel, stunned.

Just then I'm startled by rapping on my window. I literally fling myself to the other side of the seat, cautiously looking over the features of the man calling my name through the glass.

'Carrie?' He wipes away the steam of his breath with a black glove. 'Are you all right?'

I'm suddenly raging, hollering. 'What the fuck are you doing? What are you trying to do, kill us?'

'Joel Case,' he says, assuming my rage isn't personal. 'Remember? From the bar.'

It takes me a moment. The psychiatrist. Just what I need. I lean forward and roll down the window. The freezing wind rushes in, and the strange light outside suffuses the car. The black, barren arms of trees form a monstrous knot behind him. 'I saw you leaving downtown and thought I could get your attention.'

'You frightened me. I didn't know who you were, and the roads are so slick.' I hear myself reprimanding him. I recognize his expression from the time Hannah launched her tirade against him. He must seek out abuse, I think ruefully. Or perhaps he's one of those people plagued by problems of timing. Still, I'm relieved it's him.

'I saw you, so I turned around and followed.' He's standing about a foot away from the window now. He won't get any closer unless he's invited. 'Did you think I was someone else?'

'I don't invite people out here,' I say. 'I knew it was someone uninvited.'

He's silent for a moment. 'I'll go, then.' He starts to turn and walk off, but I call him back before he gets even a few steps away.

'You didn't expect me to know it was you,' I say. 'I was frightened.'

'I'm sorry I scared you.' His look changes from wounded to concerned. 'Are you all right?'

'I'm fine, thanks, though I might need some help out of here. My house is on the right. Do you want to come by for tea or something?'

He helps me reverse the car by pushing on its hood. He pushes off from the embankment with his foot. He looms over the car in the headlights, more attractive than I remember him looking at the bar. He's contrite, and it complements him more than cockiness. I can see how strong he is; he's in great shape for someone who must be in his late forties. His round, wire-framed glasses are the only indication that he's a doctor. He has the body of some of my father's friends, some of the cons Victor knew.

He drives slowly behind me, not too close. It's reassuring to have him following me, an unlikely feeling I have a hard time settling into. The porch light is on, and I think Gina must have come by. I walk cautiously up the path to my cottage, and practically lose my footing when I notice King break the curtains, his nose moving from side to side excitably. I hold onto Joel's arm and guide him quickly to the door, talking lovingly to King as I put the key in the lock.

Joel sits on the couch, and it takes King and me a while to calm down. I lay my purse on the chair and get on the floor with him.

'I've never been apart from him since I found him over a year ago,' I inform Joel. 'I was in Florida for the past three days.' I don't tell him I was scattering my mother's ashes.

'That's nice. I love Florida. Did you have a good trip?'

I'm still playing with King, but get up and offer him some tea. On my way into the kitchen, I call out, 'I liked Miami Beach very much.' I call King to the back door and let him out. I turn on the lights mounted to the back of the house; their illumination reaches almost to the edge of the pond. King bounds out the door and toward his favorite spot.

Joel leans back and crosses his legs when I hand him the cup and saucer. His demeanor changes; he possesses a kind of reason-ableness that doesn't seem too proud of itself. His posture conveys professional curiosity, a doctor's interrogation style. But it doesn't bother me. I only need him to be here in the room with me now, his car in front of the cottage discouraging anyone from thinking I'm alone. I don't have to try to manipulate him, to get something out of him. I can't help but notice that if his timing were different, I might be able to appreciate the questions he's asking, and the willingness he attempts to express by asking them.

I take a bus to the doctor's office. Dr Blaufarb. The psychiatrists have their offices in the nicest parts of town, a way of discouraging people whose problems have to do with money. People in Pacific Heights notice if you've been up for days. They look at you on the bus, take another seat. I notice a woman across from me, older, but perfect as a doll. Someone goes to the homes of these women and primps them; other women in white clinicians' outfits carrying tackle boxes of makeups. These women have their hair and nails done at home. You can't see what's going on inside them because the cosmetologists make them opaque. The only way to hide what's inside of me is to remove the insides. Any one of them can read my experience. Experience doesn't mark these women.

I can hardly walk the three blocks from the bus stop. I'm stooped over, out of breath. I hold onto a telephone pole, walk a few steps further, collapse over a newspaper rack. My whole body is aching, trembling.

But it's my head that's driving me; I can't stop thinking about the young, blue-eyed kid who sold me the coke and let me stay up doing it at his hotel. I can't forget how on the second night he brought the pipe and introduced me to crack. And all along he kept telling me he couldn't stop but he was sure he would have a heart attack. He must have weighed about a hundred pounds, so war-torn.

'Nobody wants to spend any time with me. They say I'm crazy. But I just have to keep going with the shit. I can't stop. But my heart; I'm so afraid of it.'

The dirt was in my blood and in my memories. How I told Victor I was pregnant, and how he said I'd need to stop using. How he shot up in front of me, and told me he was going to quit soon. He was going to be a good father to this baby. He took his syringe and buried the point into the cheap wall. It just hung there in the wall. I thought he did it so I couldn't use the needle again. I had my own, kept a rig hidden in my drawer. He said I should go to a clinic; otherwise I might be held responsible if the baby was born addicted. You should go to a clinic too, I thought. Have them check to make sure your DNA isn't as fucked up as your thinking.

Dr Blaufarb asks me into his office. It's on the first floor, and outside a window I can see people walking by, shopping. They can't see us. There's a big leafy tree taking the light out of the room. He sits behind an enormous desk.

'What brings you here?' he asks.

'I have terrible anxiety. I can't sleep,' I say to him. I'm kneading my hands. This is it, the end of it all. The end of the line.

'Why is that?'

'I'm about to lose my job. I'm afraid of my health. My relationship isn't healthy.'

'Let's start with your job,' he says.

'I haven't been to work in over a week. I haven't called to tell them what's going on. Let's not start there. Look, can you do anything for me because I'm about to go out of my mind.'

'I can't just take these feelings from you. I have to know where they're coming from.'

I want to scream I just killed my baby during a two-day cocaine run. I was sitting on the toilet with a crack pipe in my mouth when I miscarried. There was a seventeen-year-old kid sitting outside the door wondering why I wouldn't come out. I couldn't cry. I thought he was a cop and I couldn't open the door, couldn't make a sound. Bleeding. The feelings are coming from a gap in my reason, bleeding through. Can you take them from me?

'They're coming from everywhere. They won't let me sleep. I need you to help me. I need you to write me a script for sleeping pills. Then we can talk.'

I look at him, and know I've just dealt my last card. The end of the line.

You're not asking me to give you drugs, are you?

'I don't know if I can help you. I can't just write you a prescription for sleeping pills because you've asked for one.'

How did my mother do this? How did she suffer these judges?

You need to go to a clinic. What if the baby's born addicted? They can put you away for that.

'Why can't you sleep?' Dr Blaufarb asks. He can't stand my silence; he's a shrink, but he can't stand silence, wants everything explicit. Hands over my stomach, holes for eyes. *They can put you away for that.*

Outside, people are shopping. I can't tell him what prompted me, started the whole thing unraveling. *I was born with a hole in my heart*, that's what the boy told me when he brought back the crack. Who wasn't? *My mother killed herself when I was just three years old. Never knew who she was.*

I can't talk about my baby. But my baby talks to me. I can't understand it. It's too subtle for me. I only understand the kick of cocaine, never feel the baby move until my body forces it out. I'm afraid of the baby, what Victor and I could create together. *They can put you away for that.* Put you away for making a baby no one can understand. Little broken pieces of DNA, little broken baby teeth. Chicken wire wound around a baby's bed.

Afraid to look in the toilet. Afraid to open the door. I'm an eyeball on the floor, scanning the crack of the door. Looking for footsteps, patterns of darkness. Afraid to look in the toilet.

I imagine my mouth opening, a grave. 'Sleeping pills,' I say. Raspy, horror voice. My mouth is full of dirt and bones, soft baby ducks.

'What are you thinking?' Joel asks.

'Nothing,' I say, though I want to say nothingness. Hollowness. How it feels. That place always stays in you, becomes a center. You have to build around it.

'I like your place,' he offers. Doesn't really want to ask me questions about my thinking. He wants to be something other than what his card announced. But now I wish I'd paid him for the hour, could talk or not. Cannot talk about the baby I couldn't name.

'Do you work at South Wing?' I ask him.

'No. I have a private practice here in town.'

'I do casework here, never formally studied psychology. But I'd like to.' Formally study anything; not always have to rely on empathy, on my experience.

'You should. It's a satisfying field. I'll bet you'd be good at it. Casework is good experience.' He puts the cup and saucer down, puts his hands on his thighs. 'Do I get the tour?'

'I'm sorry.' I stand up. 'Of course.' I walk him through the place; it's not much to see. But he takes an interest in everything. He's surprisingly forthcoming. 'It's very nice here,' he says, as though expecting something else. 'How did you find this place?'

'Driving,' I say. 'I was just driving and decided to see what was down this road.' The simple questions throw me off. Do other people just drive down roads out of curiosity? Of course they do. Nothing unusual about that.

'It's odd that there's no granary out here.'

'There's one further out, but no, it's not attached. Someone wanted to live alone, until they didn't. They hung out a sign and just vacated it.' I open the door to the bedroom and notice the curtains blowing.

'It's freezing in here.' I wander around the bed and notice small bits of glass on the rug and near the baseboard. The window is smashed, all the glass removed. I reel back from it, turn up all the lights.

'Jesus, what happened?' Joel asks.

'Someone must have tried to break in,' I say, looking uneasily at everything in the room, as though everything had somehow become more tangible and weighted. I notice then the water on the floor near the dresser. Snow tracked in on someone's boots. Victor's boots. 'Someone was here. Someone was inside.' I announce loudly: 'I need to check the place. I've got to make sure nobody's inside.'

Joel's expression is frozen. He's not protective – a bad trait in shrinks. Caseworkers too. He'll need to be told what to do. I feel strangely certain Victor's gone, was interrupted. Nothing seems out of order, except for the window.

I reach under the mattress and quietly take the knife into my hand. Joel appears ready to bolt, but actually walks to the bedroom closet and quickly opens the door. Nothing. He doesn't comment on the knife in my hand, but seems more confident knowing I have it. I'm glad I can bring him assurance. I wonder if somewhere I hadn't been planning for this all along, just as Hannah had hoped. Or perhaps my desire to make this attack appear random and impersonal outweighs my own fear. In either case, he nods silently, ready to take this on. I wonder how I would handle this if he weren't here. I feel suddenly immobilized by the thought of what might have prompted Victor's return. The cold takes on a human presence in the room, and I need to get out of here.

We go into the bathroom. We open all the closets, unlikely to accommodate him because of the shelving. I turn on all the lights as we go.

After we check the last closet near the front door, I tell him I want to go back to the bedroom, to cover the window. I won't stay here.

'I guess this is the danger of living so far out of town,' he offers. He tries to smile, but I can see he's worn from the experience, the anxiety of girding himself for an intruder behind every closet door. I stop trying to shield him, think it's best he accepts that this is just how it is with me. I don't even wonder anymore what it's like to live without these little broken pieces of your life constantly puncturing the surface.

'I need to use something solid over the window, a piece of wood or something.'

He wanders over to the door of the bedroom, looks inside. I look around. I don't have anything to cover the hole. He walks further into the room and calls out, 'There's practically no glass in here.'

He's a detective now. Detective and shrink. I remember myself telling the cop, *nothing so unusual.* He was asking about my father, and I was already telling him about my life. I decide to remove a cabinet door from the kitchen, nail it over the window. Stuff the hole with blankets and nail the cabinet door over the window.

He walks into the kitchen while I'm busy unscrewing the door. I find myself completely focused on the task at hand, ruthlessly efficient, as though this were a way of finally eradicating the problem, simple as laying out mousetraps. The absurdity isn't lost on me; the cottage seems like it were shrinking behind me, tiny, uninhabitable. The space is alive: violated, unprotected, nothing to fight with but tiny, broken teeth.

I can't tell Victor about the baby. Can't think about it. The blond boy left the hotel room. Maybe he thinks I'm dead. Or maybe he left to cop more dope. I lay on the bed, face down. I need help. I close my eyes and see the needle plunged into the wall, hanging there. The door doesn't lock. I imagine someone walking in and plunging a knife between my shoulder blades. I lie there, not moving. I can't stay here, though. Can't stay in the room with it. What we created together – this life; I can't tell him what I've done. I can't tell him it wasn't an accident.

Joel takes the cabinet door from me, the hammer and a box of long nails. I grab a woolen blanket from the hall closet, holes in it. I fold it over, hand it to him. 'Do you want to nail this up first? Maybe it will help insulate it a little.' Something strange in my voice, as though I were taking care of a dying child. Not Joel, but my life here. I'll have to renounce it, do what's necessary to leave it.

'Sure.' He takes it from me. 'You're handling this very calmly,' he says. I wonder what he means. I'm asking him to seal this off. Seal this off from me. I don't want to come here again. I can't explain this to him.

'I just want to get out of here. I can't stay here.'

I pull the clothes I'd packed for Miami out of the bags and exchange them for heavier clothes. I throw some underwear, a sweater, a couple of pairs of pants into them. Take the bag with the cigar box and May's blanket with me, put them by the front door. I gather a few toys for King as well. I hear Joel hammering in the bedroom. I try not to think of anything, just listen to the sound of the nails being hammered in.

I go to the back door to let King in, and stand there calling to him. I note the large flashlight hanging by the door, but it's well illuminated outside. Usually King responds right away, but I hear him crying in a way I'm unfamiliar with. I call out to Joel, simultaneously running out over the yard to find King. I see him there at the center of the pond, unable to keep his balance, slipping wounded on the ice. Joel is carrying the flashlight when he emerges behind me, and the moment he shines it over the ice I can make out the circles of blood where King has tried to collect himself.

'Oh, God,' I whisper, moving instinctively out over the pond where he continues to fall, terrified and exhausted. I can see how badly his paw is bleeding. The fur around his paw is dense and gluey, the blood collecting in it like a brush. I try to gather him up, but he's too heavy to carry. I slide backward on the ice, landing with the full, fighting weight of him on my chest. Joel arrives before I think to cry out, and the two of us attempt to hold him up.

'It's just his paw,' he says, closing in on it with the light. 'But it's pretty badly cut. We'll need an animal hospital.' He makes the blood circles on the ice seem less grisly, and I recognize that they're unreadable to him, neither a threat nor a prophecy.

We arrange ourselves to hold King up and glide him lightly along the surface of the pond, human crutches. Joel hands me the flashlight and carries him over the yard.

I notice, sweeping the flashlight under some of the trees, a garbage bag dropped beneath one. I quickly make my way over to it, noting it's torn at the bottom, a large piece of glass emerging from it. I open it up and see a puzzle of glass inside. What was he trying to do? Was he just trying to give himself some time to go unnoticed? Maybe he'd been back more than once while I was gone. A few feet away I can make out the pattern of footsteps and car wheels, traces of his presence that I won't have to erase. Winter will.

The first two days are beautiful. An injection, a soft bed, only a few quiet interruptions of the nurse checking my pressure. There's no pressure, I mumble. I hear the light padding of people on the ward going to the smoking room. Specters in white gowns. 'Just rest,' a young nurse says, putting her hand on my forehead. I see the plunger of a syringe in her pocket, look closely at her tender expression. 'You must be an angel,' I say. She swabs my arm, gently introduces the point.

I'm able to replay the events that came before, put them together without too much recognition. I can pad around my own life, specter in a gown, watching it from a doorway I don't cross.

I walk into the manager's office at my job. It was the first time in over a week. I didn't call in sick, couldn't explain. Didn't have the time. I slip into work through the back door; go straight into his office.

I'm trying not to nod, but I can tell I'm missing pieces of the dialogue. I don't care. Two supervisors and the office manager sit at the table. I think: Now we've come full circle. But there's no tape recorder on the table. There's no interview; no questions need to be asked.

'We're going to have to let you go,' one of them says.

'I know,' I answer. 'I'm not doing too well, am I?' I laugh but with embarrassment. I don't think it's funny. Nights have become days. I'm tired, dead tired of it all.

'We think you need help.' I look up. Another voice. Why are they all unrecognizable to me? 'We won't file your termination papers so you can use your health benefits to get yourself into a rehab program. St Mary's has a very good reputation.'

Of course I know this. I refer my clients there. I know what's available.

'We suggest you do this, Carrie. But we need your assurance.'

The big boss adds, 'You need to do this today. Otherwise we'll just sign the termination papers now.'

I agree to it. You don't fight very hard when you're high. Even the thought of getting clean doesn't scare you. Everything is insulated, muffled. I'm told I can make my arrangements from my desk. I'm my own last case.

The woman at St Mary's wants the facts. 'What drugs?' she asks.

'Heroin,' I whisper.

'Speak up,' she says. Leslie watches me discreetly from her desk.

'Heroin,' I repeat. I can see the word run up my co-workers' backs, a spidery knot that presses them forward over their paperwork. I can only imagine their relief; they'd been so stuffed with lies. 'I'm just resting my eyes,' I'd say. Family crisis, flu, cancer. I'm surprised I didn't call in dead.

The woman on the phone pronounces it *heron*. 'You can come in this afternoon,' she says. 'Bring your insurance card, your ID.'

I call Victor to tell him I'm in a program. I call from a phone at

St Mary's, waiting for someone to bring down my admission papers. Let *them* take the notes for a while.

'You lost your job?' he asks.

Can't tell him about the baby.

'I can get another job. I just have to get clean.' I try to make it sound like it's not for me, but for us. I've killed us.

'Where the hell were you the last four nights?'

'I've been here. They wouldn't let me call,' I lie. I'm thinking: Is the blond boy dead yet? Did his heart give out? He's a baby or an angel, something you can't protect.

I can tell he's unsure whether or not to believe me, but he goes along with it, finally saying, 'I'm going to quit too. I'm going to be a really good father to our kid, you watch.' And then I hear what I've never heard from him, his crying. It makes me sick, physically sick to hear him. There's no suspicion in his tears, just some unfounded hope that the baby will change him, has already changed me. I tell him I have to go, hang up the phone and stare at it as though I were waiting for a dealer to call.

By the third day I'm off all their medications. They rouse me from sleep. 'It's time for breakfast,' a new nurse says. 'You have to eat with the others. The schedule is posted in the hall.'

I start to ready myself, approaching the mirror with some fear; I'd convinced myself I could go on not looking, and no one else would look either. Breakfast could be judgment, though. Frowned on by the circus of the sick. Another nurse leans her head in the room. 'It's time. You've got to be out of your room now.'

All of us wear our gowns, except the outpatients. They seem advanced, a higher form of life, full of energy and an intimidating mirth. They perform a number of tasks. One monitors the coffee; one organizes chairs, turning them from the television set to the breakfast tables; one helps an old lady sit down beside me. Her gown is wide open at the back, and her crepe-like skin is mottled and scarred. They should have a hall of fame for the really old ones. How do they wake up each day under the crippling weight of impossible needs, impossible odds?

I'm not hungry, can't eat under these lights. I ask a nurse where the phone is. She casts a withering look at me. 'There are no phone calls for the first week,' she says. This is the part of the job she likes. 'This is your time to concentrate on you.' The only comfort I have is knowing that the lie I told Victor – that I couldn't make calls – has its basis in truth.

Over the next days, I watch the others settle into their incarceration, grateful for food and quiet. Their faces bloom; the contours fill out in front of me. Even the old lady's lines fill out. She eats from my tray. I remain unshakably sullen, adjusting the slice of orange peel in my mouth, interested in nothing else on my tray. Thoughts of Victor – of returning to him – ruin whatever semblance of order the place attempts to instill in our disordered lives. There are meetings and education seminars; everything is mandatory. Even our attitudes should be open and sunny. My counselor frowns over the desk.

'I don't know what you're running back to, Carrie,' he says exasperatedly. 'You need to cut your ties. If you go back to your old associations you'll go right back to using. I guarantee it.'

I know these things. I say these things to my clients. Does it sound this hollow?

I'm nursing this alien, larval sense of self. It won't come out under the scrutiny of these counselors. It has no trust and no defenses. It's full of guilt for wanting to exist at all. It isn't sure it wants to exist, will probably never want to exist. I sit in a chair, watching others take shape.

After a week, I walk to the phone on the first floor. 'Get me out of here,' I say. 'I'll wait downstairs.'

Joel removes a piece of glass from King's paw and places it on the living room table. The wound is small, but it gushes disproportionately. 'It must be an artery,' he says. He calls the twenty-four-hour veterinary hospital while I tie a kitchen towel around the cut. We can bring him right in. I'll have to ride with King, holding him as best I can on my lap. He seems to panic less when I hold him, especially now that the wound is tied off with cloth.

Joel helps me settle King onto the blanket I've used to cover the backseat; I slide in beside the dog, pulling most of his body onto my lap. I ask Joel to take my suitcases, the things I've set beside the door, and put them in the trunk. We pull out of the drive, leaving the house with all the lights on, a sentinel with a shattered eye.

'How is he?' Joel asks over his shoulder.

'Quieted down,' I say, stroking him and thinking: He's quiet for me. I look out the window when I hear what sounds like stones on the roof of the car. Hail. Its battering becomes a regular rhythm on the roof and windshield. I look at the glowing meters on Joel's dashboard, the blood on the sleeve of his shirt.

'I'm sorry,' I say. Then, with an intensity that seems inappropriate, embarrassing even, I'm crying, gasping for breath, my nose bubbling with clear snot. The hammering doesn't let up; it's like tiny fists beating at the car. I know why Victor's come and what he found no trace of. The little fists pound away at us.

'Don't worry about it,' Joel answers. 'I'm just glad I'm here to help.'

I still have the hospital ID bracelet on my wrist when Victor and Bobby pick me up. They make me sit in the backseat. Bobby hands me an army knife to cut myself free. I throw the bracelet out the window.

I figure Victor's brought Bobby along because he has drugs. I'm right about that, but there's more in their alliance. Before they pull the drugs from the glove compartment, Victor advises me they can take me back to the hospital, that I should think about this.

'You were doing so good,' he says.

'How would you know how I was doing? You never visited.' Not that he could.

He turns around. 'You're going to have to slow down sometime, babe.'

I stare into his face, incredulous. There's a kind of listless condescension in his eyes. You're going to tell me about slowing down? And then it occurs to me he is acting concerned, acting like someone who knows that a pregnant woman shouldn't be shooting heroin. And from now on he'll be measuring it out for me, wearing his conscience like a stolen suit. 'Tell me you brought something for me,' I say, looking away.

He turns back around and sits still, as though he's not going to give me anything. I'm supposed to hide my need from him, as though he were a doctor, too important to be treated as a mere dispensary. I'm supposed to plead for his approval, allow him to turn the spotlight on me, my pathetic, trembling needs. Not when I can see that his eyes are still pinned, see how he's turned right back to his old associations, the guys he knows from the penitentiary, pool halls, and bars. I suppose this henchman in the front seat is offering him details on fathering. *Daddy.* No child could fall for that.

'You make me laugh,' I say. There's something in my voice I brought back with me from the blond boy's hotel room, something he can't recognize. It's a dead voice, a sacrifice.

'I just came out of rehab and now you're going to lecture me. Let me out and I'll take care of myself. I don't need you.' I tighten my grip around the door handle. I'll jump.

'You know I'm just worried about you,' Victor says. 'I'm going to need to clean up too. I know that.' I see him looking at me, fretful, in the rearview mirror. For a moment he resolves into the person I met in the office years before, repentant, earnest, too much of both. Sure, there's a father in him. Someone with answers they can't live by, a string of jobs with terminations he has justifications for, an open invitation to visit his parole officer anytime. Nothing so unusual.

'Give her her shot,' he says to Bobby. Bobby opens the glove compartment. It's been set up all along. I don't express any gratitude when he hands a syringe back between the two front seats. I take a belt he offers and slide my sleeve up and my body down, out of view of passing cars. And what I don't get is how he plans to hold this over me. But I do get very, very high. Enough to make my absent body feel inhabited again, this time by something I know.

They want to see Janine's house. We are rushing up onto the

bridge, and I think I owe them this information. They don't have to press me for it. Right now I'd be sitting at St Mary's in a group confessional while a group of lost souls turn piss-gold with new revelations about themselves. By giving Vic and Bobby directions, I pay for my freedom, my evasions. If I tell them where they can find Janine, I won't have to tell Victor what I've done to the baby, his hope. Not yet. And the homes here are magnificent, the kinds of lives you want to see into, and can't believe.

Janine is far away, fortressed in these hills. We can't touch her. Victor and his friend don't recognize the prohibition, but I know I can't touch her. And I think of Victor's mother in her large house, turning in the doorway and wisely locking it.

I feel exhausted by the time we carry King into the hospital. He's quickly attended to while Joel and I sit in the waiting room, strange framed photographs of animals on all the walls: blurry, eight-by-ten close-ups of dogs and their dirt-streaked muzzles, the red eyes of skittish, squirming cats. The place is almost like someone's home, and for a moment I wonder if the vet lives here, in the back of the shop, arranging his sleeping hours around pet emergencies. I wonder if these animals on the wall have all been treated here, satisfied customers.

'I hope spending time with you isn't always like this,' Joel laughs, rubbing my arm, trying to bring me into the room with him, reminding me he hadn't intended an evening of emergency rescue. The vet has assured us he can sew up the wound and King will be fine, though he'll be sluggish from his loss of blood. I become morose under Joel's kind but uninformed gaze. For him, the worst is over, tragedy neatly avoided.

'No, it's not always like this.' I want to add: It's been worse, much worse.

'I know we probably have a bit of a wait here, so I thought now would be the right time to ask you to dinner. Maybe sometime next week, if you're not busy? I expect you're going to be pre-occupied with all that's gone on tonight.' He shifts uncomfortably in his chair, trying to direct his comments more intimately by turning toward me. My mind lights on the word *preoccupied*, but he quickly attempts to make up for it. 'I understand how traumatic this must be for you, so I don't want to pressure you.'

The gallery of animals, I notice, are only slightly less offensive than if their heads were cut off and hung there. I realize I haven't taken my eyes off of them, and force myself to look at Joel. His persistence is flattering, but I'm not confused about who I am and what tonight will precipitate.

'I can't lead you on, Joel. It's just not going to work out with me. I've got too much happening in my life right now, problems even the best shrink couldn't change.' I see him visibly recoil at the word *shrink*; I can't tell him it's his most attractive attribute. I might have run to him before, as though he could carry me the way Bill had. If he'd only come into my life before it became impossible to share.

He looks despondent for a moment, then stares at the door, thinking, slapping the gloves in his hand. He won't humiliate himself, and I'm glad for that.

'Well,' he says after a while. 'I guess I did a good deed tonight. I wrote my ticket to heaven.'

'You'll experience great rewards. Strangers' pets will follow you wherever you go.' We both laugh, though with reserve, maybe even discomfort.

'I guess I'll need to take you back,' he offers.

'I'd appreciate it.'

I can see this will be awkward; waiting around with me and finding some neutral language between ourselves, some words unattached to the future, to his intentions or my past. He'd love to leave now, come to terms with the bloodstains on his shirt, a sacrifice I can see he's regretting now. But I need him to drive me wherever I'm going next. I notice the payphone and excuse myself temporarily.

For a moment, I consider calling Frances at home. I need to tell her I'm not coming in tomorrow. She'll be angry with me, but perhaps I can get some sensible advice from her, maybe ask her if I can stay with her. She has managed that office for years, unaffected by the sordidness of clients. Their stories don't penetrate her. Gina and Hannah have lived too close to chaos; it seems safer to confide in someone impervious to it. But after the first three digits of Frances' number, I imagine her saying, *Don't get dark on me. Don't tell me how you got here.* And I think: I can't bring this into her life, I can't explain this. I call Hannah.

My voice is very steady on the phone. I attempt to tell it simply, to talk as though this were the aftermath. I want to present it the way Joel perceives it, an ill-timed intrusion. But she knows it's more than that. For Joel, this was the premature end of his seduction. In a more profound way, it will be the end of my relationship with Hannah too. She knows I'll leave, that I'll go back into hiding, and whatever we've come to count on in each other will also be abruptly terminated.

Still, I find myself reluctant to tell her about running into Joel and his part in helping me, her irrational jealousy suddenly more weighted than the thought of us saying good-bye.

'Can I stay with you?' I ask.

'Of course,' she answers. 'Any idea when you'll be here?'

'Soon, I hope.' I look over at Joel, pacing the lobby and discreetly looking at his watch.

When I arrive at Hannah's, she has her bags laid out on the bed, half-packed.

'Are you going somewhere?' I ask.

She cuts me a quick look and continues folding clothes. 'I didn't expect King. I thought he'd still be at the hospital.' He moves tentatively to the foot of the bed, his bad paw still hanging limply, and lies down on the floor, nuzzling his bandage.

'I had to bring him,' I say. 'I don't know what I'm expecting, but I thought he should be safe as long as I am.'

'What *are* you expecting?' she asks gravely, moving my bags deeper into the apartment and locking the door. 'I want to be prepared, Carrie. I don't want any secrets.'

'I expect he'll try to find me. I don't think he's come to wish me well,' I say. I stand in the doorway, wondering if I'm welcome, if I shouldn't just get a ride to my car and leave town.

'What does he want?' She seems to ask this of herself, as though he were pursuing her.

'I took money from him, and I called the cops on him. There's more to it than that.' I feel almost like I owe it to her to tell her about the baby. It's because I don't want to have to confront him alone. I never wanted to confront him alone. 'He thought I was pregnant when I left. I don't even think he's here for me. I think he's here for the baby. But there is no baby. I never told him. I made the decision on my own.' It's like she senses how exposed I feel standing in the doorway, talking about this.

'Carrie, I'm sorry. C'mon, sit down over here.' She puts me into a big chair in the corner of her studio. I can watch her pack in the low light.

'Can you bring me that bag? There's a blanket in there that my grandmother gave me.'

She carries over the blanket, looking at it but not commenting on it – that it's a baby blanket. I put it over my legs and rest my hands under it. She stands looking at me for a long time, her head cocked as though she's thinking.

'What is it?' I ask.

'I guess it's too late to tell him,' she says. 'Even if he wants the baby, he also wants to hurt you. He must want to hurt you, or he wouldn't be following you and breaking your windows. He doesn't sound like he's here to start a family.' I notice she has a hard time keeping her voice level even as she tries to announce this with certainty.

'But what if he is? I mean, what if he broke in because nobody was home and he wanted to make sure we hadn't left town already? He didn't damage anything. He didn't steal anything.'

'C'mon, Carrie. He stole your sense of well-being. He's stolen mine. You don't think we should stay here waiting for him, do you? I think we should go to Sioux City and stay at my parents' house. I have some things I need to attend to, anyway.' She begins to move around the apartment, picking up some papers from the phone table, a sketch pad. Last-minute items she puts in her purse.

'I've really foisted this on you, haven't I?' King looks up, panting, then resettles. I continue talking in her direction, though I'm not sure she's listening. 'I can't run from him indefinitely. I know that. I know what he's capable of. I just can't imagine him being so angry as to try and hurt me, though.'

Even as I say it, I know I'm trying to forget the image of Janine, push her down.

She stands in front of me, and I see she's furious.

'Obviously, I'm worried about this. You know I just went through this. I wish you'd told me what was going on, that you were being stalked. I mean, I just got out of the hospital. It's too much.' She turns back to the bed and continues packing.

I want to ask her why she changed the terms of our relationship. She determined we were better off as friends. None of this would have come so close to her if she'd continued to see me at the office.

She starts talking with her back to me. 'Your dog could have died, bled to death, if you didn't get him to the hospital in time. Don't you see how little his intentions matter, how he could kill without meaning to? You really think you can negotiate these things?'

'I don't want to negotiate anything,' I say testily. 'I'm trying to figure this out.'

'Listen, Carrie,' she says carefully. 'I didn't finish telling you what went on between Stefan and Ellen, but you should know. It has something to do with what you're going through now.'

I sit there shaking. I can't tell if she's asking for permission to go on, but I don't offer it.

She faces me for a moment, then turns her attention toward King. She talks unemotionally, looking at my wounded half instead of me.

'Stefan called me when it was too late. You see, Ellen returned to Iowa City, but she never called again after she'd called to ask me to apologize to her. That was it. I didn't hear from her again. But I did hear from Stefan. He called to tell me that his studio was broken into. He thought it was Ellen. I told him it could have been anyone. But I knew it was her. We'd done it together. I knew how she could climb a tree and make her way into one of his upstairs windows. If she knew a building wasn't alarmed, she'd work her way in, one way or another. About a week later, he called to tell me that it happened again. This time she'd destroyed a series of paintings he was about to show at his gallery in Chicago. They were portraits she'd modeled for, but he'd corrupted them in a way that I knew deeply affected her.

'Her face was easily identifiable; no question it was Ellen. Had they just been portraits of her face, they might have been considered beautiful. Disturbing, but beautiful. Her expressions were troubled, affecting. Like they were drawn from his memory of her at the cemetery in Burlington. But they were done before that, as though he'd predicted her hurt, her confusion over his betrayal. Those expressions were haunted, devastated. But what he did was paint her head onto the naked bodies of young girls. There were these adult faces and expressions imposed on these thin, small-breasted figures, these tiny bird-like bodies. There was something pornographic about them, though I couldn't take my eyes off them. They captured the impossibility of Ellen's agenda, but they were also demeaning, heartless. I don't think you could look at them and not feel compromised. Ellen blacked out the faces from each canvas. She hadn't stood naked in his studio to have her *psyche* revealed in these paintings. It was brutal. Worse than anything her father had done to humiliate her.

'Anyway, Stefan called me over to see the damage. He was angrier than I could tell on the phone. He didn't say hello when I arrived, just swung the door open for me and guided me to the wall where the works were hanging, leaning against the wall, and sitting on easels. They were all exhibited: a whole show blacked out.

' "I wanted you to see what that bitch did," he said. "That fucking little cunt thinks she can destroy my work. I'll kill her." He repeated it, like it was an academic decision. Now I realize he brought me there to make me part of it, to punish me in place of her. But at the time I thought all he wanted was to find out how she broke in. That's what he asked about, saying he'd bolt the windows if I knew how she got inside.

'I told him I knew how she once did it – from a second-floor window in the adjoining studio. There was a tree she climbed. It was simple. She accessed his studio by an adjoining door.

'I remember him sitting there, covering his face with paint-flecked hands, asking himself what he was going to do for this show. How could he ever get his work back? And I left him inconsolable, though I wanted to console him. I just walked out.

'It wasn't long before he called the last time, saying it was an accident. That she'd broken into his studio and he happened to be there. They were apparently yelling at each other on the top of the stairs, and he pushed her, but he hadn't meant for it to happen. It was so strange, Carrie. I could have predicted it. I could sense it before he ever said a word. And when it went to trial, it was my testimony about that visit – the fact that I'd told him how she'd entered the building before – that sort of cinched the case against him. It was just too odd that their struggle occurred upstairs; it appeared to everyone that he'd been lying in wait, that he intended to break her neck when he pushed her. So you see how close accidents and intentions can come together. You don't want to try to negotiate that.'

She turns to her suitcases and closes the latches on them. She lifts both bags by their handles and begins to make her way over to the door, where she places them beside mine. She turns and looks at me, smiling uneasily. 'I have to admit, Carrie, I look at you and wonder how you could not have known what to expect. I'm truly surprised you have nothing planned.'

'How could I? I didn't know he'd be released. I didn't know he'd come after me. These were just possibilities.' I feel defensive again, *responsible*. I want to ask her if I should have firearms, a map of the cottage with schemata for various confrontations all worked out.

'I'm just surprised,' she says evenly. 'If someone came this far to fuck with me, I'd certainly consider killing them.' I realize her warnings against negotiation have nothing to do with a desire to avoid conflict; I begin to wonder about her suggestion to leave town, whether she doesn't have some other plan in mind.

'How long do we go to Sioux City for? I need to call Frances and tell her I'll be out of the office.'

'That's up to you. How long do you think he'll wait around for you? Maybe we ought to leave something in the cottage that suggests you've left for good?' She has filled her purse and is leaning against her sink, drinking a beer. She has taken on a challenging casualness; *I'm ready for whatever you suggest.*

'The question is whether it's worth going back there. It's already getting dark, and I'm not sure what to leave that would suggest I've left town for good.' I hope the dark will discourage her. There's also a blizzard expected if the dark isn't discouraging enough. I get the distinct feeling she wants to make this some kind of match of wits. Victor doesn't use wits. He works from desperation; I don't think it's wise to leave signs and wait for him to uncover them. He doesn't put things together.

'Well,' she considers, 'you could leave some airline information on a slip of paper. You could mess the place up like you'd been looking for things. The dog's gone. Maybe he'll believe you've left for good. Let's face it, you can't afford to come back in a week if he's still haunting the place.'

I think of Ellen. What did she want going back to that studio? What hadn't she destroyed already? But Hannah's impatient. She knows that people just get stuck; they become attached to what's not working. It's a puzzle they have to finish. She puts the bottle in the sink, loudly, to tell me that she's ready for me to be ready.

'What if we encounter him?' I ask.

'I'll take my car,' she says, 'so that it's clear there's at least two of us inside. That should discourage him.'

Her confidence is perplexing; it's as though she were reading safety tips for a walk in the woods. If you encounter a bear, bang pots and pans.

That's when I remember I haven't told her about Joel, that I left my car at home when we took King to the hospital. Whether I like her plan or not, I'll need to get back to my car. I decide not to mention him. Why bring that up again? I need her now, and I know that she requires a kind of exclusive trust between us, not unlike the bond shared by Gina and Rachel.

'You'll need to drive me back. Gina took me to the vet and dropped me here.' Still, it bothers me to lie, actually to fear her reaction. Why am I protecting her when I'm the one in trouble? On the other hand, she's seems to know just how deep that trouble goes.

We drive back out to the cottage, and as I make my way along the same roads I'd driven earlier I feel intuitively that this is wrong. I quiet my sense of alarm by telling myself we would have come this way anyway. The cottage is where the town collapses, thins out, and becomes cornfields and – in the winter – barrenness. I think this is the way we'd get to Sioux City if we kept driving.

Hannah turns to look at King stretched out over her backseat, and her gentleness with him reassures me. Now that we're on our way, her face seems less inscrutable than it looked in her apartment. Her kindness to King is her way of asking me to trust her.

'Shouldn't we just drive straight to Sioux City?' I ask. 'I don't think I want to go into the cottage again.'

'If we can make him believe you've left town, we can buy ourselves time. We'll go in and out. You leave the note, I'll pull things out of the drawers. Do you still have the envelope your air ticket came in? Something like that lying around will help.'

Somehow, it sounds more reasoned now. It sounds like a plan we've actually considered. Buying time. This makes sense to me. It's why I drew the jewelry out of the safe deposit box before I went to Florida. I didn't even look at the pieces, still in their soft cloth envelopes. I reach into my carry bag on the backseat and find the airline ticket envelope, itinerary, and receipts still there in the pocket. I dig deeper and feel the cloth envelopes with the jewelry coiled inside them. I run my fingers over them; their stones make me think of the crested back of the baby alligator on my desk. Someday I'll ask Frances to send that to me. I know she'll fire me; she needs me now, and I'm leaving her. Though my absences are legitimate – my mother's ashes, and now Victor – I'm sure it will look like so many excuses. She'll see through me, noticing the job references I never had, the clients who know more about me than she ever did. She'll either let me go angrily, or she'll ask questions. I'll use the jewelry to buy my way out of explaining, disappear again, start again somewhere else. On and on.

There's a long flat stretch of land followed by the hill – large for Iowa City – before you get to my cottage. Whenever I drive the flat distance, I always feel uneasy, and now it occurs to me why. It is not how close the stars feel, or how the land stretches out flat and limitless in either direction. It is not about monotonous options, some great yawning vacancy. It is simply that the road is too exposed; it's too easy to imagine the electric arm of God interposed here, the loud crash of judgment spread out over these fields.

'It's really coming down now,' Hannah says. Snow is falling like something dumped from the back of a truck. She slows down and puts on the headlights.

'This is really bad, isn't it?' I ask. But I can see in the way she looks out the window an excitement about the ludicrousness of this endeavor, with all the elements pitched against us. We drive slowly over the hill. There is not another car in sight. The road is flanked by black ice; the headlights swim through it.

'I'm thankful I got chains last winter,' she says.

King recognizes the hill and gets excited. He lifts his head and barks sharply. I wonder if he'll fear the pond now, and if it matters. He won't run here again. I look out the window in a state of quiet absence. The cottage is in view, my car in front like a piece of equipment left abandoned in a postwar photograph. For a moment I think we can get away with this, leave the scene untouched, ghosts sweeping through a village. I remember the sense of elation I felt leaving San Francisco, placing the call to

the police and driving off. There was a sense of wonder behind it:
Can it be this easy?

'Pull behind the cottage,' I say. 'I want to check the window
and see if it's still boarded up. Let's circle the place entirely and
look for tracks. He left tire tracks and footprints earlier.' The place
is transformed now. The lights are on, but it might be years since
anyone's lived here.

The snow is falling too hard to try to find tracks; what was there
a few hours ago is now filled in. The window is still sealed. We let
the engine settle and listen for a moment to the sounds outside,
and I wonder if the owls hide when the wind is this furious.

We walk out toward the cottage; I hear King's barking until we
enter the back door. 'Where are the knives you were hiding?' she
asks.

I feel oddly ashamed that she actually saw my crouching by the
bed and slipping a knife beneath the mattress. It's the shame of
recognizing what I considered preparedness. Go out into the
world with nothing but a kitchen knife. It's just like me. I see a
crouching madwoman, hair like a million disconnected thoughts,
ready to pounce on a hospital rat.

I go into the kitchen and find myself crying, rummaging loudly
through the drawers, opening them all and slamming them shut.
Let him know I'm in my house. I want to draw every thrift store
plate from the cupboards and crash them on the floor. Not his to
destroy. I'm practically strangling the knives as I hand one over
to Hannah. Ready if the rat should arrive. She pretends not to
notice the tears.

'Call the airlines and find a flight, an early flight. I'll pack your
bag.' She looks at me sternly, and I realize she is saying these things
for his benefit, as though he were hiding here. Play it for real. Her
expression is insistent, almost maniacal.

I stand in the kitchen with the phone to my ear, calling information. He hasn't cut the lines the way they do in movies. Still,
I'm uncomfortable with my back to the living room. I turn
around, conscious of not twisting myself in the cord the way I
normally do. I call the airline and write down the information for

a 6 A.M. flight to Chicago, a big city I mean to avoid. I hear Hannah in the bedroom, opening drawers. I haphazardly drop the envelope with the flight information on the floor. I do it as though he were here, which enables me to feel oddly disengaged and above my own actions. The cottage feels like a set of props I'm familiar with, my lines spoken for an audience I can't see.

'I think we should go now,' I advise. 'Let's go to your place until it's time for my flight.' I say these lines so convincingly I worry she might remind me where we're really going.

We leave by the back door. I don't look around one last time. I lock it. Hannah warms up the engine and we begin to pull out. That's when I notice headlights on the hill of the main road. I point them out to her; she's strangely expectant, as though the distant beams were something prophesied. She stops the car, doesn't turn on the lights. We both recognize that the vehicle on the road is not moving either. It looks stuck.

A rumbling from the cottage roof makes us both jump as a mattress-length sheaf of snow slides off the eaves and breaks over the hood of her car. I clutch her arm, my eye still focused on the unmoving headlights stuck at the top of the hill.

'That's him, isn't it?' she asks. Her voice is dark with calculations. We watch as a figure leaves the car and wanders toward the front of it.

'He'll need help,' she says, staring out at him as though she can place these thoughts into his head. 'It looks like he's fishtailed coming over the hill.' She puts the car in reverse as she says this, then maneuvers slowly toward the front of the cottage.

'Let's quietly avoid him. Don't turn on the lights,' I say. I realize my heart is pounding even as I try to calm her, to suggest that we can slide out of this, characters slowly walking backward out of harm's way.

We pull up to the road where we can better make him out, looking at his tires, trying to dig the snow away from the front wheels. It's the car that we'd seen pull up before, a brown car, nondescript, wide. 'I can't tell if it's him,' I say flatly. 'I'll need to see him walking.' He's wearing a ski mask, but he's may be the right height.

She slowly drives onto the main road, moving in the direction of his accident.

'This isn't the way to Sioux City,' I say, turning in my seat to look behind us. Nothing but the accumulation of consecutive storms, massive snowbanks, and roads glistening with ice as black in the moonlight as coagulated oil. I turn around and see him wiping his gloves on his pants, his woolen mask pulled from his face. 'That's him. Jesus, that's him.'

'Slide down in your seat,' Hannah says, biting her lip, her intentions clear, or blank, on her face. I want to tell her not to do this, that we can drive off and avoid this. But we are operating on some vague recognition, more powerful than any thought of retribution, his or ours. It sweeps over us with the obliterating power of the snow and the darkness.

I slide down, seeing his gait again, the way he uses his palms as though he were making his way through water. He's drawn out to the road, waving us down, though she's driving recklessly fast now, no headlights. Or perhaps he's pressed to the side of his car, noticing too late this barreling black weight. I hear the hard thump of his body and the chains as they come down on him. She brakes, and with my mouth open in shock I hear his body dragged beneath a second set of wheels. We almost lose control but manage to drive to the top of the hill, and there's nothing, no cars, only the vast dispersal of snow and a darkening, like the closing of an enormous eye. I sit there crouched, cowering.

'You need to check him,' she says. 'You need to feel for a pulse.'

I look at her and see nothing in her eyes, only a quiet certitude that is both persuasive and silencing.

'I can't do it,' I say.

'Do it now. Don't wait.' Her hands are still on the wheel. She's ashen, unable to look back. I open the car door out of a surprising sympathy I feel for her. I don't know if she's going to cry, whether she's even aware of what she's done.

I step out of the car and walk down toward the body twisted in the snow. I can't figure out what is anatomically wrong with it, what makes his body look inhuman there. I have the disturbing feeling that he can't be killed, that this is his real shape. I imagine something supernatural in the inconceivable twist of his torso and neck – and that he is lying there in wait. I remember a painting I'd once seen or just imagined of two devils battling on a snowy road. Two devils vying for dominion on a road like this. I stand beside him for a moment and look quickly into his eyes. I don't look at them long enough to recognize horror or anger. I don't search out his motivation for coming. The pupils are still. I take off my glove and reach down to touch his neck, to feel for a pulse, and there is only cold, the rapidity of it as it encloses him. There is some horrible irony in the stillness of his blood. Its coursing and its contents had been his sole preoccupation. He had never strayed far from the current. I put my glove back on and stand up. Hannah is standing beside her car.

'Come here,' she says. 'I want you to look out. If you see anyone coming, get into his car. I'll pretend I've stopped to help you.'

She walks over to Victor's body and rechecks his pulse. I look past her. The night is jammed with stars. The lights of his car eerily illuminate the mound of what looks like very fine glass off the side of the road. His palms are starting to fill with it.

She turns the car around and we drive toward Sioux City. We discuss what has happened as though we hadn't any option. Each time we talk about it, it's like trying to shake off a mantle of snow, to shake the chill out of our bodies, out of our blood. Hannah maintains we did what had to be done. When she uses the word *we* I don't resist her, but I think if the police were to find out about us they'd know; it was her car and she was driving. I cannot disentangle her altruism from her opportunism. They presented an intersection, and we entered it fast and blind. I don't need her to illuminate it.

I let her talk, but my ears feel like they're full of cotton. I can feel his cold skin under my fingertips. I look at her and want to see the life in her; she seemed elsewhere on that hill. Somebody else.

There's a gulf between us, each of us attempting to share the experience, but unable to make it real for the other, or to make it unreal. I am uncertain if I should thank her; perhaps it's best not to suggest she'd acted on her own. But then, perhaps she hadn't. I touched him and I did not bring him back to life. The more I accept that he's dead the more the word *we* settles down in my chest.

We discuss how the elements were in alignment: the storm, the hill, the darkness. We witnessed his car in trouble with the sharp eyes of owls. We acted like owls. And so we discuss the details, our involvement no more premeditated than nature, and so absolved.

9

We stop at a small motel in Greenville, its dim VACANCIES sign like an eternal and exhausted offering. We feel achy after the hours of driving, the events. The motel seems strangely appropriate; it seems almost to sink away from the roadside, a kind of battered shell. We are not put off by the gravity of its drabness. The woman in the office is watching a black and white television, the sound up too loud.

'You ladies look tired,' she says, lifting herself from the chair and putting both arms over the counter, her thick bracelets clanking on the glass top. She is clearly commiserating.

'We've been driving through the storm,' Hannah says.

'Just to get here?' The woman laughs, her voice pitched as loud as the television.

'We're on our way to Sioux City to visit my parents. I don't think I can keep my eyes open any longer, though.' I feel I'm watching Hannah for the first time; her earnestness and ease are qualities I've never noticed in her. I wonder if she engages strangers all the time; if three years from now she won't tell someone in a supermarket that she once killed a man, vehicular homicide. She killed him without particularly wanting to, but she knew her friend needed to be free of him.

I feel emptied out of fear, one way or the other. Who would believe her? Who would care? She'd be another person with too much on her mind, no one to tell it to. Not the right person to tell it to, anyway. And what would I do if I didn't know her and she told it to me? Exactly what I did. I'd recognize her. I'd give her an opportunity.

Hannah takes the key, and I nod to the woman as we leave the office.

'Lock your doors,' she says. The woman's face looks suddenly like a mask, bleached out by the yellow fluorescent tube above her. Her lips are smiling, but her eyes are severe, warning.

'What do you mean?' I ask. My voice sounds ragged, abrupt.

'I tell all my guests to lock their doors.' Her face quickly becomes as stern as her eyes. She doesn't like questions. I feel Hannah's hand on my arm, trying to draw me out of the door. But for a moment I can't move.

I find myself staring at her as though something were speaking through her. 'I think that's odd,' I say, and I feel my lips trembling.

She looks at me inquisitively, cocking her head to one side as though allowing my words to drop into her ear. 'There's nothing odd about it,' she says slowly, deliberately. 'People think they're all alone out here. But you're not. You should always exercise caution.'

'Thank you,' I say finally. I drop my eyes from hers and close the lobby door behind me. She's still watching us quizzically.

We walk down the hallway abutting the parking lot, the lights dim, fixtures filled with the accumulated carcasses of insects. The ice machine buzzes and stamps beneath a stairwell. Our room is beside it.

Hannah doesn't say anything but looks at me while she opens the door. There's a light smell of mildew when we enter. Hannah goes directly into the bathroom. I put my bag down and immediately pull the cord on the heavy drapes, shutting them entirely. I grab a handful of its fabric and put it to my nose. That's where the smell is coming from.

I walk back out to the car and take King inside, careful to close the car door quietly. We didn't investigate the question of pets here, and I don't feel like negotiating with the lady in the office.

King is still barely able to walk, so I carry him back. I put him down near the heater, and he practically collapses in front of it. Then I go back to the door, lock it. There's a chain, and I use that too. I put my forehead to the door, and suddenly I'm crying. It's a deep sobbing I find hard to keep down.

I'm like a little girl dragged off with a suitcase someone else has packed. I find myself running not just from figments but from the law. I close my eyes and I'm touching his throat. He pronounces me guilty, a judge who occupies every cold hotel room along the roadside, the vacant eyes of every waitress and hotel clerk driving home after their shift. We're not alone out here. I know the woman's right; there are judges.

When Hannah emerges from the bathroom, I'm sitting on the edge of my bed. She is already in a T-shirt and panties, drying her hair. 'What's wrong?' she asks.

'Nothing.' I start to make my way to the bathroom.

'Do you mind if I watch television?' she asks.

I'm surprised she wants to do this. 'Just not the news.'

Later she's watching something like the home shopping club. But they are only selling dolls – large porcelain ones – not for children.

'Thank you,' I say finally. And I mean it, regardless of the outcome. She doesn't say anything, just nods sleepily. She is still watching the set, the large hand turning over the seal of authenticity. The doll's head is ornamented with silver satin and cheap glass beads. I fall asleep with the voice of a woman saying, 'This is something you can keep on cherishing and cherishing.'

We drive toward her parents' house. The storm has been less destructive here, but the roads are tricky, the trees hung with icicles. I think about what she's said about her father, how he'd lost the use of his body from his waist down, and how his temper took the place of his manhood. Perhaps Hannah had, as well.

She'd promised that if her father died, she would take care of her mother. But he didn't die, and so she couldn't do a thing for either her father or her mother. Her father saw to it that she remained outside the conflict. She was never in a position to address his loss; that was something for his wife to comment on. That was bad enough.

These towns have a sullen quality about them, populated by frugal, haunted people. People who lost or never had options. It's like going back in time, with humble, small homes dressed for Christmas, long streets with shop signs in fonts that signify an America I was born too late to see.

Despite my ruminations, I feel less uneasy today and think it's because I'm exhausted. No dreams, just a restless shifting of tonalities and shadows.

The past seems to recede too, as though you could lose it in the right car. And though I know this is an illusion, it is one of the few that brings me comfort. Hannah, on the other hand, is returning here. I know that she has come to collect something, to pick up some piece of her past she isn't done with.

She's better after we stop for breakfast. She appears less drawn and her compulsion to talk about last night is lessened. That talk carried us over what felt like endless blank miles. I thought the sun would never rise and the roads never end.

Over coffee she says, 'I don't want to spend a lot of time with my parents. We don't need to, and I think it's less stressful for them if we leave tomorrow.' I want to propose our staying in a motel again. I'm not sure I can get right back in the car and turn around. I'm not sure I want to go back. But I don't say anything. Best to wait.

In the car she becomes animated, pointing out the monuments: the Howard Johnson's; the auditorium with its Indian head mosaics; the abandoned storefronts of downtown; and later, on Nebraska Street, the old Central High School, its windows broken out and its stone walls covered in black soot; the old synagogue, shingled and dilapidated and vaguely Gothic.

Her parents' house is small with a small lawn where the snow is mounted knee-deep. We pull up into the driveway and stop before the garage. There are no trees on any of the surrounding lawns, as though landscaping meant the removal of anything but grass.

'I'm glad you came with me,' she says, turning off the ignition and looking straight ahead. 'I need you here. I need you to just go along with me while we're here. Can you do that?'

I nod. 'Sure,' I say.

'I'm going to say some things that will probably surprise you, and I need you to just stay on your toes and go along with it. Promise me you'll just go along with it.'

'I'll go along,' I say.

She steps out of the car before I can ask her what to expect. I know now that we have not come all this way to hide out. She has come to finish something. This is what we'll do for each other. The finishing business.

Her father answers the door, almost agile in his chair. He's wearing bottle-thick lenses that make his eyes seem enormous. They are full of distrust, perhaps incomprehension. Hannah bends to kiss him, and he turns his cheek up. It is almost entirely subsumed in gray stubble. She introduces me as Ellen.

'Ellen? Oh, you're Ellen. Come on in,' he says. 'We've heard so much about you.'

'I hope you don't mind King,' I say. At first the dog surprises him, but his face comes alive when King licks his hand. 'I love dogs,' he tells me. He speaks softly, not like the angry man Hannah described. Then again, he's old now, reconciled. We hang our coats on a rack next to a small piano; it's covered with at least ten different-sized frames. He begins to tell me about the family; there are great-grandmothers and his grandfather; austere, almost regal women in furs; a boy with beautiful hands at the piano. Hannah is standing in the yard as a child; she makes the yard look enormous. I look from the picture to her face, but she turns quickly from me. There's dust over all the surfaces, and I have to keep myself from lifting one of the frames and wiping it clean.

'Is that you?' a voice calls from the kitchen. Hannah's father guides us in. Her mother is sitting at the table, feeding an infant from a bottle. The child's eyes are closed, but his mouth is working feverishly. Without a word she hands the child, bottle still in its mouth, to Hannah.

'We've taken good care of him for you,' she says to me. 'I guess you want to hold him. Alex,' she coos, 'your mother's here.'

I take him from Hannah, searching her eyes for some kind of prompt. Her eyes are full of a sadness that could as easily be shame. They're chilling. We all stand around the child, doting on him. The child is oblivious. Anyone can be his mother. I feel claustrophobic in this circle of adoration; my thoughts are too stained, my heart too agonized by this deceit I have to play out. I know the child is Stefan's – that Hannah couldn't kill him – this child that is either the unexpected or planned outcome of her confused seduction.

'Ellen's better now,' she tells her mother. 'She's ready to take him back to Iowa City.' I wonder if she's told them I was in the psychiatric ward, whether she's projected her entire story on Ellen. I don't say anything, just look down at the baby as though he's my excuse for everything that may have come before. If I was mentally too weak and had to be hospitalized, it was only because the child seemed too perfect; I wasn't equipped. Finally, I look into her parents' faces. 'Thank you for taking care of him,' I say.

'We're happy you have him now. He's a beautiful baby,' Hannah's mother says. She looks exhausted. She stands up and shuffles toward the refrigerator, barely lifting her feet.

'Do you mind if I walk with him?' I ask. I break off from them and walk out the back door into the yard. I pull the blanket up over Alex's mouth. I look into another house, another kitchen window. I think I can make someone out behind the screen, a woman no doubt. Probably washing dishes. It surprises me that Hannah doesn't follow me out into the yard. Instead she remains talking with her mother, watching me from the window, clumsily adjusting to the baby's fitful movements.

We go to an early dinner with her parents. It is a difficult procedure – and one that I imagine is irregular – to get them out of the house. I carry the baby. There are a few families already seated at tables around ours. The place has a large salad bar, adjoining rooms separated by brown accordion doors. The waitress, who must be in high school, immediately comes over to look at Alex. He is asleep in my arms.

'He's adorable,' she whispers. 'How old is he?' I look into her eyes for a moment, the question skipping over my mind but not landing.

'Thank you,' I say to her. There is something in my voice that keeps her from asking again.

Hannah's parents, on the other hand, don't ask questions. Perhaps they thought this child was Hannah's, and they are just grateful now that she hasn't lied, grateful there was a real mother out there. They accept me as some kind of proof, something incapable of concealment or falsehood. And though I haven't had a moment to pull Hannah aside, to tell her how startling this charade is, I've already grown used to it. I step into the role of uneasy mother with no great effort; I feel slightly possessive and slightly intimidated by the child, and these feelings seem natural. I dip a cloth napkin into my water and rub his cheeks clean, and his sparkling green eyes – so much like Hannah's – are full of delight. I listen to their conversation while I tend to the baby; Hannah tells them about a job she has applied for, how well her painting is going. Finally, she tells them she may have to cut the trip short, that I need to get back to work.

I look up in time to see her parents quickly glance at each other. There is relief in their eyes, as though being in their daughter's company has required them to acknowledge a part of themselves they don't want to revisit. They act as if they'd reached some kind of tenuous truce, a mutual forgetting. I imagine Hannah's awkwardness, her mannishness, is too present for them to ignore. Their resolve to get on with life no matter how unfortunate leaves very little room for her. Hannah understands this too well.

I can see that she respects their bond; she seems to watch them with a bleak satisfaction. It's familiar, even if it's not warm. It occurs to me she'd be happy to stay with them if she could, that it still hurts her to acknowledge their preference to be alone.

She holds her mother under the arm as we make our way out of the restaurant. It's cold, but it's not snowing. Her father manages his wheelchair with difficulty, gritting his teeth at times but not asking for help. Alex is sleeping, drooling pearls along the edge of the blanket. I carry the bassinet, wondering whether Hannah's mother made the blanket for him or if they bought it. I wonder if I should offer to give it back to them, if it's a family item, something meaningful.

Hannah has to help her father into the car and fold the chair, put it into the trunk. He sits in the front seat, winded.

'Thank you for dinner. I had a nice time,' I say to the back of his head as I lift Alex onto my lap. He begins rolling the radio dial, looking for a talk station.

'We don't get out often. We're just very happy this baby is with his mother. Hannah's mother became quite attached to him. I hope you'll take him back to visit us.' He turns up the radio. We drive back with barely a word spoken. I look over and notice Mrs Fisher blotting her eyes with her scarf. I feel agitated by the hoax, by the promise I've made to bring him back here for visits. I can't even look at Hannah. I look out the window instead. I imagine myself a new mother, seeing the world in all its abrasive wonder for the first time, not the faintest idea how to keep my child from expecting too much of it.

Hannah asks me to stay in the car; she tells her parents we're going for a ride and not to wait up for us. Her mother offers to take Alex inside, but she says we'll take him along.

'He's asleep already,' her mother persists. 'Let me put him to bed inside.'

'Ellen wants to spend time with him,' she says. Her voice has an edge to it. Her mother steps out of the car, and Hannah opens the trunk, carries the chair over to her father. I also leave the car to embrace her mother. Her parents enter the dark carport, but before they disappear I notice Hannah's mother turning a last time, her eyes reluctantly gazing at the bassinet in my hand.

I move Alex into the front seat between us. 'Now you understand why I had to come here,' she says. 'I told my parents it was Ellen's baby. I couldn't tell them what happened.' I move Alex out of the direct line of the heater. His cheeks are stippled red.

'I told them Ellen was in the hospital with depression, and asked them to watch over him. They've had him off and on for two months. But he needs some stability now.' She says these things flatly, as though effecting these new conditions requires nothing more than clearly stating them.

'I hated that,' I say to her. 'I hate faking, pretending I'm someone else.'

She says nothing, but I can tell she's angry at me.

'I don't know how you can do that to your mother. That was really hard on her. She was crying.'

We drive into the parking lot of the old Central High School. At night, the structure is terrifying. Its blackened stone makes it look like an enormous crematorium. Hannah shuts off the headlights and we sit silently for a moment; we've come up against a wall of darkness.

'What are we doing here?'

'Let's go inside,' she says.

The whole place is boarded up; there are some weathered signs promising restoration for the following year, but no indication that anything is yet under way. I find the place more than forbidding. It seems impossible to imagine children inside its high walls. It's like a prison, designed to dwarf and intimidate. The windows – all broken out now – offer no relief to the facade. They propose a deeper blackness.

'C'mon,' she says. 'Wrap Alex up and let's go inside.'

'I'm not taking him in there.' I hear something like outrage in my voice. What is she thinking?

She turns on the seat, looking first at me, then him.

'All right,' she says, taking the handle of the bassinet. 'I'll carry him.'

'What are you doing?' I ask impatiently over the hood of the car. 'It's cold in there and he might get hurt.' But she's already slammed the car door and is nearing the chained doors of the school. I follow her, though the whole thing feels strangely overdetermined, as though I were back in an old dream with the onus to correct something. I catch up to her as she makes her way around the side of the building, and she smiles at me, faintly, as though she's pleased I've decided to come. There's a low window covered only by a loose board. I take Alex from her, silently and without prompting. I look at his sweet face; how a child born from so much remorse could look so untroubled.

She puts her foot against the side of the building for leverage and, pulling the board away, slowly draws the long nails out of the stone.

'We don't have a flashlight,' I say. 'This is stupid and dangerous.'

'Trust me. I do this all the time.' She puts the board down and knocks the shards of glass out of the frame. Turning to look at me, she adds, 'Once we get upstairs, we'll have moonlight in the windows. This is a great place. You'll see.'

She hoists herself up and over the window ledge; then her face reappears, framed by shadows. She passes her hands out to retrieve the bassinet, and I hand Alex over to her. There is something ancient about the transaction, the shrouded appearance of her face, and my making this offering through the wall. And then I, too, climb inside.

Once our eyes adjust, it's easy to find our way to the stairwell. The place is damp. There are puddles underneath the busted windows, and wooden chairs stacked against the walls. I'm worried about things roosting in here, or kids squatting, endangering the baby. I try not to think about it. I become interested in some of the old desks, the bookshelves stacked with paperwork and files, information nobody claimed.

Hannah seems to know where she's going. She moves confidently through the dark halls, and Alex looks like he's sleeping still. I watch her carrying him aloft, guiding him over these forgotten, broken things.

She turns to me before a large window in one of the classrooms on the second floor. 'You see,' she says. 'Perfect light.'

I walk to the window, and the face of the moon is spectacular. The light of it falls like powder over her shoulders, and over her knuckles, tightly clenching the plastic handle of Alex's bed.

'Thank you for what you did today, with my parents. I'm sorry it was so hard for you.'

'It was all right,' I say. *You killed Victor. I owe you one.*

'I want you to keep him, Carrie.'

I stand still, sensing the magnitude of this. She has chosen this place to ask this of me; her words fall resoundingly, chillingly, in here.

'I came here after I first had Alex, and I knew I'd come back here. I thought of leaving him here and just letting the cold take him out. And then the opportunity with Victor happened, and I thought if I acted on that, you'd understand what I was going to ask of you.'

'I don't know anything about being a mother, Hannah.' She's taken him out of his bassinet, and is holding him before her like a heavy package.

'You know not to take a baby into a place like this,' she says. 'You know he could get hurt; he could fall.'

Her implied threat makes me outraged. The anger momentarily keeps me from noticing the creepiness of her suggestion, her fixed, flat gaze.

'Even if I could keep this child,' she says, 'I could never be honest with him. I'm responsible for his mother's death and I helped put his father away. If you take him from me, it'll be like Ellen has taken what was rightfully hers. I think that's the only way to make things right. You could care for this baby, Carrie.'

'You're wrong,' I say. 'Ellen will never have what's rightfully hers. And if you give up Alex, you'll never have the experience of your son's love. You have to accept him. You can be a good mother to him.'

'My killing Victor gave you the chance to move on. I gave you that chance. I can't move on with this baby,' she says, annoyed. 'I need you to take him. I'll abandon him otherwise. I will.'

'I can't just take your baby, Hannah. You have a responsibility.'

She cuts me off. 'I have a responsibility to Ellen. I'm responsible for the dead.'

I imagine holding the baby – how much greater the responsibility to the living.

'Now I've done something for you,' she continues, 'and I need you to think about how much is at stake for me. I can't mother a child if I'm sitting in jail.' She takes a step forward, holding Alex in front of her. 'This is his last chance, Carrie. Trust me.'

I hold out my hands and collect him. I bring him close to me, bewildered. At first I think it's Hannah who confuses me, but I understand her. It's my own thoughts that I'm confounded by. They seem for the first time to be purged of fear. I look at Alex and wonder if this wasn't the child Victor was looking for, the one I'd lost. Courage. I was looking for courage in his face.

I stand in her parents' hallway speaking to Frances on the phone. I tell her I won't be working there any longer. I'm trembling as I say it, afraid of her reaction. She wants to know what's happened, but I insist it's a personal matter. I don't try to explain it.

'What do you want me to do with your things?' she asks. She's controlled and diplomatic, but I know she's angry at me, even though she'll be leaving soon and her memories will quickly dim.

'My friend Gina will collect my things. Just put aside the pictures and stuff on my desk.'

'I'll box it up,' she says. 'I'll do it this afternoon. I need to have that desk cleared.'

She makes it sound as though my replacement were already hired.

'I'm sorry,' I say. She's quiet for a moment, and I realize that what she thinks matters to me.

'I hope you're not in trouble, Carrie.'

'I don't think so,' I answer.

'I think you are. But I know you're not asking me for help,' she says. 'I'll miss you.'

Hannah is holding Alex at the end of the hall, pretending not to listen. She doesn't like holding the baby; she fights her attachment to him with a monstrous will. But I feel expansive and open, like anything is available to me. I ask Hannah if she has a map. I need to look at one right away, trace my finger over its branching lines.

I hold Alex while she searches for her father's atlas. I think of the ocean, its swimmers rushing out to embrace it, trusting that its force will be benign, its currents will return them. And maybe Alex has had a grandmother all the time, waiting in a room by the beach, knowing this was all his and all ours if we wanted it.

Hannah knows I'm leaving. I can't bear to live on that small stretch of road any longer. Judgment has been passed on our lives. Hannah thinks I can take her memories from her. I know she's wrong. We can't predict how relief will finally come. We can never predict.

The god of endings has asked me to oversee only the beginnings.